# Frumious Bandersnatch

## A Cryptid Horror Anthology

Three Ravens Publishing
Chickamauga, GA USA

Credits:
Cover design by: J. F. Posthumus
Edited by: David Hensley

WILLIAM JOSEPH ROBERTS PRSENTS: FRUMIOUS BANDERSNATCH by William Joseph Roberts/Three Ravens Publishing – 1st edition, 2025

Ebook ISBN: 978-1-966507-49-9
Trade Paperback ISBN: 978-1-966507-51-2

# Table of Contents


So, I Hear You Eat Houses......................................................................1

Ol' No. 5 .................................................................................................15

The Cutting Room Floor...................................................................... 41

Frogs of Rain .........................................................................................55

Mr. Guthrie's Familiar ......................................................................... 71

Saints and Monsters ............................................................................. 83

Dark Tooth............................................................................................107

Last Bus to Travina .............................................................................125

Composite..............................................................................................131

Homunculus ..........................................................................................145

The Wine King......................................................................................167

The Murderous Grasshopper ............................................................173

The Velvet Hammer.............................................................................201

# So, I Hear You Eat Houses

By: Lyman Graves

Ned found the bar nestled in a fold of semi-occupied neighborhood between Claiborne Avenue and the Interstate. To the west lay ghostly traces of the old Hunter's Field; to the east, haunted shadows of St. Roch Cemetery. Though not the worst corner of New Orleans for an able-bodied man to visit in daylight, as late afternoon wore on it paid to walk there with a sense of direction and purpose. Ned came with no doubts about his aim, whatever consequences awaited him.

The individual not so much tending the bar as guarding it wore an ambiguous physique, which probably hid crushing muscle beneath exterior fat. There was no clue as to the giant's disposition, intelligence, gender, or anything apart from the challenge in the black eyes flashing toward the door as it swung shut. Ned, who hadn't touched a drink in seven months, gestured to a random bottle on a shelf. Failure to behave like a good customer might drive the proprietor to draw the firearm that surely sat waiting for action under the bar. Ned overpaid with damp bills from his pocket and made for the far corner, leaving the freshly poured shot where it sat. His host turned away, likewise unconcerned about the drink, to mop the backbar mirror with a filthy rag. Formal transactions complete, Ned could be left to his own affairs.

The alcove where the old buzzard sat, sipping torpedo juice at a slanted card table, wasn't a proper back room. A loose partition of spare wood and pest-gnawed Fiberfill obscured it from the main bar. Whether such a barricade was to give the lone drinker privacy, or to spare other patrons the sight of him, didn't interest Ned. A pyramid of rusted kegs and moldy PVC tubing against the far wall indicated he was in the house nook for stowing garbage, human and otherwise.

Ned helped himself to a seat on an upturned bucket. The man at the table didn't welcome him, pushing an unfriendly sigh through flared nostrils. Age-yellowed skin like ancient newspaper clung to his joints and hollows. The shock of coppery hair wisping around his rootlike ears confused the image. The man was like something grown on the lightless underside of a log, something struggling daily to hold itself together in a solid shape. Ned spent an unhurried minute studying him, offering no introduction.

"Don't have no music in here 'til Thursday," the old man grumbled at last.

"Say what?" Ned replied, flicking sweat off his eyebrows in the sweltering stillness.

"They don't hire your kind, anyhow. No punk rock."

Ned couldn't keep amusement out of his voice. "That what I look like to you, old-timer? Punk rocker?" A savvier old crank would have pegged him as an unremarkable Gen-X longhair.

"What you look like, boy, is one kind of rat-fart nuisance or another." The old man sat back to show his full height, gaining maybe a quarter-inch. "How's about you pick your unwiped punk ass up off the bucket and carry it back to the Quarter where it belongs."

Ned shook his head slowly. "You got me wrong, man. I'm here on business, right at this table."

"What business?" A gurgle came from one of the old man's organs.

Ned leaned over the table. He couldn't help injecting his answer with mock drama. "I've got some property I need looked over."

In the following silence, Ned listened to the feeble click of a ceiling fan hung precariously off-balance above them. He hadn't noticed it before, since it wasn't doing a damned thing to relieve the tomblike atmosphere. Outside in the street, two dogs began a nasty snarling fight.

"You made a mistake," said the old man. The change in his demeanor was plain. There was no need for a countersign to show they understood each other. The coot was nervous; let him play stubborn if he felt like it. Ned was in no hurry as long as he could set the hook.

"Let me show you an old Indian trick," Ned said, drawing a crinkled photo from his pocket and sliding it across the tabletop. From the momentary jump of the old man's hairless brow, he recognized the high-grain black and white image. Ned spoke two new words, a name, with chilly confidence.

"Balthazar Cull."

The old man eyed him. "Yeah?" he croaked. "What's it mean?"

"Friend, it means you." Ned tapped the photo with a finger. "It means him, too. Wasn't easy getting a snapshot from your younger days, before you aged into the fine old specimen I see before me. Balthazar Cull, meet Ned Brooks." He offered a hand.

The old man wrinkled his nose. "You saying you know me?"

Ned put his hand away unshaken, and gladly. "No, sir. I introduced myself to you just now, didn't I? What I know, Mr. Cull, is your work."

Old Cull took a slow, painful-looking swallow from his glass. "I'm retired," he wheezed.

"Ah, hell," Ned said, unfolding another item from his pocket - a newsprint photo, smudged and brittle but clearer than the portrait. The shot was high-angle on a suburban block recognizable from its layout of sidewalks, half-demolished low fences and sheds. Anywhere a house ought to have stood, the rubble of a foundation slab spiraled and sank to a central pucker of loose earth. It looked as if someone had flushed each lawn, sending the attached home swirling down out of sight.

"There you go," said Ned. "Good ol' American gumption."

"What's this supposed to be?" Old Cull's ribcage creaked as he shifted in his seat.

"East Chicago. Or East Saint Louis, I forget which. Made your mark on a mess of towns, didn't you, Mr. Balthazar Cull? Make the deal, do the job, book the next one when you need the scratch." He leaned on his elbows and stared into the withered scowl. "North Braddock, Pennsylvania. Pontiac, Michigan. Neighborhoods on death watch, laying fallow on land that some developer's having big wet dreams over. You're the man they'd call, right? Most times, I bet the folks in those houses were too busy paying double mortgages, praying the lights wouldn't get cut off, to see the end of the road coming. You could fix it, though, like nobody else. Make sure they'd sell up or hoof it out of Dodge, and quick."

The skin of Old Cull's face rippled in an unsettling way. There was no use denying a history too big and deep-rooted to keep buried. "I'm not… in the business no more," was his halting reply. Ned watched the masterful scorn bleed out of his sallow features.

"No kidding?" Ned scoffed. "I thought old pros like you never quit, just learned to slither a little slower. It figures you'd be skulking around the world's biggest bowl of hurricane gumbo. If some Big Swinging Bulldozer Man's got urban renewal on the menu, who better than Balthazar Cull to make the roux?"

Old Cull squirmed at each intonation of his name, like an arthritic half-drunk Rumpelstiltskin. "I look like I'm… working… to you?" he croaked with a weary gesture at their surroundings. The edge of one sallow hand cut swirling wakes of dust in a stray sunbeam.

"Nope," Ned said with a shrug. "Just now it looks like you might be free for a job."

"I told you, I don't—"

"One house," Ned growled. "I'm not asking you to clear the Seventh Ward. This one's out of state anyway. I'll even drive."

Old Cull was loading up a fresh protest, maybe gathering strength to swing his unlabeled bottle, when Ned pushed a yellow brad-fastened envelope across the table. It was big enough to mail a hardcover book, and bulging. Old Cull had been paid in similar parcels long enough to guess at the considerable sum inside. Calculation froze his hostile features, except for the wattled throat which gulped as if swallowing something hard.

Watching Cull's performance of mulling the offer over, Ned saw a man who looked hungrier than any living thing ought to be. He looked exactly the way Ned wanted him.

The town was Moseley, Arkansas – a crusted wart on Texarkana's knee. Ned never mentioned it by name. They'd sat in silence for six rattling hours up I-49. Ned's Atlantic Blue '92 Mercury Topaz lacked a radio - boosted by some shitbird in a Piggly Wiggly parking lot more than a year ago. The car itself, loose at the joints, clattered like a mouthful of floating dentures. Ned checked more than once to make sure the road vibration didn't shake his passenger apart at the seams. Old Cull stared so diligently at nothing, not even the passing absence of scenery, Ned was afraid the son of a bitch might die sitting up in an act of spite.

Only as they jogged onto Route 67, ambling past the regional airport, did the first road sign stamped with "MOSELEY" appear. Ned heard a grunt and hiss from the seat beside him.

"Still with me, old fella?" he asked. "You think there's been nothing to see up till now, just wait till we get there. That kind of nothing is really something."

Old Cull didn't respond, swiveling to face the dark expanse ahead of them. "I been here," he said as if waking from a doze. "Worked the town once before."

"I wondered if it would ring a bell," Ned half-whispered. In truth he wondered no such thing. Maybe "when," but never "if." By the time he accosted Balthazar Cull in his rank lair, Ned was dealing in certainty.

"Strange thing," said Old Cull in the same dreamy murmur. "I never worked the same town twice before."

It made sense. His method of doing business made it risky to operate more than once in a single area. Localizing a phenomenon brought undue attention. Ned had picked through dozens of municipal journals, not to mention countless crypto-boner Web forums to find the handful of deserted-street images he needed. The irregular distribution of sites across the continental States made it hard to draw connections - a third-rate conspiracy theory among amateur chasers of the unexplained. In an age when many strange occurrences attracted cults of hardcore truthers, Moseley's peculiar case never captured the popular imagination.

Ned hadn't counted on the novelty of doubling back to former haunts as a lure for Old Cull's interest. If his fossilized intellect sensed anything suspicious in the coincidence, he showed nothing. Perhaps, after dull and dormant years, he was up for a contest of wits. More likely, Ned presumed, he was merely broke and starving for the old satisfaction of doing the one thing he'd ever been valued or rewarded for.

It was pointless educating the likes of Balthazar Cull on Moseley's history, although Ned could lecture on it from nearly two dozen years of study. The town's focal point throughout most of the Cold War was an expansive and robust government facility. During those years Moseley housed the families of numerous contractors and military personnel in basic comfort. Whether Gorbachev and glasnost, *Exxon Valdez* or the high hopes of young Governor Clinton had a lick to do with the price of federal pencil-pushing in Greater Texarkana, 1989 saw the formal shuttering of the complex, ending its slow death one bureau at a time.

As the federal tide receded, the Arkansas Department of Transportation circled on black-asphalt wings, planning an extravagantly wide new stretch of expressway. Failing to invoke eminent domain, the State Highway Commission engaged the services of Balthazar Cull. Though the man's name and how to reach him wouldn't appear in any official register, corporations and governments retained their own special methods of getting in touch.

Cull's unorthodox approach allowed him to drive out the bulk of the target populace more quickly than any sanctioned methods. He worked without leaving the usual traces of slum clearance, obfuscating his process even from those who hired him. Those who learned more than they should were not inclined to discuss it later. Tunneling through pages of official denials and mires of conjecture ended up costing Ned a great deal.

The aborted Moseley mega-highway construction stood as a shrine to vanity and statehouse graft. The short-sighted project budget expired a handful of miles down the road, where a crudely erected spur shunted it back to the existing route. The twice-blighted town of Moseley lay starved to a lonely remnant of its population.

The Mercury cleared a dark stand of trees. Three quarters of a mile ahead, the diffuse glow of sodium-vapor lamps revealed the main overpass like the spine of some colossal half-buried horror.

"Our exit's just up here," Ned mumbled. "We don't go over… that."

Old Cull gave no sign of hearing.

The house was near the exit, on a short lane alongside three more built from a developer's so-called "custom" catalog of half a dozen hybrid styles. Frankenhousing, Ned called it - part of a final not too sincere stab at resurrecting Moseley. Vast, inappropriately colonnaded, patched with allegedly chic brick veneer that looked like psoriasis, the house was the ideal of bargain-bucket palatial. Anyone with an eye for architectural vulgarity would picture the miles of cheap cornice work inside. Siding distressed by gritty winds added to the skin-disease look. Mildew from seeping pipes and leaking gutters jaundiced the eaves. Even so, it was the only house in sight with its roof, doors and windows all intact. As they approached over the half-dead, half-overgrown lawn, Ned's fingers curled into fists.

The house perked Old Cull up right away, evaporating his moribund surliness. He'd expected some garden variety tract home, not such a garish treasure to draw him out of retirement. Good taste didn't factor in his estimation of worthiness, while sheer size did seem to play a part. He stared at an upper window, computing something. A liver-colored tongue tapped the lipless, whiskered upper edge of his mouth. Ned waited.

"Three days," Old Cull said at last. "To prepare. Fourth night, I'll be back ready to go."

"Three?" Ned barked, playing indignant. "You know I'm not paying a day rate."

"Big job for a single property." Old Cull assumed the placid tone of a professional in his element. Although he'd dropped his confrontational posture, securing earnest money for the work failed to warm his demeanor.

"You want it done in a night, I gotta be set first. You want to torch it instead, sort it out your damn self. I don't refund no deposits."

"Easy, old-timer," Ned said. He made a show of weighing his alternatives, as if any existed, then turned up his palms. "I'll leave you to it, then. You… ah," he paused in the motion of turning to leave. "You need a ride anywhere? Got someplace to crash for three days?"

Old Cull's face tightened in distaste at the tone of the questions. Ned's grasp of the services his money bought sat like a bad smell between them.

"I'll let you know where to leave the rest of the money," Old Cull said.

"You want my number?"

"You can find me, I can find you." The reply was assurance and threat delivered in one. As Ned gunned his car engine, Old Cull shambled off the opposite way down the block, seeking shelter away from dawn's prying eyes.

It came on the third night. That had always been the plan, never a fourth night, in case Ned got the urge to sneak back and watch the work.

The thing living as Balthazar Cull never minded shedding its frail human skin, although the long confinement brought rusty aches as it stretched out to its full dimensions again. Stagnant fluid sat pooled in segmented joints long out of use. Bunched and compacted flesh, lined with tender creases, unfurled and swelled to an abdominal chamber forty yards across. Ropy capillary clusters unclotted, spilling gouts of thin yet nourishing blood into a vast open circulatory system. Radular muscles flexed and lubricated, engorging with readiness to feed. Rings of bristly pedipalps fidgeted around a central pair of scissoring antlion mandibles as large as twin folding saws.

It moved across the derelict lawns of Moseley under cover of night, without the intrusion of working streetlights or concerned neighbors. Two days prior, the lifelessness of the subdivision prompted Balthazar Cull to wonder what made the target property such a stubborn holdout as to require his intervention. Now, as unthinking ganglia drove the creature's black spade-shaped carapace toward ground zero, such questions no longer mattered. Olfactory pores received the essence radiating from the house. Though the scent registered as unusually sharp and pungent, the thing's appetite following a long hiatus overrode any tremors of instinctual caution.

It made a slow circle of the lot, heedless of fence rails as they splintered under its advancing bulk. Choosing an entry point with sweeps of its oral feelers, it turned its back to the house and reared up against the moonless night sky. Plunging downward with the speed of a predatory insect, it punctured the dirt with the razor spur on its dorsal plate.

The body oscillated, sliding into the earth like a camping shovel. Positioned squarely under the foundation, the creature fastened supple guiding tendrils to the corners and spread the elastic hood around its maw, priming the way to its cavernous gut sac with pulses of peristalsis.

The dissolving agent secreted by the creature's mandibles was naturally concentrated to soften the most unyielding elements. The foundation, consumed first, would fracture into hefty gizzard stones to help with the rest of the house. The method allowed the consumption of bulky matter with negligible excretion. After a brief period of torpor in a pre-selected hideaway, the creature would either die or emerge with renewed strength. So late in the life cycle, the gamble assumed higher stakes. It hadn't counted on surviving to molt again, but Ned's proposition jump-started its ambition to try.

After nearly two hours of steady consumption, the creature's digestive churning developed a dull edge of pain. An acrid, over-salted flavor disrupted its pleasurable feeding. The house grew gamey and sulfuric, inviting a new and frighteningly alien sensation. The thing was growing sick on its food and would soon need to vomit.

This posed a problem. In its compressed bipedal Cull form, it could mimic human functions well enough to swallow grain alcohol and live on little else. With full feeding apparatus deployed, the process was only meant to run one way. The massive tract could absorb virtually anything, shedding only traces of jellied waste on the inner lining of its molt. Without standard mouth-to-cloaca plumbing it was more or less an armored, sentient gastrovascular cavity. Every internal surface bristled with hooks and barbs designed to draw material down. Even though it wanted to disgorge the descending mass, the swallowing reflex was too strong. The system did not tolerate counterflow.

"Hot damn almighty!" The blue Mercury sat in a driveway three houses down, obscured by a mound of uncollected garbage bags. It wasn't the first seventy-hour campout in a car for Ned Brooks. The ground rocked with furious tremors as the creature sensed his presence.

Ned bounded up the curb and over the mangy non-yard, his easy manner gone. At the edge of the quaking pit, he dodged falling debris from the caved-in house. Half-coherent curses, held in too long, spilled from his lips.

"Chow down, you fuckwaste. Chomp on it. Work them jawbones, big boy. Soo-eee!" Although fully lucid, he sounded dangerously drunk or worse. "I took a lot of crummy-ass government work just to chase down reports about you. You're one hard-to-track methodical monster. Ever get chased up a windmill before?"

The sagging structure vibrated with a sudden, low vocalization from the mass beneath it. Whether questioning Ned's bewildering rant or merely warning him to withdraw, the thing in the ground meant to be heard. Ned gave not one shit.

"I've got a complaint and nowhere to file it, amigo. You missed a detail on the Moseley job back in '89. Did I mention I'm from Moseley? I'm not just some sketchy landlord here. This is my story, understand, about when you took a contract on our house."

A jagged corner of pavement pushed up against Ned's boot sole. He stepped to one side without looking down at it.

"You're a planner, I gather. So stop me if you've heard the one about the family supposed to be out of town when a hungry thing came crawling up their lawn." He leaned toward the hole in a confidential posture. "Did you know only my Mom was away? Gone to bury some crazy aunt my dad and me'd never met. My Dad caught the flu, and I said there was some school thing I wanted to go to — total bullshit, but Mom understood I'd be a nightmare on the trip with just us two. I got to stay over with a friend so Dad wouldn't get me sick."

The ground beneath the sidewalk distended further, until a small wedge of cement broke loose. Ned kicked it lazily into the pit.

"You were done and gone by the time I came home that Sunday. Nine-year-old kid actually feeling homesick after a night away. Guess what I found when I got to the end of my street. Or… guess what I didn't find. My house, and my dad, who must've been conked on enough cold and flu dope to give a horse amnesia." Ned blew his nose in a hard stream onto the grass. "I barely remember what I did those three or four hours till Mom got home. No way to call her on the road back then. All I could think of was knocking on neighbors' doors, hollering about my gone house, and my gone dad."

Ned wiped his face with his shirttail. Whether queasiness or heavier emotions played the larger part, his nostrils and tear ducts ran freely.

"Here's my question: Did you botch the job, or were you just curious what it would taste like with somebody home?"

There was no telling whether the creature in the pit understood, not that Ned minded. What he shouted was for himself; the thing at his feet would grasp the essential points of what was happening to it.

"You'd be amazed, or maybe you wouldn't, how many different ways a bureaucrat can shrug at you. They cooked up geology reports to show rubes like us how a solid house could have a freak sinkhole open underneath it. As for my old man, they shrugged again when we said what a good provider and daddy he was. A man running off from his home in broad daylight, they as good as told us, was even easier to explain than the planet swallowing the odd home. Some desk troll in the payout department conveniently forgot to carry a zero, and Mom got a hell of a kick on the settlement. God bless her, she tried to give some back, and the adjuster told her to keep it considering the 'unfortunate coincidence' of a husband gone AWOL at such a tough time."

Ned paused, grabbing ragged breaths, as a badly-serviced engine rumbled into earshot over his left shoulder. A battered Chevy Nova — vivid yellow and scored with brown rust, like a banana going bad — halted at the street corner eighty yards away, its interior so fogged with smoke that Ned couldn't have described the driver in any detail. Their most likely business at that hour in that place was to meet with a dealer, or a hooker. Possibly they'd mistaken Ned's parked car for a rendezvous point. The last thing they'd expect would be to catch a sweaty drifter shouting curses at an actively collapsing house, which was exactly what it must look like from down the block.

Ned bared his teeth, like Nicolas Cage or Gary Busey did when they played crazy people in the movies. That got the Nova moving. It bounced over the curb in reverse, then turned the opposite direction to speed away into the dark. Ned resumed his angry sermon.

"Mom didn't get far. Couldn't let go of what she'd lost. Ain't it funny, me explaining this to you? Lucky for her, the next wave rolled right into town — cookie-cutter developers come to suck on the carrion. They peddle these gaudy cheapo dream homes, you know? Of course you do. People too stunned or hard-headed to move away got their pick of newly groomed lots, with a stunning view of ArDOT's godawful overpass to nowhere."

The funk of hot rubber left by the Nova's tires, mingled with the skunky tang of the driver's weed, wafted under Ned's nostrils. The local authorities weren't likely to receive any panicked calls about his odd nighttime behavior. Not by anybody that high, fleeing at that speed.

"Mom was so looped out on shock and grief, she didn't know what else to do with her big insurance windfall. The state, or whoever, even threw in some kind of bogus disability pension. Once I got out of there I sent money back, whatever I could spare, so she always had enough to live on. Money's not what she needed. I just couldn't stick around to be her tether to reality. Not how I was raised, and it's my burden to make peace with. As if you give a damn, you ugly bugsack."

Miles away, too far to matter, a siren shrieked across the night. Ned listened as a second siren joined it, then licked his lips as the twin wails faded away together, bound for some other disaster.

"Trust me, after ten years you'd have cut and run too. You ever see those TV programs about hoarders — people too depressed and scared to go outside or throw a pizza box away? Well that's the cutesy-pie version, cleaned up for broadcast. One whole room of her upstairs was dead Christmas trees and old strings of lights. Broken lights, not working ones. You couldn't get through the door. We stuffed our trash through a narrower crack every New Year's. How none of those trees ever caught fire and burned us out is a Christmas miracle. Couldn't have got out if there'd been a fire. I was more or less bricked up in my room by diet soda cans and shipping boxes. I came and went through my window like a fucking squirrel."

He looked down at a buckling frame of wood and glass, perhaps the very same bedroom window.

"I can tell you about living with undiagnosed and untreated. Hell, I left home with plenty of my own issues. Difference is, I know I've got it. Never needed a doctor to recite it in Latin for me."

Ned gulped oxygen to steady his thumping heart. A tremulous groan filled the quiet — maybe a wall folding under stress, maybe a guttural plea for him to shut the hell up. He gagged on a gust of odor from the house, then steadied his breath and continued.

"Mom couldn't shoulder all her problems, but she never did anything halfway. When she turned shut-in, she went for the blue ribbon. Wish I could've shown you what you were fixing to bite down on. Guess it would spoil everything, huh?"

A flatulent gush from under the house punctuated Ned's talk. Twenty feet from where he stood, the soil rose in a low dome as big around as a rain barrel.

"How do you like it? My widowed mother's dream house, bought with blood money. Have a big taste. Are you into all the sour-wet newspaper yet? The plumbing leaked all over it. Mom didn't mind, just left it to sit and let the silverfish do their thing. Always hated those little bastards, ten times nastier than a cockroach, and I bet she has ten times as many in there since my last visit."

The soil bubble burst, releasing warm noxious gas. Ned grimaced as his throat released an anxious chuckle.

"A real modern wonder… being stuck inside doesn't even slow people down. Ten of anything you want in economy clamshell packs. Two-day delivery or free returns. Name me one useless household gizmo that's run on QVC since 1996, I guarantee Mom could tell you where in the house she kept a lifetime supply."

Another, larger swell of dirt pushed up along one side of the property. Watching it grow, Ned barely heard the words he'd rehearsed a dozen times in his mind.

"I tried to get her out, get her help, and when she ran me off I'd come back every few months to check in. I'm one of those who moves around. Lots of short-time jobs and research in my downtime, connecting the dots, moving among the public library's homeless. Mom never wanted to hear about you, or any of my theories about finding you. It's been lonesome work."

The condenser unit for the air conditioning system slid noisily on its concrete pad, tilted askew by the oblong bulge of earth.

"Funny, what spoils most houses is people smoking in them. Mom didn't really do self-control, but she wouldn't touch tobacco and didn't have more than a Bloody Mary a week. Now, those Big Chief Chicken 'n' Gravy dinners, that's what you'd call one of her vices. They stack up neat in a chest freezer, with mashed potatoes and peas and a brick of peach cobbler in cute little compartments. Mom could sock those away, brother, and half a Dream Divine Cherry Cheesecake any lunchtime or dinnertime of the week. Every day was Thanksgiving around here for the last decade or so. And between meals, forget about it!"

The AC unit fell into the hole with a crash. Ned watched the heavy fan housing tumble end over end toward the center.

"Call me crazy, Cull… I think your snacking flaps or whatever I'm staring at just turned a shade greener. You must be into the dirty dish room. Anything you feel squirming between the empty trays, call it extra protein. Ha!"

Ned recognized the signs of a vast mechanism straining to reverse its action. The creature, he thought, must be working against its own biological safeguards. Bony spines buried in drywall and timber pulled loose from soft-looking follicle beds. Fissures opened all over the mass he could see from his vantage point, widening to long V-shaped slits and releasing volcanic moans. As pieces of house fell away to the sides of the pit, pieces of monsters sloughed off with them. An agonized whine like electrical turbulence filled the air. The sphincters of the colossal flayed throat sucked impotently at the air above.

Ned spoke softly, his tirade burned out. "Took my time working through my own grief. Once I was done, and managed not to kill myself, I needed to be sober. I came back one last time, not glad but steady on my feet. I didn't get far inside the house…got sick three times before I got out again. If she'd still been in there suffering, I'd have burned it down. Lucky for everyone, her heart gave out or her liver burst or sweet Jesus alone knows what. I got close enough to be sure she was gone."

The fizzing respiration slowed. Presuming the thing could still listen, it was time for Ned to wrap things up.

"Figure you enjoyed my old man so much," he said with perverse relish, "you wouldn't want to miss having the pair of 'em. I don't guess there's any way you'll see her… oh, God forgive me… I can't let you finish without knowing she's still inside somewhere."

The creature gave a thunderous retch, clawing at the pit's edges. The vibration shook a dark boulder of matter loose from a shelf of jagged second floor. It plummeted into the pulsing red funnel of throat, washed on a surge of blood into the central opening. With its mandibles and guide-feelers torn free in the act of belching a wall aside, the creature's great mouth could not slow the putrid mass down. Once human, the obstruction lacked most recognizable human features after untold months of decay in the fetid labyrinth of the house. Even partially rotted, with skin as purple and blubbery as a seal's, the body must have weighed eight hundred pounds. The fleshy ruin slid into the raw gullet, sealing it like a cork. Sounds of painful suffocation followed, sending prickly waves of revulsion over Ned's scalp.

Thrashing so violently that sidewalks ninety feet away buckled and cracked, the scavenger tortured its joints until they gave way. Chitin snapped, loud as a twenty-one handgun salute, and when upward resistance fully ceased the house's upper story and roof collapsed, mashing the remains of the late Balthazar Cull into the pit.

Silence fell for a time over Moseley, Arkansas. Ned kept a solemn vigil. He doubted anything could remain alive under the leveled house. It simply wasn't clear to him what came next.

The dull stench of the ruptured house lingered, a problem only time could fix. With his blood cool again, Ned felt its oppressive thickness. When he was ready, a bundle in brown paper waited on the passenger seat of his car. Carrying it like an infant in trembling arms, he watched as puffs of pollen from the downy petals made yellow smudges on his jeans. All his life he'd called them daffodils, which they basically were, yet in some rare moment of normal conversation his Mom told him her favorites were a special kind called jonquils. Ned remembered how she'd filled the house with them, before her accumulation of dry neglected plants added their compost aroma to the atmosphere of despair. Caring for them, while she was capable, had been her last true comfort.

The flowers were all Ned could think of, an offering to release him from the last of his obligations. He placed them against the curb, steps from the edge of the pit, where somebody or nobody might see them in the morning.

Climbing aboard the Mercury, he brought it to grumbling life without another glance back. He pulled out of the driveway with a screech of tires and steered into the sunrise, leaving the dust of his hometown behind for good.

# Ol' No. 5

By: David Hensley

*Late last night and the night before,*
*Tommyknockers, Tommyknockers*
*knocking at the door.*
*I want to go out, don't know if I can,*
*'Cause I'm so afraid of the Tommyknocker man.*
—Stephen King

The setting sun dipped behind tree topped western mountains taking nearly all of the fading winter light with it. I rumbled through the rusted chain link gate into the compound of Abbot Coal's Number Five Mine and parked my '66 Riviera in front of the guard shack. Normally my sleek black coup stood out among the battered assortment of pickups, blazers, and broncos favored by the men who worked the Number Five. Normally I would arrive right around the same time those grime encrusted men were climbing into vehicles for the ride down the steep walled valley, or holler as they called it, to homes in and around the small town of Hemlock Bluff. Normally I'd have to endure half hostile stares from every living soul in every vehicle that rolled through the gate.

When I first started working for Abbot Coal, I thought it was my car that made them stare. I'd put a lot of love and TLC into her over the years. Her gleaming black paint, custom exhaust, and fifteen inch mag wheels polished to a high shine made her a real peacock among the pigeons. It wasn't the car. As it turns out, company security men are not popular in the holler.

No such problem this night. There would be no oncoming or outgoing shift. The mine was shut down due to a string of safety incidents, the last of which, a collapse, left four men injured and six more presumed dead. The entire crew, including the administrative staff that worked in the big building, walked off the job and had yet to return.

I killed the motor on the big Buick, grabbed my lunch pail and large green Stanley thermos, and opened the heavy door. Silence. It was more than a little unsettling to have complete silence greet me. Normally the sounds of heavy equipment and the machinery that processed the coal would be growling and clanking away as the oncoming shift continued the business of wresting the black rock from the earth. I stepped out into the cold evening. Nothing drops the temperature in these steep walled valleys like the sun sinking behind the western ridge. One minute sunset is painting the eastern side of the valley in gold. The next it's twilight, getting dark and cold damned fast.

I looked around the silent compound. Over in the admin building or mine office or whatever the locals called it I could see one light burning in the site manager's office. His window looked out over the compound. I guess it was so he could keep an eye on the work. But what do I know? I'm a security guard, not a coal miner. Hell, a week ago I was an operative for The Company.

The door of the Buick closed smooth and easy with just a nudge from my hand. Twenty years old and the doors didn't sag a bit. God, I loved that car. I turned and headed for the steel steps of the small single wide trailer that served as the guard shack. As security posts went it wasn't half bad. It certainly beat the hell out of standing pier sentry in the icy rain or flight deck integrity watch in the North Atlantic.

I checked the stove pipe sticking out of the trailer's roof. No smoke and the trailer was dark. Damn. It looked like Mr. Abbot hadn't found a replacement for the day shift security man. The one we had, Mike Hollis, had walked off the job with the rest of the crew. It made sense. Mike was a local boy and his brother was one of the men presumed dead in the collapse. That would explain why the site manager's light was on. Mr. Abbot was keeping an eye on things until I arrived and checked in. It was going to take at least an hour for the thin-walled trailer to warm up. Damn.

A loud popping rumble dragged my attention from the novel I was reading. That sounded like Tom Hollis's Dodge. I glanced at trio of closed-circuit television monitors on the left-hand end of my desk in time to see a late seventies Ram Charger with a dented tailgate slide to a stop outside the office building. It was definitely Tom's.

"Shit." I dogeared my page and tossed the book onto the desktop.

A stream of pickups rolled through the gate, past the parking area, and stopped with their headlights shining on the steel railed deck that served as porch and public address platform for Mr. Abbot.

The phone rang; not one of those new cordless models with the gentle electronic burble, this was one of those old rotary phones, square and heavy with a ring like a fire bell. I lifted the receiver from the cradle.

"Evans?" Mr. Abbot's voice came through harsh and tinny.

"Yes, sir."

"What the hell is going on out there?"

"Looks like trouble sir." I cradled the receiver in the crook of my neck and shrugged back into my coat.

"Then handle it. It's what I hired you for, to handle trouble." The line clicked dead. He'd hung up without waiting for my response.

"Yes, sir." I dropped my receiver on the shiny black cradle. "Maybe I picked the wrong week to stop drinking."

By the time I made my way from the security trailer to the rear of the half-moon of pickups parked in front of the mine office two groups had formed. One, comprised of Tom Hollis, his son Mike, and three men I recognized as equipment operators gathered on the deck. The second, larger group, clustered around the base of the deck and the foot of either set of steps. From the looks of it Tom, his son, and those operators were all that stood between Mr. Abbot and an angry crowd of miners. Tom and his boys gripped pick handles, and a pair of operators held the top end of the steps on either end of the rusted steel deck.

"…not doing this." I caught the tail end of whatever Tom was saying to the group of angry sounding coal miners. I did a quick count. Fifteen or so. Six against fifteen is bad odds. Even if Tom and his boys held the high ground so to speak.

"Get on out the way, Tom." A voice like a jack hammer cut through the murmur and grumble of the crowd. I couldn't see the speaker from where I stood but his voice was unmistakable. Gus Harmon. What Gus Harmon lacked in height he made up with fuckery.

"Ain't happening," Tom gripped the rusty rail and stared out at the crowd. I doubted he could see me standing in the back, not that it would matter anyway. "Get back in your truck, Gus, and go home."

"You're gonna stand between that Company Man and what he's got comin'?" Gus asked.

"I'm standing between you and the unemployment line, Augustus Harmon."

I eased my way into the back of the crowd while Gus and Tom debated the pros and cons of what Mr. Abbot did or did not have coming to him.

"What's the deal?" I asked the man to my right. He was a head shorter than me with his hands jammed deep in the pockets of his denim coat, the sheepskin lined collar turned up against the cold. "Paycheck bounce?"

"Naw," Denim Coat spit a dark stream of tobacco onto the frozen gravel. "Gus just found out that the Company Man sent off for scabs to come in and work in our place. Said if we won't go back in the mine he'll find folks who will."

"What's he figure on doing?" I asked.

"Gonna take the Company Man down deep, let him see what's what."

I wasn't sure what that meant exactly. What I was sure of was that I couldn't let these men get their hands on Mr. Abbot. I definitely picked the wrong week to quit drinking.

Under normal circumstances, in my old life for example, that was the point where I would have radioed the support team lurking in a nearby van or truck and let them get local law enforcement involved. That was then.

Now?

Now, I didn't have a support team or a radio of any kind. I'd walked away from the old life. Moved out to a little slice of paradise called Hemlock Bluff and took a job as the night watchman for a medium sized coal mining operation. The pay was decent when you combined it with my pension, VA disability payments, and the retainer stipend The Company paid for the privilege of being able to interrupt my new life at their leisure should something go bump in the night near me. Best of all, the worst thing I'd had to deal with thus far was the stink-eye from the folks working the mine and Mr. Abbot's shitty attitude toward anyone who didn't share his last name.

"Maybe you could tell me what that means," I said to Denim Coat. He turned his attention away from the ongoing debate and looked at me.

"You're that other security man."

"I am." I nodded. "What's Gus aiming to do?"

"Stop jawin for a minute and listen, you'd know." Denim Coat spat and jerked his head toward the debate.

"…ignored the signs," Gus said. "He sent them boys back down there anyways, even after me and Ed said not to. Your boy's down there buried right now cause that Company Man won't listen to reason."

"Damn it, Gus," Tom's knuckles stood out white against the rusted railing. "It was safe. I checked the shaft myself. Roof bolts and timbers were solid. No way that collapse should have happened. It ain't Abbot's fault."

"The hell it ain't." A miner from the crowd shouted. "We told him about the knocking."

A chill ran down my spine. "Knocking?" I asked Denim Coat.

"Yeah." He spit another stream of tobacco and looked up at me. "Knocking. Surest sign there is you're in a trouble spot."

I came all the way out to Hemlock Bluff to get out of The Life. Damned if I didn't just find it waiting for me when I got here. "Let me guess," I said to Denim Coat. "Tools have started going missing, lunches getting pillaged, can't keep a radio working deeper than three hundred feet?"

"That's right." Denim Coat nodded and spit. "How—"

I didn't wait around to hear the rest of his question. Instead I started shoving and elbowing my way through the miners. I needed to get inside and talk to Mr. Abbot before this thing got out of hand.

I, as you may have surmised, am not nor have I ever been law-enforcement. The resume and background checks that landed me this particular gig all say law enforcement of one sort or another. Hell, if anyone bothered to check into my military records they would find a distinguished history as a Navy Master-at-Arms with an excellent record and service with NCIS. It's all bullshit. But having worked for The Company for a couple decades did and does come with some benefits.

All of that to say, a real cop would have gotten in front of those miners and found a way to diffuse the situation and or disperse them well before I started shoving my way to the platform. I, as I said before, am not a real cop.

Tom Hollis spotted me coming and the look of relief that washed across his face gave me another jolt. He really was trying to keep Gus and his cronies from doing something dumb. And that look said he was awfully happy to have some real help. I was going to disappoint the hell out poor Tom. To be honest, I didn't really care if those pissed off miners tarred and feathered Mr. Abbot and rode him out of town on a rail. As long as they did it after I had a talk with the man and got a look at the records concerning Abbot Coal's Number Five Mine.

By the time I pushed my way to the left-hand side of the crowd, Gus had moved on from reasoning to threats. Augustus Harmon did not strike me as the sort of man that made idle threats.

"Tom, you and your boys are gonna have to step aside now," Gus said.

I started up the steps toward a burly excavator operator. The man was nearly as wide in the shoulders as he was tall. I'd heard the others around the yard call him Iron Mike. I eyed the crowd while I waited for Mike to decide whether or not to let me through. Down there on the ground, Gus was hefting a pick handle and eyeing the platform. The rest of the crowd were similarly armed with pick handles, lengths of pipe, sucker rod— hell one lanky guy in the front had a Bowie knife hanging from his belt.

"Gus," Tom's voice was calm and flat. "If you or any of those boys come up these steps there'll be hell to pay. Now go on home."

"You letting me up there or are we waiting for the rush?" I asked Iron Mike, keeping my tone conversational.

"We'll go home once we've shown that Company Man the mine. And don't think your pet city-boy on the steps there's gonna stop us." Gus looked at me and grinned like he'd been waiting his whole life for a moment like this. Some men are born troublemakers.

"You'd best be up here before this thing gets rolling." Mike shrugged and made a gap for me to pass though. I squeezed past the big man. I'm not exactly small, standing 6'1" in my socks, and I barely came up to Mike's shoulder. I almost felt sorry for the poor bastard that tried to get past him.

"Tom." I stepped to the rail next to my daytime counterpart.

"Evening Stan." He nodded, keeping an eye on Gus and his cronies. "What's the play here?"

"Damned if I know." I shrugged. "Never had to face down a bunch of pissed off miners. Your pal Gus there looks like he's working himself up for a fight though. Maybe we ought to get inside and wait him out."

"What do you mean…" I lost track of what Tom was saying. The big lights that illuminated our little mountain valley drama had started to blink and flicker. It was subtle at first, just a flicker, a sputter like the power was browning out. Then it picked up, the big lights flashing off and on like giant strobe-lights in a Berlin disco.

"We need to get inside." I grabbed Tom's shoulder. "Everyone, now."

A rumble accompanied the strobing lights. It came from somewhere near the big trucks that stood ready to haul away loads of coal. We all watched the closest big rig shake and sway. The ground around the front wheels started to boil. There's no other word for it. It went from hard packed gravel and dirt to this jumping earthen frothing like the sea when a good wind is up. That's when the hands started appearing. Small hands and arms, like a legion of dirt dwelling children, burst through the earth all around the nose of the truck. That's when the big rig started to tip nose first into the ground, sinking like an iceberg-stricken ship. After that everyone in the yard was a lot more interested in getting into the office building than arguing the merits of taking Mr. Abbot on a tour of the mines.

We piled through the doors into the reception area of Abbot Coal's Number Five offices. Not a lot of room with fifteen or twenty coal miners crammed into the space with Iron Mike and the rest of Tom's crew. I stood looking out the glass double doors watching the last few feet of the coal truck vanish into the earth. In the twenty-five or so years I'd spent with The Company, keeping a lid on the various things that go bump in the night, I had never seen anything like this.

"What the hell was that?" Tom asked.

"Knockers." Denim Coat stepped into the vestibule looking out at the small earth covered shapes pulling themselves up out of the hole where the truck had vanished. "I told 'em about the knocking. Told 'em not to run radios down there."

"Don't start with that horseshit again Donny." The lanky kid with the knife stood half in half out of the vestibule. "No such thing as Tommyknockers, or haints, or boogers, or any other nonsense your meemaw told you."

"I'm looking at fair compelling evidence to the contrary." Gus Harmon pointed through the glass at the little figures sprinting across the compound toward the shaft tower.

"Wonder what they're running from?" Iron Mike asked.

I turned my attention, away from the small sprinters, back to where the earth had swallowed the truck. More figures were coming up out of the pit, a mix large and small smeared in black, some still wearing helmets with working lamps on them. Large or small they moved with an unsteady jerking lurch. Like marionettes on the end of uneven and tangled strings piloted by a half-blind drunk.

"Tom, Gus get these doors barricaded before those things notice we're here," I said, working my way into the crowded reception area.

"With what?" The Lanky Kid asked.

"Start with that desk and the filing cabinets." I pointed over the half wall into the receptionist's office. "Use your imagination. What matters now is keeping those things away from us in here."

"Who says you're in charge?" Gus asked.

"No one." I looked up at Augustus Harmon. He'd been a tall broad-shouldered man in his prime. Decades of pulling coal from the earth left him stooped and limping. He still had hands like shovels and his arms were knotted with muscle like cypress roots. Gus may have been a rabble rouser but most of these men had followed him here. "Things are going to get real crazy real fast and you don't want to be within arm's reach of what's coming up out of that hole right now."

"What exactly *is* coming out of that hole?" Everyone was trying to crowd into the vestibule and see what was going on.

"The dead." I started pushing my way through the small crowd. "Get the doors barricaded or we won't live to see the sunrise."

"Where you goin'?" Gus put one shovel wide hand on my shoulder stopping me cold. That old bastard had a grip like a vise.

"To have a word with Mr. Abbot."

"Sounds like a grand idea. I think I'll come along."

There wasn't much I could do to stop him, not if I wanted his help in the fight that was headed our way. "Sure, why not?" I nodded. "While we're going up to see Mr. Abbot, you think your boys could get that door secured. Those things won't ignore us for long. They can feel the living the way a blind man feels the sun."

He looked out at the flickering lights and the herky-jerky movements of the figures coming up from that hole. Then looked back at me with eyes narrowed like he was really seeing me for the first time.

"Donny, Chris. You and the boys get that door blocked off. Me and the Security Man here are gonna go have a word with the Company Man."

"Evans." Mr. Abbot met us at the top of the stairs. "I believe I ordered you to disperse those men, not bring them up here to my office."

Mr. Abbot was a disagreeable man. I'd encountered more than my fair share of his sort during my Navy days. Fewer in my time with The Company. He was of middling height and rail thin. And, even at this late hour, impeccably dressed. No wrinkles in his Brioni suit, not a single iron gray hair out of place and his pencil thin mustache perfectly limned the top half of a perpetual frown.

"Have you looked out your window, sir?" I brushed past him and continued into the tiled hallway.

"One more step and you will find yourself back among the unemployed."

I looked at my watch. 1808. Still a long way to sunrise. "If we make it to morning, you can fire me. Now where do you keep the blueprints?"

"Blueprints?" Mr. Abbot and Gus both asked.

"You know," I paused and turned to look at Mr. Abbot. "Blueprints, diagrams, the documents that tell me where your digging, how deep you've gone."

"You mean the mine plan," Mr. Abbot said.

"Sure." I turned back toward his office. "Where do you keep it."

"Map room downstairs." Gus said.

I pushed open the door with Mr. Abbot's name emblazoned on a gleaming brass placard. "A man like Mr. Abbot here, I bet he keeps copies where he can reference them day or night."

"No need to wait until morning, Evans." Mr. Abbot pushed past me into his office and stepped behind the large mahogany desk. "You're fired."

"Great." I scanned the room and found what I hoped was the mine plan. Along one wall of the office ran a storage rack about bellybutton high with a sloped top. Spread out along the top were large sheets of paper covered in lines and notations that looked a lot like blueprints to my untrained eye. I walked over to them and started trying to make heads or tails of what I was seeing.

"I said you are fired, Evans."

"I don't think he cares," Gus said.

I stared at the drawings. They were a confusing mass of lines and labels with various forms of crosshatching. I had no clue what I was looking at.

"What is going on here, Mr. Harmon?"

"Come see for yourself, Company Man."

I turned away from the drawings to find Gus and Mr. Abbot at the window peeking through the blinds.

"What is the matter with the lights?" Mr. Abbot looked from the window to Gus then at me. "What are those men about? Are they ill? And where did all of those children come from?"

I stepped to the window and peeked through the blinds. Those weren't children. They were about the size of a four-year-old kid. But, that's where the resemblance stopped. Their herky-jerky movement first too fast then too slow was hard to sort out in the strobing flicker and flash of the floodlights but I knew where to look. Oversized heads and hands, between three and four feet tall, big noses and eyes the size of saucers. They were, or had been, Coblynau. Now they were dead and animated by something that hadn't quite learned how to control their central nervous system. Same went for those men jerking around the yard down there. When whatever it was learned how to drive, we were in very deep shit. Deep enough to drown in.

"Those aren't kids." I let the blinds close. "Gus, can you make heads or tails of these drawings?"

"Sure. Can't you?"

"I demand to know what is going on." Mr. Abbot stepped away from the window.

"Fine," I said. "You dug too deep. Or followed a coal seam into someplace that mankind was never meant to find. Or pissed off a witch or sorcerer or hoodoo man and they cursed you. Pick your poison. Those 'children' are or were Coblynau."

"You're shittin' me." Gus walked over to the mine plans and started leafing through them. "Them's Knockers?"

"They were." I nodded. "Like those *used* to be men down there."

"What are you going on about. You both sound like that man, Hartley. Blathering nonsense about Knockers and warnings."

"Maybe you should have listened." I stepped to the desk, retrieved the phone receiver from its cradle, and started dialing a number I swore I'd never dial again. "Why don't you sit down and shut up while I figure out how the hell we are going to survive till sunrise."

They picked up on the third ring. "Norfolk Freight and Foundry how may I direct your call?"

"Cut the crap, Janice." I stared at the partially reflective surface of the desk. I could nearly make out Mr. Abbot's face. I bet he hadn't been spoken to in that fashion in quite a while, maybe never. "I've got a situation."

"Stanley," she said. "I've been expecting your call."

"I'm not calling for my old job back," I said. "I've got a fully developed Stage Four Necroflux Incursion."

"How many?" Janice dropped the smarmy tone.

I picked up the phone, cradled the receiver in the crook of my neck, stepped to the window and peeked through the blinds. They'd stopped coming up out of the hole where the truck had vanished. I counted as best I could. "Twenty or thirty humans and another sixty cryptids, Coblynau."

"You call that a situation?" She sounded flummoxed. "That's a mother-loving catastrophe. How developed is their control?"

I watched the men and Tommyknockers jerk and stagger around the compound. Little groups had started to gather here and there, not moving, staring toward the big steel building where we were.

"Nodes are starting to form." I stepped away from the blinds. This was going from bad to worse.

"What are your assets?"

"Twenty coal miners and a company executive."

"That's not much to contain a Stage Four Incursion."

"I'm not looking to contain the damned thing." I shook my head and sat the phone back on the desk. I'd walked away from that life nearly a year ago. Desperate stands, understaffed and underfunded were no longer my bag.

"The closest asset is Freemont and she's in Philly tracking a doppelganger. You're the man on the scene."

"I quit, remember." I looked at Mr. Abbot. He stood there glaring at me. Maybe it was his good manners that kept him from blowing his top. Maybe he was still trying to work out who I was talking to.

"You're taking a hefty retainer stipend from The Company for just such an occasion. I'm reactivating you, Stan. As of right now," she paused and I could hear the shuffling of paper, "February 6, 1988, at 1837 hours, you are recalled from inactive reserve."

"Great." I glanced over at Gus, he was still leafing through those incomprehensible drawings. "I need close air support."

"You know damned good and well air assets have to be planned for and requested months in advance of an op. We can't just whistle up a couple of F-4s. What do you think this is, Korea? Where are you."

"Abbot Coal's number five mine just north and west of Hemlock Bluff, Virginia."

"You know the drill. Contain the threat then see to the safety of the civilians."

"I'm getting these civilians out of here. I'm not sacrificing a bunch of coal miners and their shit-ass boss to shut this down."

"That is not how we do business. Threat first, civilians second."

"That's not how *you* do business." I glanced at Gus and then over to Mr. Abbot. "You want to handle this your way then get your narrow ass out here."

"Do you think you can get them out and find a way to contain the threat?"

"Don't much matter what I think, it's what I'm going to do. Get me some kind of backup in here. This is going to get hairy fast." I hung up the phone.

"What is a stage four necroflux incursion?" I looked up from the shiny black plastic of the phone. Gus was leaning against the map case with his arms crossed. "I'm guessing from your conversation it's some kind of problem with the dead. I didn't follow that bit about nodes and what not but the way I figure it we got us a problem with some kinda haint or booger out there."

"You've got the gist of it." I sat on the edge of Mr. Abbot's desk. A headache was starting to grow right behind my eyes. "A necroflux incursion is egghead mumbo-jumbo to describe what happens when some dark force from beyond pushes into our reality starts taking a bite."

"Like Lovecraft?" Gus asked.

Mr. Abbot and I both stared at Gus nonplussed.

"Hey, just cause I say words like haint and booger don't mean I can't read." He shrugged. "Granny taught me to read and write before I was old enough for proper schooling."

"Don't be ridiculous." Mr. Abbot turned back to the window. "My grandfather knew Howard Lovecraft. The man was quite mad, you know."

The lights in Mr. Abbot's office began to flicker. I stepped to the window, pulled the blinds away from one edge and looked down at the yard. The floodlights had gone dark. They stood in the open, miners and coblynau, stock still and staring at the front of our building. They almost looked normal in the light from the three-quarters moon. The terrible details of their deaths blurred and softened by distance and shadow. They looked like a crew gathered for some announcement before going off shift. With slow deliberate unison, every head turned toward the window where Mr. Abbot and I stood. A dark presence looked at us through fifty-some-odd pair of glowing cobalt blue eyes. It was in full control now.

"Time to go." I let the blinds fall back into place. "Gus grab those drawings."

"What about Company Man there?"

"He comes with us."

"Like hell he does." Gus continued to lean against the map cabinet. "That pampered prick is the reason we're in this fix."

"I've had about all of th—"

"Shut up." I held up a hand to forestall any further talk from Mr. Abbot. I looked Augustus Harmon in the eye. "We don't leave people behind for the darkness. Even if they have it coming. You want to kick Abbot's ass once we get out of here, that's your business. Until we get out of here, keeping him alive is mine."

Gus and I stared at each other for long seconds. I'd seen his type before. Hard working, tough, smarter than he let on, practical. He shrugged and turned back the map cabinet and started rolling up the drawings.

I opened the stairwell door into chaos. Somewhere between leaving Abbot's office and reaching the bottom of the stairs the thing that inhabited those blue-eyed puppets had decided to come for us. The possessed miners and their Coblynau counterparts made short work of the barricade, pushed through the entryway, and on into the reception area in a tight mass of grasping hands and hungry mouths. Gore smeared more than one of the puppets' faces.

"Move!" A large man with hands like hams shoved me against one wall and bolted up the stairs nearly trampling Abbot. Behind him panicky men spattered with blood shoved past me and pounded up the stairs. The situation had just went from bad to catastrophic. In a matter of seconds all that remained in the stairwell were Gus, Mr. Abbot, and myself. Iron Mike, Tom Hollis, Donny, and Chris backed toward the stairwell door fending off the mass of animated dead with pick handles and in Iron Mike's case a fire ax.

I looked at Mr. Abbot and Gus. Gus shrugged and ran the rest of the way down the stairs, through the door and took up a place to the left of Tom Hollis anchoring the line. He didn't have a pick handle or a fire ax. Just hands hardened by decades of wresting coal from the earth. Abbot glanced from me to the fight and back.

"Hold this door open until I tell you otherwise." I reached into my coat and pulled my 1911 .45 from the shoulder rig.

"As you say, Mr. Evans." He stepped forward, grabbed the edge of the door, and gave me a curt nod. I'll give the old bastard credit. He didn't argue or hesitate.

If we were going to have half a chance at escape I needed to break contact and find a way back to the vehicles parked out front. The question was, how in the hell do you break contact in close quarters battle with the living dead?

Only one thing I could think of. I scooped up an abandoned pick handle from the floor and waded into the fight. Just in time too. One of those little glowing-eyed Tommyknocker puppets grabbed Donny's ankles and yanked him to the floor. Immediately more of the little ones started dragging Donny away into the crowd. I opened up with the .45 shooting three of the little bastards in rapid order. Donny kicked free of a fourth and scrambled back from the grasping hands.

"Fall back to the stairs." I shouted over the ringing in my ears.

No way I could tell if anyone had enough hearing left to understand. I dropped the pick handle, grabbed Tom, and shoved him toward the stairs and continued firing until the slide locked back. Hitting the mag eject I risked a quick glance around. The others were still hotly engaged, backing in an ever-tightening semi-circle toward the stairwell door. I kicked away one another of the little ones, retrieved a fresh mag from my coat pocket and slid it home.

One by one we fell back through the door to the stairs until Mr. Abbot, Iron Mike and I were the only ones left. My slide locked back, empty again. Pulling my third and final mag out of my coat pocket, slid it home, and thumbed the slide release.

I tapped Mike on the shoulder and jerked my head toward the stairs. He nodded, used the end of his pick handle to shove another grasping puppet stumbling into its fellows before slipping past Mr. Abbot onto the stairs. That left me and the old man to face the grasping mob. I glanced at him, nodded and emptied my last mag into the heads and faces of the oncoming mob in a near continuous roar of gunfire.

Mr. Abbot retreated to the stairs, I felt him grab the back of my collar and pull. I followed, backing through the tightening gap. My slide locked back, and the door closed. I reached down and turned the deadbolt lever before thumbing the slide release and holstering the smoking weapon.

"What?" I asked for the third or fourth time. Firing a .45 indoors without earplugs plays holy hell with your hearing. It wasn't the first or even the third time I'd had to do something that damned dumb—only the most recent. My ears were still ringing like a bastard.

"I said," Janice shouted. "You have an air asset arming and fueling at Naval Air Station Oceana."

"I thought you said that wasn't an option."

"I called in a favor."

"What did you get?"

"Intruder…" She paused for a moment. My stomach dropped.

"That's an airstrike, not close air support."

"No choice, Stan." Even through the ringing in my ears I could hear the resignation in her voice. I'd heard that tone more than once over the years—usually when being overrun and calling in danger close strikes. She'd written us off as casualties already. "You know the deal. Containment first."

"How long?"

"Three and a half, maybe four hours."

"Radio freq?"

"The usual VHF, UHF stuff. What do you have there on the ground?"

"Hey Gus, Tom," I waved the two miners over to me. "Are there any radios handy?"

"Like walkie-talkies?" Gus asked.

"Sure." I nodded.

"No walkie-talkies but we've got CBs in the trucks and the dozer," Gus said.

"Tell your bomb jockey to have his ears on, I'll be on channel thirty-nine, that's two-seven point three-niner-five on the HF radio."

"I'll pass the word. And Stan?" It was hard to tell but I thought I detected a pensive note in her voice.

"Yeah, Janice."

"Watch your ass. You can't cash retirement checks if you're dead."

"Right." I dropped the receiver in its cradle. "We need to huddle up, make a plan. Gus, Tom get everyone in here."

"Who said you was in charge?" Gus gave me a hardassed stare.

"No one." I shook my head. "Fact of the matter is that we need a plan if we're going to get out of here before an A-6 Intruder flies into this valley and blasts it to rubble. I'm the guy with the most experience getting out of these situations in one piece. You can take my say-so or you can take your chances with what's down stairs. Your call."

We gathered in the conference room across the hall. Gus spread one of the drawings from Mr. Abbot's office on the big table. Chris, the lanky kid with the big knife, held a flashlight so we could see. The power having finally given up somewhere around the same time the puppets broke through the first stairwell door. The ringing in my ears had died down enough I could hear them pounding on the door at the top of the stairs. It was a fire door, constructed of sturdy steel, they weren't getting through that for at least another twenty minutes or so.

"Now, what the hell do you mean there's an A-6 coming?" Gus looked up from the drawing and stared at me.

"It's a navy attack bomber."

"I know what an A-6 is." Gus pulled the right sleeve of his denim jacket back to reveal the globe and anchor tattoo of the United States Marines.

"I was with Third Battalion, Fifth Marines for two tours in Nam, fought the reds in Korea and the Japs in the Pacific before that."

"Will wonders never cease." Mr. Abbot said. "I was a second lieutenant with the second raider battalion, all the way from Guadalcanal to Okinawa."

"Great," I said. "We can have a reunion after we get the hell out of here."

"You still ain't answered my question." Gus let his sleeve drop. "And, come to think of it, who the hell are you to call in close air support, security man."

"I used to work for Virginia Department of Game and Inland Fisheries." I flashed him a grin. "And that's not a close air support mission headed our way. It's a sterilization strike. That A-6 is going to come in here fully loaded with 18,000 pounds of ordnance and scorch this little valley clean of everything living or dead. When that bird gets done the only thing left is going to be rubble and ash."

"So, we need to not be here when that happens." Tom Hollis said.

"That's right." I looked around the table. About half the men who'd been gathered out front were left. "We only have one way out of here and that's down the back fire escape."

"If those things ain't got it blocked off." One of Gus's boys said. He looked half out of his mind with fear.

"First order of business then is to scout our exit," I said.

"I'll handle that." Mr. Abbot raised his hand.

"I'll tag along." Gus eyed Mr. Abbot. "In case there's trouble."

"Good." I nodded. "Next order of business is arranging transportation and exfiltration." The problem was that anything with power in it when those animated puppets came pouring up out of the earth was going to be stone dead. Which meant every vehicle between the hole and the mine office.

"Hell," Chris spoke up. "There's a whole mess o' trucks out front."

"No good." I shook my head. "Notice how we don't have power in here?"

"Yeah." One of the other miners nodded.

"The thing that is puppeting your dead friends out there generates a negative energy field that makes electrical systems unreliable at best. The closer to the mass of puppets something is, the worse the effect."

"So, no trucks?" Donny asked.

"Nothing you arrived in," I shook my head. "Hell, nothing that had a charged battery in it when they passed by."

"What if the battery wasn't hooked up?" Iron Mike asked.

"Probably would be alright."

"The dozer's got a short to ground that drains the batteries overnight. We unhook the batteries before we go off shift."

"That would work." I nodded. "Where's it parked?"

"Other side of the processing plant." He tapped a spot on the drawing with an index finger the size of a bratwurst.

I stared at the drawing. It was starting to make sense now. Which was good news. The bad news was that the dozer was on the opposite end of the compound from us. We would have to transition an awful lot of open ground to get there. The alternative was to try and get far enough away on foot before that A-6 came growling up the valley and pounded us to ash.

"Gus, Mr. Abbot." I looked at the two old marines. "Get going on that recon. Everyone, make sure you're armed and ready to roll."

Gus and Abbot may have been more than a decade past their prime, but they managed to do a proper reconnaissance. We slipped down the back steps and skirted the compound, moving behind tool sheds and other outbuildings along the fence line, keeping quiet. Not that silence mattered all that much; the thing animating those puppets sensed life the way a blind man can sense the sun.

The problem, near as I could ever tell, was that on our side of the barrier between our universe and theirs they were at least half blind. More like an old blood hound with failing eyesight. It could sense us, where we were in general but not proximity, once we were more than twenty yards or so away. Separated by distance, it could only sense where we had been and the general direction in which we currently lay. Which meant it flailed around in a horrific game of existential Marco-Pollo hoping to get close enough to pick up our trail once again.

We made it to the dozer well ahead of the puppets' flailing search. Iron Mike got busy hooking up the batteries while Gus, Abbot, and I posted up in the shadow of the processing plant to keep a lookout. I checked my watch, we had about an hour and a half before the Intruder would be here at the earliest. Plenty of time.

"Hey, security man." Guss whispered and tapped me on the shoulder. "This looks like trouble."

I looked up from my watch.

The puppets stood in the open, between the mine office and the processing plant, probably fifty yards away. They no longer blindly bumbled about looking for us. Instead, they stood facing east swaying in the pale moon light; the men who'd went down in the lobby adding to their numbers.

"What are they doing?" Abbot asked.

"They've got the scent of larger prey," I said.

"How is that?"

"See the direction their all facing?" Gus asked.

"Yes." Abbot nodded.

"Town's that way, Company Man."

"Then we have to stop them." Abbot slipped back behind the processing plant and headed for the dozer.

I caught up with Abbot about halfway back to the dozer. I put a hand on his shoulder.

"Hold up a second."

"Yes." He turned and looked at me, then at my hand.

"You do remember that an A-6 is going to roll in here about an hour and a half from now and bomb this place flat?"

"Yes." He nodded.

"If we get close enough to engage them then they will stay engaged with us. We have no place to hide, no way to break contact and separate ourselves from them before the airstrike gets here."

"I know." Abbot nodded again. The motion short and curt. His tone and body language had shifted. I could see the man that lead marine raiders forty years ago. "Tell me, Mr. Evans, what happens if those…puppets make it into town?"

"They will kill every living thing that they can get their hands on and the entity that inhabits them will inhabit everyone they kill. Hell, if they get close enough to the cemetery it'll inhabit everyone ever buried there."

"It seems to me that our little group here is a small price to pay for stopping that atrocity, yes?" Abbot stared at me.

"Cheap at twice the price." Gus clapped me on the shoulder. "Hell, I didn't spend half my life fighting the Japs and the Reds to let some damned haint come along and wipe out my people."

I'd quit The Company and moved to the tiny town of Hemlock Bluff to get out of the desperate last stand business. And yet, here I was, getting talked into another one by two old marines. This was definitely the wrong week to give up drinking.

We gathered in the shadow of the dozer. I looked at my team. One equipment operator who could have been a stunt double for Andre the Giant, two old marines, three coal miners and me. Seven against a hundred or more corpses animated by some hungry entity from the universe next door. There wasn't one chance in a hundred that we were going to live through this.

"We need to grab and hold their attention for at least," I looked at my watch, "an hour-and-a-half, give or take a little.

"What happens then?" Chris asked. I couldn't see his face, not huddled here on the dark side of the dozer. I couldn't see any of their faces.

"A navy bird drops enough ordnance to kill everything in the holler," Gus said.

"Don't that mean us too?" Donny spat another stream of tobacco juice. How he managed to keep a dip in this entire time was beyond me.

"Yes," I said.

"I didn't survive two tours in 'Nam just to get blown to hell in my own damned holler." Donny spat again.

"If we don't pin them here, they will go to town, Mr. Powers." Abbot's voice was low and hard.

"My wife and kids are there." Donny spat again.

"Everyone's families are there, Donny," Tom Hollis said. "I don't want to die here anymore'n you do, but it beats letting folks get torn to hell by whatever those things are. I'll do it."

"Hell, I always knew I'd die in a mine," Chris said. "Just didn't figure on it being today."

"Look," I said. "It won't take all of us. Probably won't take but one or two. They aren't exactly thinking beings. Once a warm body gets close enough, they'll go for it like ants on a sugar cube."

"And if they catch that warm body?" Gus asked.

"Well…once they're done," I looked at Gus and shrugged, "they move on to the next, and the next until there aren't any more."

"I'm staying." Iron Mike put one shovel sized hand on my shoulder.

"Same here," Tom Hollis said.

"Well shit," Donny spat again. "You stayin', Gus?"

"Yep. Me n' the Company Man here," He jerked his head toward Mr. Abbot's thin outline. "We come to an agreement."

"Alright then." I looked around the circle wishing I could see their faces, meet their eyes. Men making this kind of sacrifice deserved that much at least. "We'll go after them with the dozer. Treat it like a tank. When they start to overrun us, we fall back on the mine."

The dozer lasted long enough for Mike to push up a berm between the puppets and the road leading east, down the holler and into Hemlock Bluff. As soon as they turned their attention on us the old dozer began to sputter and cough. Mike turned the heavy blade toward the advancing mob of puppets and started rolling forward. I think he was hoping to crush a few before the Dozer conked out. It didn't matter. By now, thing that inhabited the dead miners and Coblynau was completely at home and was pouring energy into them making them faster, stronger and more nimble than they had been in the mine office. They swarmed around and over the front of the dozer, fast.

"Fall back toward the mine." I slapped Mike on his hard-hat as I bailed out of the cab.

The dozer sputtered and died. Mike slid out of the seat and out the right side of the cab seconds ahead of six or seven puppeted Coblynau.

Damn, those things were getting faster.

We ran along one still tread, laying about us with our improvised weapons. Me with a busted drill rod and Mike with a massive wrench he swung one handed, crushing skulls and swiping puppets from our path like Ajax before the walls of Troy. There were a lot more dead miners than I'd initially seen come up out of the hole. Some were skeletons clad in scraps of meat and work clothes from back around the depression. Ol' Number Five must have claimed a lot of lives over the years. Good news was, we most definitely had their attention.

Mike and I backed toward the shaft house making a fighting withdrawal and doing a fair job of it. It didn't matter how much quicker our adversaries had become, they were still half blind and guided more by appetite than intelligence.

I risked a glance over my shoulder.

Nearly there. I could see Chris and Donny waiting to slam the door shut and give us a chance to hole up.

I turned back to the problem at hand in time to see several of the puppeted Coblynau duck under Mike's wrench and hit him in the knees. He adjusted his swing to deal with them and several more leaped onto his broad chest clawing and biting at him. I ran into the growing pile of puppets swinging and stabbing with my drill rod. It was no use. They swarmed over the big man like Army Ants on a goat carcass. It was all I could do to fight free of the grasping hands and snapping teeth. The big man went down punching and swinging that big wrench and cursing a blue streak.

Nothing engenders panic quite like being overrun. Worse, it's a tricky situation. In some cases, the right move is to stand and fight, in others it's run like a bastard jack-rabbit. If you stand when you should've run, you die. If you run when you should've stood, you die. I hadn't lived this long by picking wrong. Of course, there is a popular theory among my former co-workers that my continued survival is more a matter of luck than skill.

This had been a jack-rabbit situation when we were back on the dozer. The puppets were starting to swarm past the mound where the big equipment operator had been. I bashed one of the little ones caving its skull in and kicked another away before turning and sprinting for the shaft house door.

Being on the wrong side of forty for a few years now—and not quite as diligent in maintaining my physical fitness as I probably should have been—the only reason they didn't pull me down was Gus, Donny, and Mr. Abbot. The two marines and Donny stepped out of the shaft house and stood shoulder to shoulder bashing puppets with pick handles like they were in a batting cage. They separated long enough for me to pass through their line. Tom and Donny pulled me through the door. Mr. Abbot and Gus followed close behind.

"That…" I bent over and rested my hands on my knees gasping for air. "Was too damned close." Maybe there was something to that luck theory.

"Not unlike facing down a banzai charge." Mr. Abbot jammed a length of lumber against the rough planks of the door. Tom and Chris followed suit with several more.

"I ain't seen nothing like that since the Toktong Pass with Fox company back in '50 Gus said. There was a snap-click, and several bare bulbs came on illuminating the space.

"Shit." Donny spit a stream of tobacco juice into the dust of the shaft house floor. "Like being back in the Ia Drang with Sargent Major Plumley. Really wish that old bastard was with us. Then we'd show you jar heads a thing or two."

The two marines stared at Donny for half a second then Mr. Abbot threw back his head and laughed. Gus started chuckling and it wasn't long before Donny joined them.

The puppets were hammering the plank door of the shaft house and rattling the corrugated tin that covered its sides like a living hail storm from hell, knocking coal dust free to float in the now flickering lights. With a crack of splintering planks, the wall around the door started to give. The overhead lights began their mad strobing flicker.

Glancing around, I spotted the only line of retreat left to us. A large expanded metal cage that dangled over a hole into the bowls of the earth. I looked down at my watch. At least an hour and twenty to go before that bomb-jockey would be here and put all of this to an end. Way too much time.

"You know," I said. "They have this thing down in Australia where they put on SCUBA gear and get in these big metal cages with big hunks of raw meat tied to them. Then they lower the cages into the water and film the sharks coming to feed."

"Sounds like a dumbass way to die if you ask me." Chris shook his head.

"In the cage?" Tom asked.

"Yep." I nodded. "This shack won't hold for long and we still have a solid hour and twenty before our avenging angel gets here."

The shack held out longer than I had thought. We only had about fifteen minutes to go when they burst through the thin plank and tin walls of the shaft house. We'd spent a long hour and five minutes dangling over that hole in the earth listening to the puppets hammering and clawing away at the walls. The lights gave out somewhere around the half-hour mark, so we spent the rest of the time dangling in the night, telling war stories—mostly to keep our minds off what was coming. We were doomed men doing what doomed men have always done—killing time till it was time.

The puppets swarmed over the cage reaching with their hands, fingers poking through the gaps like hellish sea anemones. We crowded to the middle keeping out of their hungry grasp. More and more piled against the cage pressing and crushing their fellow meat-puppets tight against the expanded metal.

I checked my watch only ten minutes to go. This was going to work.

That's when it all went terribly wrong. In all the flailing and banging around one of the puppets must have inadvertently banged into the switch that activated the cage because the motors that controlled its descent whirred to life and down we went. A small army of recently and not so recently dead miners and Coblynau piled onto the cage as we descended into the hole making grotesque thumps and thuds as they landed.

"Son-of-a-bitch," Gus grunted.

Son-of-a-bitch was right.

The Company rescued us. When I say rescued, I mean they unearthed us, dug us out of the collapsed mine. I'll probably never know for sure what really happened.

My best guess is that the puppets damaged the hoisting gear or the cable or the braking mechanism who knows. What I do know is that we ended up falling in lurching jerking stages to the bottom with those blue-eyed pricks still clawing and grabbing for us the whole way. We managed to force the cage door open and retreat into the mine. Gus and Tom led us into a space they called the lamp room, not far from the bottom of the shaft. We holed up there determined to stay alive long enough for the navy to bury us with 18,000 pounds of ordnance and fire.

We sat there and waited for the puppets to break through the door. My watch must have gotten banged up in one of the falls because it had stopped so I had no way of knowing how long we sat there waiting for the world to end. That's when the knocking started. Little clicks and clacks like someone banging rocks together. First behind us then to one side or the other.

"Told you they were real," Donny said. I don't remember much of anything after that. None of us do. One minute we were down there in the lamp room with our mine lamps starting to flicker. The next, we were being pulled out of the hole where those puppets came up.

Donny and Chris both swear that the Knockers pulled us out of there after the bombs collapsed everything. Gus, Tom and Mr. Abbot have no clear memory either. Well maybe not Gus. When I came out of the debrief the old marine kept giving me the side-eye like we were sharing some kind of secret. I suspect the Coblynau felt bad for dumping those puppets in our lap. Or maybe we did what they wanted us to do and helped them deal with the puppet incursion. Who knows?

What I do know is that I'm back to work for The Company. Mine security is way too dangerous for my tastes. I started my new position three days ago as Middle Appalachia Chief of Station, located in the bustling metropolis of Hemlock Bluff. I have an office above the barber shop and a company car. Which is good, because that A-6 blasted my baby to scrap metal when they laid in the air strike. God, I loved that car.

# The Cutting Room Floor

## By: Derek Dunn

Darkness. Then light—feeble, yet sufficient, illuminating the deserted alley. Two concrete walls disappearing into the night sky. In the distance, sirens blared, horns honked, and dogs barked; but in this forgotten corner of the city, even the rodents were sleeping—*or hiding*. The air was still, save for the pitter-patter of rain on the metal dumpsters. Tiny splashes glistened on the blacktop like twinkling stars in the heavens.

A heavy boot—scuffed and worn—landed in a frothy puddle, breaking the silence like a thunderclap. The boot belonged to a man wearing jeans two sizes too large and a discolored white tee. He trudged to the nearest dumpster, lifted the lid over his head, then dropped it onto his back as he leaned in. Rummaging through the contents, the man didn't see the lid of the adjacent dumpster rise. It crept upward, reaching the height of a tin can before it stopped. The man delved deeper into his dumpster, feet no longer touching the ground. He let out a resounding whoop, possibly finding treasure in another man's trash. From the other dumpster, a gray skeletal limb emerged. Razor-like claws extended from the appendage, resembling neither hand nor foot but some monstrous combination of the two.

Nick Hernandez turned from the forty-two-inch plasma above the editing bay to watch the other two men in the room. It was the first time either of them had seen the edited scene. Nick had labored all day on the sequence, studying the storyboards and script notes, cutting various takes together. It was a pivotal scene. The one in which the titular monster made its grand entrance. To succeed as horror filmmakers, they had to instill fear in the audience, and this was their first opportunity to do so. This moment would set the tone for the rest of the film. Ricardo had been very clear on his vision, and Nick didn't want to disappoint the ambitious director. But he also wanted to put his own stamp on it. He may have had only one feature credit to his name, but it wasn't for lack of talent. *The Chupacabra* was slated for a wide release, so this was his time to shine. Nick needed to make a good impression, not just on the men in this room, but on every producer around town.

Ricardo De Luna, the film's director, sat beside him, back rounded, shoulders slumped, eyes hidden beneath the brim of his tweed cap. He twisted a ring around a finger on his right hand, both legs shaking. Nick grew more anxious the longer he watched him. From past observations, he knew a subtle, closed-mouth smile would indicate approval. So far, no smile.

Nick glanced back to the screen, rubbing his eyes. The monster crept across the wet pavement on all fours. Only its hairless, leathery legs were visible. Back to Ricardo, a slight scowl on his face. Had Nick used the wrong shot? Or was it the creature effects? He hadn't really questioned the monster's appearance before, but it did look like nothing more than a scrawny dog—slightly mutated or deformed. Perhaps he shouldn't have used that shot after all. Nick thought he'd created a suspenseful sequence, even throwing in some eerie temp music to add tension. But now, watching the scene with these two men, he doubted every decision.

Phil Newhart sat on the far side of the room, leaning back in his cushioned swivel chair, a clipboard in hand. The seasoned producer held a pen between two fingers the way one might hold a cigarette, inches from his pursed lips. Had this been the young Phil Newhart, Nick imagined he would indeed be sitting there with a cigar in hand, smoke escaping his mouth, the room hazy, faces indistinguishable. Even without the smoke, Nick couldn't read him. The man never smiled. His brow was furrowed under shaggy strands of gray hair, his eyes squinted. If Nick hadn't seen that look on Phil's face countless other times, he would have construed it as disgust. Watching the old man was pointless.

Phil had produced dozens of horror flicks since the late seventies. Nick grew up watching his sleazy B movies on late night cable while his parents slept just down the hall. Films like *Carni Clown*, *Jack's Lantern*, *Honeymoon Night Terrors*, and *Animal Hospital* were childhood favorites. Working for the legendary producer was a dream come true. And fortunately, for Nick's sake, it wouldn't blemish his resume. In the changing world of horror, Phil had abandoned his schlock roots and was now aiming for higher production value. Highbrow was in. Shock was out. In an attempt to rebrand himself and revive a dying career, he'd handpicked Ricardo De Luna to be his savior.

The hot-shot Mexican director was a bit of a computer whiz. He'd made a short film at the age of twenty-two about a Chupacabra terrorizing a family in an isolated farmhouse. With little to no budget, he'd managed to create exceptional CGI creature effects. The authentic looking monster, based on Latin American folklore, garnered much praise, and the three-minute film became a huge hit online. Phil had convinced the studio to throw millions of dollars at him to turn the thing into a feature.

Now, after a month-long shoot and one week to assemble the first cut, the film was coming together. Nick could finally dig into each scene and work his magic. It was his favorite part of the process. After all, films were made in the cutting room. Nick hadn't cut film—not in the physical sense—but he still adhered to that old adage. In fact, there was no film to cut for *The Chupacabra*. It'd been shot digitally—on location in Southern California, far from the farmhouse of Ricardo's short film. That setting had been replaced with an urban ghetto. The story now followed a migrant mother seeking shelter and protection for her two children, the carnivorous beast on her tail.

Nick watched the monster's front legs rise from the ground. The homeless man, still combing through the garbage, shrieked in pain. In the blink of an eye, he was yanked backward. The dumpster lid fell with a bang, and the man landed face first on the blacktop. He sluggishly turned his head, fear mounting in his eyes. The Chupacabra stood over him, growling. Saliva dripped from its fangs. Beady yellow eyes narrowed on the man, his face frozen in terror. A blur of motion. A snarl. Blood splattered across the screen. A wide shot, the camera pulling back, allowing the viewer to watch the Chupacabra gut the man, his body twitching and jerking in the filthy rainwater.

Nick stood and hit the spacebar on the keyboard. He considered hitting the lights too but decided against it. He'd never used the overhead lights in here, opting for the ambiance of the desk lamp instead. He fell back into his seat, stifling a yawn, hoping one of his superiors would break the silence.

Phil hadn't moved. Ricardo was leaning back, his arms and legs crossed, still staring at the image paused on the screen. Finally, the director turned to Phil and said, "So, what do you think of the monster?"

"It's not the worst thing I've seen."

Nick restrained himself from laughing. It was an ironic comment coming from Phil—though Nick doubted it was meant as such. Sure, the man was a legend. Many of his films were cult classics; but none were award-winning, and some were downright awful.

*The Roaches of Rio Grande* came to mind. It was a science fiction western from the early eighties featuring a forgotten western star and a soon-to-be forgotten centerfold model. They played—appropriately—an aging rodeo star and a prostitute stuck in a small Texas border town in the aftermath of a failed scientific experiment. Giant cockroaches were crossing the border from Mexico and causing mayhem throughout the Southwest. It was laughable at best and cringeworthy at worst. In today's politically correct world, it would have never gotten the greenlight. Copies still existed, but the film had largely been swept under the rug in recent years. Nick wondered if the social commentary had been intentional or if Phil and his crew had really been that ill-advised. He also wondered if Ricardo had seen it.

"It doesn't look right," the director said, scratching the stubble on his chin. "It doesn't look real."

"Well, I've never seen a real Chupacabra." Phil chuckled. If he was attempting to lighten the mood, it didn't work. Ricardo uncrossed his legs and leaned forward. He took a deep breath, paused as though words were on the tip of his tongue, then released all the air from his lungs.

"Is it supposed to look like a dog?" Phil said. "I thought it was supposed to be a big, scaly lizard creature, with bug eyes and shark teeth."

"We were going for more of a canine look, something more familiar, less alien."

"That's not what it looked like in the short film."

"We've talked about this," Ricardo said. "I don't want it to look the same."

"But that's what people are expecting."

"No, they're not." Ricardo removed the cap from his head. Dark knotted hair fell over his eyes. "Most people who watch this won't even know about the short film."

"Well, if you're going for dog-like, I think you've succeeded. That thing looks like a rabid Greyhound."

"It looks like a puppet," Ricardo said sharply.

"That's because it is." Phil matched his director's tone.

Nick didn't think it was that bad. It did look like a practical monster rather than a CGI one. But that was a Newhart staple. Phil was responsible for some of the most memorable—and often cheesiest—creature effects ever put on film. *The Chupacabra*, however, as Ricardo repeatedly reminded the crew, was aiming for a darker, grittier look. The tone was meant to be much more serious than previous Newhart productions.

"I mean…" Ricardo said, more coolly than before. "It's close. It's just not complete. There's not enough detail. There should be more spikes on the back, and the face…" He shook his hands in frustration, unable to articulate his vision.

"Well, you're the one who shot this. Why didn't you say anything before?"

"There wasn't time. The props team didn't deliver the final creature until the day of the shoot. I thought we could get some wide shots, shoot as much coverage as possible, then fix the rest in post."

"Fix it in post?" Phil looked as though he'd just heard the most preposterous thing ever. "That was your solution going into this?"

"That's what I do. I'm a special effects guy. I kept telling you we should have used CGI from the beginning."

"And I told you that horror audiences want to see the real thing." Phil tapped his pen against the clipboard, emphasizing his words. "*Trust me*, I've been doing this since before you were born. Your little CGI effects are great for YouTube, but that's not going to translate to the big screen."

"So, what do we do now?"

"We edit around it, right Nick?"

Nick sat up, surprised by the mention of his name. He nodded—or at least started to. He didn't want Ricardo to think he was taking the older man's side, but he definitely wasn't going to disagree with him.

"That's the magic of moviemaking," Phil said. "We don't need to see the whole monster. Maybe this is a case of less being more."

"Since when has that been your philosophy?"

**The room fell silent. Nick** eyed the door, wondering if he should leave the two men to duke it out. But to his surprise, Phil remained calm. He looked into the young director's eyes, letting his gaze do all the talking. **This obviously wasn't his first rodeo with a hot-headed director.**

"I mean, this is a monster movie," Ricardo said. "You should know better than anyone that people want to see the monster."

*Good save*, Nick thought.

"Then show it to them. It's not bad. Sure, it looks like a dog. But it will be the scariest dog they've ever seen."

"I can't. Not like that." Ricardo leaned forward and looked Phil squarely in the eyes. "Just give me time to add some effects."

Phil released a long breath. Nick imagined a thick stream of smoke fleeing his lips, blasting Ricardo in the face, a visual reminder of the old man's authority. Phil squared his shoulders, laid his pen on the clipboard, and met the director's eyes. "We're already over budget as it is. We have no money left for additional effects."

"So, this is just about money to you?"

"Love it or hate it, that's the business you're in."

"So as long as we stay within budget, you're fine releasing another crappy film?"

Nick slouched in his seat, hoping it would swallow him whole. Ricardo had gotten a pass on the first snide comment. Nick wasn't sure he'd be so fortunate this time. Phil lifted the pen, clasping it firmly between his fingers. He held it up, the pointed tip aimed at Ricardo's heart. Nick half-expected the old man to stab Ricardo. Apparently, the director did too. His chair rolled back, bumping into Nick's.

"I hired you because you made a great film," Phil said. "Not because of your CGI work. Your short film had more heart, passion, and energy than most Hollywood films today. That's what's going to make or break this movie. Not that monster."

Phil inched closer, the pen trembling in his hand. "So," he said, spittle flying from his mouth, "I suggest you keep your ego in check, consider what we have, and make the most of it." He reclined in his seat, the pen safely in his lap once more. "The footage looks great," he said encouragingly. "The monster's fine. We've hired the best crew in the business…"

Nick doubted the accuracy of that statement. He was honored, to be sure, but clearly, no one would have included him in a who's who of Hollywood filmmakers. His only feature credit was *Nighthawks*, a neo-noir mystery film following the misadventures of three Latin American teens in the San Fernando Valley. It was extremely low-budget, extremely independent, and had done little to advance Nick's career. When he landed *The Chupacabra* job a year and a half later, Nick was ecstatic—but equally shocked. It was less shocking, though, when he attended the first production meeting. Of the department heads, the only one who wasn't Hispanic—other than Phil—was David Elliott, who'd co-written the film with Miguel Sanchez. He wasn't going to complain, but Nick knew it was his name—not his merits—that had secured him the job.

"Okay," Ricardo said. "I'm sorry. I was out of line." He ran a hand through his greasy hair. "We'll cut around it. We'll get creative with the sound design—"

"Of course, you will," Phil said, standing. He was a short man, even shorter in his old age. His brown blazer hung loosely from his hunched shoulders, as though it might slip off his slender frame. "You two figure this out." He patted Nick on the back and stepped past him. "It's looking good, son. Keep at it."

The compliment caught Nick off guard. "Thank you…sir," he said, smiling. Praise from Phil Newhart warranted celebration—but not now. Ricardo was pulling himself up to the keyboard, ready to get to work. Still, Nick couldn't resist a discreet fist pump.

Phil walked slowly to the door, a slight limp in his step. Though it would have suited him, he held no cane. Once he'd left the room, Ricardo turned to Nick and said, "Oye. Tengo una idea." Nick wanted to roll his eyes. Sure, he was *half*-Mexican, but that didn't mean he spoke Spanish. His father was a Hernandez, his mom a Miller; Nick was raised in the Denver suburbs with his white cousins. *Nick* wasn't even short for **Nicolás. It was just Nick.** He was about as Mexican as sour cream on tacos.

"Okay," he replied in English. "Let's hear it."

"I think we can still save the movie."

"Do you really think it's that bad?"

"I just need some time to make the monster more real."

"Okay, but you told Phil we would just cut around it."

"Phil's out of touch. He doesn't know what he's talking about."

Nick didn't completely agree with that sentiment, but he supposed his loyalty should first lie with his director. "So, what do you need me to do?"

"Nothing."

The curt response hurt. He wasn't needed, just like those times he wasn't needed for pick-up basketball games as a kid. But he was already a part of this team. Now was his time to shine.

"Not yet, anyway," Ricardo added, softening the blow. "Take the weekend off. I'm going to stay here and work on the monster. When you come back Monday morning, I'll have something you can work with. It will look way better than that awful puppet."

"Okay," Nick said. He'd been staring at screens all week and needed to get his eyes on something else, **preferably the underside of his eyelids. But** could he rest while Ricardo was here, undoing the puzzle he'd pieced together all week?

Monday morning couldn't have come any sooner. Nick arrived at the studio before sunrise, which was not unusual for him. What was unusual, however, was Ricardo's car in the otherwise empty lot. Hadn't the guy worked all weekend? Why was he here so early? Nick exhaled a sigh of disappointment. Now he'd have to work with the director looking over his shoulder.

The door to the editing suite was unlocked. White light spilled over the desk from the LED lamp. There were signs of Ricardo: empty take out boxes, soda cans, a crumpled bag of Doritos, crumbs, the smell of body odor and stale food—but no Ricardo. "Come on, man," Nick said, reaching down to lift a swivel chair off its back. Ricardo may have been a filmmaking genius, but he was a slob. This was just the thing a diva director would do. Make a mess and expect some intern or assistant to clean it up. Well, Nick was no one's assistant, but he wasn't about to work in this mess either. He grabbed a small trash can and swept the crumbs off the desk. There were still chips in the bag, so that could stay. Looking around, Nick half expected to see Ricardo passed out on the floor. He wasn't there— but something else was. Candles. About a dozen of them, placed in a circle in the middle of the room. Some lay on their sides. Others stood upright, bound to the floor by melted wax.

*Huh*, Nick thought. *What was Ricardo doing in here? Did he have a late night rendezvous, and things got a little wild?* The scene might suggest such a thing, but Nick couldn't imagine it. Not Ricardo. The man was a workaholic. He wouldn't have time for pleasure.

Nick sat down and rolled himself to the desk. "Seriously?" he said, his shoes sticking to the hardwood floor. Nick felt like he was back at the old dollar theater he frequented as a teen, the one that apparently had no janitor. He spread his legs wide, placing his feet safely beyond the sticky mess. *One more thing to clean up.* But not now. First, Nick wanted to see what Ricardo had done. As he waited for the machine to boot up, Nick reached for the Doritos. Beneath the bag was a book he hadn't noticed before. It was a composition book. *El Conjuro* was written on the cover in bold, black ink.

Nick flipped through the pages. They were filled with handwritten text, all in Spanish. Was this a translation of *The Conjuring* script? It wasn't written in screenplay format. So, maybe Ricardo's notes on the film? He had mentioned it as a major influence.

The dual monitors came to life, casting a stream of light across the room. Nick set the book down and glanced at the editing timeline. It had been left open, set to the beginning of the scene they'd reviewed on Friday. Nick hit play.

Rain fell on the dark alley. The homeless man's boot splashed in the puddle. He dove into the dumpster. The lid next to him opened. It remained open … but nothing happened.

Nick bit his lip, a blank look on his face. He scrolled back a few frames and played it again. The creature's arm should have emerged from the dumpster—only it didn't.

"What in the world?" Nick said. He double-checked the clip to see if it had been altered.

It hadn't. This was the original footage.

He let it play on.

The homeless man rummaged through the dumpster, whistling a cheerful tune. Close-up of the wet pavement, the camera panning, following the movement of…

Nothing?

The monster was gone. Its legs should have been creeping across the pavement. But they weren't. They had completely vanished. Had Ricardo removed them? Why would he have done that? The close-ups were fine. The legs looked good. It was the rest of the body he'd complained about.

Nick continued watching. The homeless man was yanked from the dumpster, dropped to the ground, then left convulsing, no attacker in sight.

This was too weird. The edit hadn't been changed at all. The footage wasn't altered. The file names remained the same. It was all as Nick had left it. The scene played out as before—only the monster was gone, as though it had never been captured on camera.

Nick reached for his phone. He needed to check with Ricardo about this. If he had removed the monster, where was the new one? The footage was useless without it. He dialed Ricardo's number. It went straight to voicemail. After leaving a quick message, Nick continued scrolling through the timeline.

"No way," he said, his eyes growing wider. The monster was gone, completely erased from the entire film. Every scene was there, unchanged. The actors, the sets, the props—all of it there, moving and being moved, acting and being acted upon, all as though an invisible force were present. It wasn't possible, was it? Ricardo couldn't have done all that in one weekend. And if he had, then why? He'd taken the monster out of his monster movie. Even if Ricardo didn't like the puppet, some of that footage was still usable. Nick was left with so many questions but not one answer.

His phone buzzed, just once.

A text from Ricardo? No, an email notification—from Nick's bank.

He called again. No answer. As Nick hung up on Ricardo's voice recording, the plasma screen flashed. A video started to play. But the footage was not from the movie. It was footage shot in this room.

Ricardo was sitting in a chair, his eyes closed, candles lit in a circle around him. An image of the Chupacabra was displayed on the monitor before him. Ricardo uttered a phrase. Something in Spanish, Nick thought, though he wasn't sure. The screen flickered off, then back on. The Chupacabra was moving—not on the screen, but out of it. Ricardo didn't see it. He was repeating the phrase again and again, his eyes still closed. Nick wanted to shout at him. Tell him to stop. But it was no use.

The monster crawled over the desk, studying Ricardo. It rose to its hind legs, its beady yellow eyes narrowing. This wasn't just any Chupacabra. This was the puppet. The one from their film. Only it was real. It was alive!

Nick felt sick to his stomach. He couldn't help Ricardo. He couldn't look away either. The monster sprung forward, knocking the chair back, sending Ricardo to the floor. It reared its head, shrieked, then plunged into Ricardo's shoulder. Blood spewed from the wound. The man screamed, his arms flailing. The creature's jaws clamped tighter. It held fast, unwavering, until the man struggled no more. With flesh still in its mouth, the Chupacabra looked up, peering through the screen, locking on to Nick's eyes.

The screen went black.

Nick's heart raced. He couldn't move, his stomach too heavy. He would never be able to unsee what he'd just witnessed. What was that, anyway? A supernatural snuff film? Surely it was just Ricardo testing his CGI monster. But it was the puppet, not the creature the director had envisioned. And where did that video come from? Who'd played it just now?

Nick tried Ricardo's number once more.

*Bang!*

He dropped the phone and whirled around. Something was back there. In the darkness. By the metal shelves. Though his legs felt like jelly, Nick lunged toward the near wall. He flipped the switch; the place lit up like the red carpet. Through squinted eyes, Nick searched the room. It was so small in the light. So lifeless. His eyes scanned over the dusty shelves, cabinets, and cables until settling on a tweed cap hanging by the door. It was Ricardo's. His favorite cap. He wouldn't have left without it.

"Ricardo, are you in here?"

Nick stepped toward the tall cabinet on the back wall, then stopped short. His shoe was stuck. Stuck in—

*No, it can't be...*

He stumbled backward, almost falling, the world a blur around him. The floor was red. Smudges under the desk, around the candles. Spots here and there like giant paw prints.

Nick should have run, but he couldn't. His eyes were glued to the display screen. It was playing another video. He was there, on the screen, standing as he was now, the room a reflection of its current state. He tilted his head. The image mimicked his movement. This was live.

A cabinet door opened behind him. Nick turned. The door stood ajar, but nothing was there. He looked back to the screen and froze. The monster was right behind him, standing on its hind legs. Nick closed his eyes, hoping the thing would disappear. *This can't be real*, he thought. *It can't—*

The Chupacabra released a deathly, guttural growl, its hot breath stinging the back of Nick's neck. This was real—as was the chance he would die right here, in the same spot as Ricardo.

Finally, Nick found the courage to move. He raced for the door, but the thing was too fast. Its claws dug into his calves. Nick screamed and fell to the floor, then rolled onto his back, lifting both arms in time to block an attack. He couldn't see the monster, but it was there, drooling all over his face. It was growling, yapping at him, hungry for more blood.

Nick grabbed it by the shoulders, using all his strength to hold it back. He kneed it in the stomach. The creature whimpered and pulled back, giving Nick a chance to kick it. Rising to his feet, Nick glanced at the screen. The Chupacabra was crouching a few feet away. Nick grabbed the chair and swung it in the monster's direction. The makeshift weapon could fend it off for a while, but how could he defeat it? The thing wasn't real, not in this world anyway.

*What if…* He looked at the plasma screen again, not to find the monster, but to take aim at the screen itself. He hurled the chair, shattering the display panel. The video disappeared. The Chupacabra, however, was still growling.

"Crap," Nick said, taking a step back. Maybe that wasn't such a good idea.

He fell back to the floor, the monster upon him once more. Nick threw punches, landing a few, but the thing wouldn't relent. Its claws tore into his shoulders. Nick screamed. His arms trembled. Fighting against the pain, he held the creature back. But it was too strong. Its rancid breath grew heavier on his sweat-drenched face.

Looking up, he saw the hard drive attached to the computer. It was within reach, but Nick's arms were the only things keeping the Chupacabra from dissecting his face. He couldn't hold it off forever though. This was his chance. He took a deep breath, reached one arm out as fast as he could, then yanked the hard drive free. With no time to spare, Nick slammed it against the monster's head, beating it again and again. The Chupacabra withdrew little by little, until finally, Nick freed himself of its grasp. Rising to his knees, he lifted the hard drive high over his head, then brought it down on the hardwood floor like a hammer. It cracked. Pieces spilled out. Nick jumped to his feet and stomped on it.

The door flew open; a security guard walked in. Nick gave him no heed. He continued crushing the hard drive, smashing it into smithereens.

"What are you doing?" The voice was Phil's. He stood behind the guard, gaping at the scene before him.

"It's okay." Nick took a knee, trying to catch his breath. "It's gone."

"Are you crazy? What have you done?"

"I destroyed it."

Phil clenched his fists, the veins on his neck looked ready to burst. His eyes darted across the floor, examining the remnants of the hard drive, the ruined fragments of his film.

"Get out! Get him out of here."

The security guard grabbed Nick by the arm and lifted him up.

"You're through here. I'll make sure you never work in this town again!"

Nick didn't protest. He left the room willingly.

# Frogs of Rain

By: Douglas Goodall

**K**insey sat in her patrol car at the Sonic Drive-In, waiting for her order. She watched the carhops skate by and wondered why they never strayed from the steel umbrella. She would, if she worked here. She'd skate right under the edge of the awning, in that contrived waterfall, until she was soaked. The rain pounded on the back of the patrol car, but only a little mist wafted in the open window. It wasn't enough. It was never enough.

A waitress, one of the Ward kids, skated up with her tray and stuck it on the car window. Kinsey thanked her, tipped her, and waited just long enough for her to turn around. Ignoring the burger and fried pickles, she grabbed the slushie and rubbed the condensation on the sides of her uniform. Then she sipped a little of it. It was cool and refreshing.

The worst drought in decades struck last summer. To Kinsey, it was torture. She stopped eating at places like this and just went home for a half hour bath. Then last month it rained gently every weekday afternoon, like clockwork. There was no rain for a few days, but there was a tension building in the air, growing almost painful over the weekend, and today it was finally released.

Kinsey had finished her burger and was nibbling at the fried pickles when she saw someone stumble into the parking lot. A young man, soaking wet, dazed and possibly intoxicated, wearing a white shirt with pink vertical...no, bleeding enough from his forehead that the rain isn't washing it all away. She reached for her radio. "Car 4, at the Sonic on highway 30, 10-52, got a man here with a head wound. 10-6."

"10-4."

She had to move so many times. Finding another job was easy. No one checked references or school records. But she wished all the city police, county sheriffs, and highway patrols used the same code. Kinsey got out and approached the man, who was talking at the passenger window of a parked car. "I need—I need a...a...tow truck," the man was shouting to a car full of stunned teenagers, "or a...a...tow truck."

"I'm Officer Swanson, you look like you need help."

The kid – once she got closer, he looked like he was still in high school – turned and stared at her. "Help, yeah, my car, uh, the frog ran off."

"Why don't you come and sit in my car," Kinsey said. "An ambulance is on the way."

"No, I don't need a…a…tow truck. Dad's gonna be pissed. Can't believe a frog." He was mumbling, and it was hard to make out what he was saying over the music. The Sonic was blaring "Simply Irresistible," but it was losing to "I Told You So" from the teen's Cutlass.

"I can call a tow truck for you. Please come and have a seat in my car, okay?"

He shook his head, then shook his whole body, like a dog. "I didn't do it."

"I'm not saying you did anything, sir. It looks like you hit your head."

"Yeah, yeah," he said, touching his forehead. "All the way out the window."

He took a stumbling step towards the patrol car, and Kinsey took his arm, guiding him gently into the back seat. She reached for the radio again and asked for an update on the ambulance. It was on its way. She got out her first aid kit, opened a pack of gauze, and went back to the rear door. She pressed the gauze up against the young man's head. "Here," she said, "lie back in the seat. Can you keep this pressed on your forehead?"

He pressed it to his head, then took it off and looked at it. "Maybe I need an ambulance," he said, and pressed it back on his head. There were abrasions on his hands and small rips in his shirt.

"There's an ambulance on the way. Can I see your driver's license?"

"What? Oh, yeah." He reached into his pocket and handed her his whole wallet. He was Edward Snider, nineteen, from Cincinnati. "Don't you want to get back in the car? Kinda funny talking to you squatting in the rain."

"Don't worry about me. Can you tell me what happened?"

"I was driving, and the frog just jumped out. It was huge. Big and sad. I swerved and went all the way out the front."

"You mean through the windshield?"

He nodded a little.

"Where were you headed?"

"Going to see my dad."

"Where does your dad live?"

"Salem."

"You didn't take the interstate?"

"No, too many cars. Makes me nervous."

"Have you been drinking?"

"I had a 7-Up in my car."

"Where did the accident occur?"

"The frog jumped out on purpose. Wanted me to hit him."

"Can you tell me where your car is? And what kind of car is it?"

He pointed back down highway 30, the way he came. "A Chevy. Riverside Red."

Kinsey heard the ambulance and was happy to release him to the paramedics' tender mercies. She stood in the rain as long as she could, breathing deeply and naturally, and then drove up highway 30. She found the wreck just past the bridge over Rag Creek. No one else was around. She didn't bother with a flashlight.

Edward was lucky to be alive, even luckier to be driving a Sting Ray. He'd run off the road and hit a tree, probably going at least 60. The front was wrecked, but the doors were closed, and the windshield was intact. The top was on, but slightly open. There was a dent and blood on the top frame of the windshield. Edward must have hit the top and forced it open on the way over the windshield. Kinsey tried to visualize how that happened, and decided it was a matter for the Sheriff. Beyond the front of the car, there were shallow tracks where he must have landed, and footprints leading up to the road. The rain was lightening up. Too bad.

She was about to head back to her patrol car when she smelled something. Her nose was always better in the rain. She turned and walked downstream, following Rag Creek as the rain nourished it. Usually sluggish, the creek reveled in the fresh rain after so long a dry season, and the current rushed as much as it dared.

She found what she expected. A girl. Young. Normal. Freshly dead. Wearing a shirt and sweater, but no bottom. Her legs wrapped around a thick tree root, and even the rising waters wouldn't wash her away soon. Her hands were missing. The edges of her forearms were ragged, as if they were bitten off. Kinsey went back to her car and called it in, both the body and the car. Her bath would have to wait.

She went back down to the creek and looked under the bridge. There were handprints and footprints in the mud. Some were human, a bit on the small side. Some were wide, thin, splayed. She didn't need to be a detective to see what had been going on.

She wanted to strip and soak in the river, to revel in its renewal of life. But she just stared at the prints until the rising water washed them away. Sometimes it was good to be alone, but sometimes it was good to imagine you weren't alone.

Once the first deputy arrived, everything was routine. Sheriff Merritt was a jerk when he got there, but she was used to him. He yelled at her for contaminating the scene, as if she could have done anything else. The Sheriff would handle the investigation. Speeding tickets were more her business. She didn't get home until the wee small hours. She filled the tub, poured in some salt, stripped down, and sighed as she slid under the water, careful to keep one leg on each side of the divider she'd installed.

She woke, still in the bath, to her alarm. She had to go on duty at noon. She dressed, first the leggings, always leggings, then the silk scarf. They were her greatest expense but an absolute necessity. She clipped her fingers and put on gloves. Only then did she put on a fresh uniform.

She arrived at the hospital an hour before her shift started. The nurse at the front desk told her Edward's room number and that his doctor would meet her there.

Edward was awake and bandaged. He seemed startled when she arrived. "Uh, am I in some kind of trouble?"

"How are you feeling?" Kinsey asked. "Do you remember me from last night?"

"No, I was....my car ran off the road. I can't remember the accident very well, and then nothing until this morning. Isn't that odd, like I was here the whole time, but part of my life didn't happen. So how are you feeling?"

"I'm doing well, thanks. Can I—"

"It's just you're breathing kind of funny."

Kinsey tried to breathe deeper and slower in the sterile, conditioned air. She got out her notepad. "It's just asthma. Can you answer some questions?"

"Sure, sure."

"So you're from Cincinnati?"

"Yeah."

"And why did you come down here?"

"I was going to visit my dad."

"Did someone contact him and tell him what happened?"

"Yeah, he was here this morning."

"Good. So what made you lose control of your car."

"Uh, I don't know. Maybe a deer? It ran in front of my car, and I swerved, and they said I hit a tree."

"Last night you said it was a frog."

"I'm not crazy," he said. "The doc said I must have imagined him."

"Well, humor me. What did the frog look like?"

"Uh, he was." He stared out the window. "Look, the doc said I just hit my head pretty hard. I must have dreamed it."

Kinsey put her notepad away. It made people more comfortable, but she'd remember it either way. "I'm asking because someone else saw footprints, sort of frog-like footprints, but they were huge. If you saw something strange, I won't think you're crazy, and I won't tell the doctor."

"Okay," he said, turning his head to one side and staring out the window. "Well he was sort of a man and sort of a frog. About five feet tall. He walked on his hind legs, like a man." He turned to face her again. "They were like frog legs, you know, like backwards."

"Uh-huh. Go on."

"He had a sort of frog-like face, and not much neck, but he had a head. Like you know a frog's head is all part of its body?" Edward moved his hands down the sides of his head. "He had a wide sort of frog-like head, and a big mouth, but he had a head. He reminded me of..."

"What did he remind you of?"

He didn't respond at first, only looked up at the corner of the room. Kinsey waited.

"In Loveland, back in Cincinnati, someone there saw a frog-man. A few other people said they saw it, too. They started calling it the Loveland Frog. I didn't think...I thought it was a joke, I mean my friends used to joke about it sometimes."

"Well," Kinsey said, "if it's the Loveland Frog, he's a long way from home. And he jumped into the road in front of your car?"

"Yeah, I saw something on the side of the road and wasn't sure what it was. Then he jumped right in front of my car." Edward leaned forward in the bed, hunched over, and put his arms on his knees. "I think he wanted me to hit him. He was looking right at me. He looked...I don't know, kind of sad? It's a miracle I didn't hit him."

"It's a miracle you survived. Do you remember much of the crash?"

Edward lay back down and shook his head. "They said the car was totaled. I thought my dad would be more upset about it."

"Did you see a young woman there?"

"What? No. Just the–" Edward cleared his throat and rubbed the back of his neck. "The frog."

"Did you hear any screams or smell anything strange?"

"No. I had the windows up. It was raining."

Kinsey stood up. "Do you know anyone here other than your father?"

"Not really. Not well. He moved down here just a year ago, after the divorce."

The door to the room opened, and an older man peered around. "Officer Swanson?" he asked.

"Yes."

"I'm Doctor Pittman. You had some questions about this patient?"

"Yes, thanks," Kinsey said, and turned back to Edward. "Get well, and don't drive so fast next time, okay?"

"Okay."

Outside the room Kinsey said, "Did you run any toxicology on him?"

"Yes and no. He wasn't drunk. The lab here at the hospital can't test for much. We can request a comprehensive panel if you need one, but it will take a week or more. He didn't strike me as being under the influence, just confused. He hit his head quite hard."

"How bad was his head injury?"

"The cut was deep and he has a concussion. A rather serious concussion, but he's out of the most dangerous phase. I think he'll fully recover."

"Good to hear. Well, if he wasn't drunk or on drugs, I don't think he'll be charged with anything. Thanks for your time."

Kinsey left the hospital and saw it was almost noon. She went to her car and went on duty. There were no calls, so she sat in the car, filling out reports and writing down Edward's responses from the interview. It was cloudy again, and Kinsey looked out the window, wishing for rain. On days like yesterday she loved the job. She could wait around a corner or drive the major roads, with the window down, until the dispatcher called or someone went by speeding. Then she'd pull them over, get out and relish the rain. If only the ticket book was waterproof, it would be perfect. That was half the problem with paperwork. She couldn't do it in the rain or in the bath.

Early evening she drove to Jessie's Deli and went on break. It was a popular place for both the county police and the highway patrol. Cheap, fast, and close to the major roads.

"Kinsey! Come on over," Saul Saunders said. He worked for the Sheriff's Office. She liked him, but she worried that he liked her.

After their food arrived, Saul said, "So you're the one who found the body last night?"

Kinsey nodded. "Yeah."

"Do you think the car accident is related?"

"No, I interviewed the kid. The driver. I was interrupted before I got into that line of questioning, but I don't think he killed her or even knew she was there." Kinsey fidgeted with her straw. She rubbed her hands down the condensation on the iced tea, then dried it off on her side. It was better than nothing. "Any idea when she died? I didn't do more than look at it in the dark, but it seemed fresh."

"Yeah, the coroner's report isn't out, but Jim told me she died in the afternoon. Probably drowned, but she has some strange marks on her ribs and legs." Saul drew in a breath and let it out slow. He started bouncing his knee, shaking the table slightly. "I interviewed some people today, but the closest houses aren't that close. No one heard or saw anything."

"Did you ID the girl?"

"Yeah, Jessica Davis. Lilly's kid. Was going to graduate this year."

Kinsey put her sandwich down. "Lilly's kid? That's a shame."

"Yeah," Saul said and looked out the window. "Had a rough life, probably, and then this."

"I know. Her mom called a few times when Jessica went missing. Said she was disappearing after school. It started last year, but then she went to visit her grandparents all summer. A month or so after school started, she was going somewhere afterwards, not coming home until five or six. Lilly didn't know where she was going. Probably didn't care. Sorry, that was cruel."

"No, I understand. She cares, but not enough to clean herself up."

"And now she has less reason." Saul looked at his half empty plate. "Hey, you're off work tomorrow, right?" Kinsey froze mid-bite. "So am I. Want to go to the history museum in Millburn? You like weird stuff, and they have a Native American exhibit. Jim said they have some weird stuff."

"As long as it's not a date."

"Not a date, I swear," Saul said, raising his hands in surrender. "I don't know what you don't see in me, but you made that clear."

Kinsey let out a long breath and smiled. "I'd like to go, then. Gives me something to do."

"How about after lunch? Like 2 PM.?"

"I'll see you there."

When her shift was close to its end, she drove back to the bridge. She went off duty, got out, and walked down to the creek. The car had been towed. There weren't barely even tire tracks left. Only a few flashes of red in the grass showed it was ever there. The sky was clear, and the creek was back to its usual quiet self. She heard the soft trickle of slow water and the occasional fish popping up to the surface. There were no new handprints under the bridge.

She woke in the bathtub again, but she wasn't working today. No need for an alarm. She lounged about and snacked on crackers and sardines, eventually dressing in the casual clothes she only used to get groceries.

Saul was already at the museum, waiting by the door. "I'm glad you came," he said. "I wanted to see this exhibit, but, you know, didn't want to go alone."

"I get it."

He looked at her hands. "It's cool how you always wear gloves. Elegant, you know?"

"I'm not trying to be fashionable," she said. "I just like them."

The exhibit had the usual arrowheads, recreated pottery, and dioramas of glass-eyed savages staring at nothing. She found it fascinating how eager people always were to mold the sparse artifacts into a sanitized narrative, one in which the monsters were just myths, and people long ago knew less. Kinsey knew better. One display caught her eye. It was a collection of tobacco pipes, each one carved into an animal. There was an owl, a raccoon, and a frog-man. She read the panel.

These pipes were found in the Burford Mound after a flood, and are similar to those of the Hopewell Culture in Ohio. Archaeologists believe they were used in shamanic and funerary rituals. These animal motifs are common to carvings throughout North and Central America.

"Thinking of taking up smoking?" Saul asked.

"No, just looking at these pipes. They're interesting. Detailed."

"Yeah, I've often wondered if there was some connection between the mound builders and the Aztecs and Mayans. The frog pipe looks like a Tlaloques."

"A what?" Kinsey asked.

"A Rain Dwarf. A kind of half-frog that helped Tlaloc bring the rain. It's an Aztec thing. Tlaloc's always creeped me out, but I was real interested in him as a kid."

"Kids often are."

"Into Tlaloc? No, I was weird."

"I mean, into things that creep them out."

"Oh, yeah. The experts don't think there was any connection. But they look similar. And that's not all."

Saul preached on the many links between North and Central Pre-Columbian America. Kinsey nodded and smiled. As they were leaving, Kinsey felt a tinge of regret. She enjoyed the museum trip and even enjoyed Saul's company. But she knew what would happen if she indulged.

Harvey Merritt interrupted them. "If it ain't Saul and McKinsey, McKinsey and Saul. You on a date or what?"

"No," said Kinsey, "we're not—"

"Sheriff Merritt. We're not dating," Saul said. "We just met here."

"Just met here," Harvey said, "uh-huh. No, you wouldn't date a fellow officer, would you, not even a Sheriff. You're too good for us. Too pretty."

"Hey," Saul said, "that was uncalled-for."

"And you, Saul, I'd think with a murder on our plate, you'd be following up leads, even on your day off."

"There's not much to follow up on, Sheriff. We talked to all the neighbors, all her relatives, half the high school. We're waiting for the coroner's report."

"We're not going to solve it with that attitude," he said, and stormed into the museum.

"Your boss always cheers me up," Kinsey said.

"What did you do, turn him down?"

Kinsey nodded. "Exactly. Almost my first day on the job. How do you stand him?"

"He mostly stays out of the way, unless the media or some bigwig gets involved. He doesn't have to be nice or even do a good job. He just has to kiss ass and get re-elected."

"I guess."

"I had a nice time," Saul said. "I won't press you, but let me know if you ever change your mind."

"I won't," she said, looking down. "As much fun as it would be to piss Harvey off."

"You don't want to get him really pissed off. Well, I'll see you at Jessie's Deli tomorrow or Friday."

"Sure, see you there."

Kinsey wanted to go home but stopped by the library in Millburn. There was a long line of people, mostly parents with children, waiting to check out, so she wandered the aisles until she spotted an older woman rolling a cart of books.

"Sorry to bother you," Kinsey said.

"Oh, it's what we're here for, you know. You can call me Mrs. Shaw, though Mr. Shaw passed years ago. What can I help you with?"

"Uh, do you have any books on the Aztecs?"

"Aztecs? Well it wouldn't be here. Don't you know how to use a card catalog?"

Kinsey shook her head. "I didn't go to a regular school. I was an orphan."

The librarian held her hand up to her chest and took a step back. "Regular or not, you should have learned to use the card catalog before you graduated."

"The orphanage didn't have a library," Kinsey said. There weren't graduates either, she thought, only survivors.

Mrs. Shaw shrugged. "Come along. I'll show you how to use it."

She led Kinsey to the card catalog and explained how it worked while expertly flipping through it. "This is a small library, you know. You can't expect too much. Now if you wanted to know about Egyptians, I could help."

"Do you have a large Egyptian collection?"

"Goodness, no," Mrs. Shaw chuckled. "At least not here in the library. I have quite a collection at home. I can read Egyptian—Old, Middle, and New—and in heiroglyphic, heiratic, and demotic."

"That's quite impressive," Kinsey said.

"It's just a hobby. Ah, here we are. Aztecs." Mrs. Shaw examined several of the cards in detail. "Now I remember. We had books on the Aztecs, but they were all checked out by William Ward."

"Do you know where I could find him? Or when they're due?"

"Bill ran away from home years ago. He must have taken the books with him. They weren't at his house or with his school things. My youngest was in his class. His sisters are all nice, just lovely young ladies, but he was a weird kid. He'd eat anything for a quarter. Banana peels, bugs, a whole egg, shell and all. We do have one book on the Aztecs. I don't know if it would be of any help. It's in the children's section."

"It's better than nothing," Kinsey said.

"I'll have to get it for you. It's not on the usual shelves. Martha reads all the kids books we get. Some of them are not really suitable for children. She puts them in the back in case someone wants them, but she doesn't want them just out where anyone can see them."

The librarian led her through the children's section and unlocked a closet door. She rolled a trash can out of the closet. The closet held cleaning supplies, but there were a few shelves and maybe a hundred books. Behind them in the children's section, another librarian was in the middle of reading a book to three kids. Kinsey couldn't help but listen. The book was about a frog telling a fish about all the wonderful things he saw outside the pond. The fish tries to be a frog, but can't breathe. The frog pushes the fish back in the pond and the fish says the frog was right. "Fish is fish, and frog is frog."

"But what if the frog isn't a frog?" Kinsey whispered.

"Here it is," said Mrs. Shaw, holding out a book. The title was *Appalling Aztecs.*

Kinsey flipped through the book, which was true to its title. It had many depictions of human sacrifice and severed body parts. There were two pages on Tlaloc. The first was a large, stylized drawing of five versions of Tlaloc pouring out water and sometimes little red things. Fish? Maize? Below each Tlaloc sat a woman, mouth open, staring upwards. Water poured into the woman's mouth. On some panels she looked pleased, while on others she looked distressed. The next page had four figures, one on each corner, which had green skin, a fat somewhat frog-like body, and a stylized head. And teeth. Definitely teeth. The text only said that Tlaloc was a god of rain and agriculture and that the Aztecs sacrificed humans to him to make the rains come.

"I can see why Martha put this one in the closet," Kinsey said, handing it back.

"We have the whole set."

"The whole set?"

"Murderous Mayans, Riotous Romans, Gruesome Greeks, Eerie Egyptians," the librarian whispered.

"Well," Kinsey said, returning the book, "I'd keep them in there if I were you."

"Sorry I couldn't be more help. We can loan out more books on the Aztecs from another library if—"

"No, that won't be necessary. Thanks for your help."

She couldn't help but go back to the bridge. The sky was clear, and the sun hadn't quite set. But it was still, quiet, eerie. She went down underneath the bridge again. There were no handprints, but someone had written on the concrete of the bridge, shakily in mud. "The price of rain." Just below it were two severed hands, crossed over each other.

She reached down into the mud herself and stared at the wall. What could she say? She wrote on the wall and washed her hand off in the creek. There was a stillness to the air. She thought she was being watched. She looked in the creek, and all around, and dipped her head under the water. But she didn't see anyone. She wondered what he must be like.

That Friday she ate at Jessie's Deli. Saul came in and sat next to her. "Hey, Kinsey. Did you hear about the girl? The one under the bridge?"

"No, I'm not part of the investigation."

"Of course not, but they found her hands."

"Yeah? Where were they?"

"Under the bridge."

"They weren't there the night we found the body."

"Yeah, the killer must have taken them back there. Then he wrote, with mud, on the wall."

"What?" Kinsey said, feeling cold. "What did he write?"

"The price of rain," Saul intoned. "You're not alone."

"Creepy."

"Very."

"So you think it's a psycho? I thought it was just...you know...a high school girl. I figured it was a rapist who then killed her."

"Well the coroner said she'd had sex recently, probably right before she died. But there wasn't any human sperm."

"Uh," Kinsey said, noticing his grin. "And, um, non-human sperm?"

"Maybe a fish or amphibian. They had to send it to another lab. It will take weeks to get results."

"It's probably not related," Kinsey said. "I mean, a fish didn't kill her. Probably just something in the creek."

"Yeah, yeah. Weird, though, huh?"

Kinsey nodded.

"Maybe we have a gator."

"Maybe. It would explain the hands being bitten off, but wouldn't a gator eat them?"

"I guess. Hey," said Saul, "it's a bit early to ask, but do you want to go caroling this Christmas? Our church does it every year. You have a very rich sounding voice. I bet you're a great singer."

"I have a horrible voice," she said.

"Maybe you just need some practice. Like my mom couldn't carry a tune at all until...no? Okay, okay, forget I asked."

Weeks passed. Cold, dry weeks. The murder remained unsolved. Kinsey visited the bridge a few times a week, but didn't find anything new. She saw Saul more and less than she liked. It was cruel to nurse such hopes, either in him or herself.

One night as she was driving towards the Rag Creek bridge, something jumped right in front of her car. She braked, swerved, and missed it. Luckily, she also missed the trees and came to a stop. She pulled off the road, just before the bridge, and put the emergency lights on. She ran down to the bank of the creek.

"Listen," she said, standing in the beam of the headlights, "I won't hurt you. I just need to talk to you." She untucked her shirt and began hastily unbuttoning it from the bottom. "I understand. I know you don't think I do." When she unbuttoned her shirt halfway, she began unwrapping the silk scarf from around her waist and chest. "You can't drown me." She lifted her arms, showing the red and swollen slits all along her sides. She turned slowly around, and the third time she heard a splash. He was there.

He was as hideous as she dreamed. Short, fat, with green skin, eyes too far apart, and much too wide a mouth. His skin was splotchy, and his arms hung almost lifeless. She let her arms down. "Can you talk?" she asked.

He shook his whole body left and right. "But you can write," she said.

He leaped away from the light, and she heard a rusting, then a snap. He returned holding a stick. There was plenty of mud to write on.

"Were you trying to kill yourself?" The frog bowed a little. "Because of what happened to the girl?" The frog bowed again and stayed that way. "Was it an accident?"

The frog wrote, "Careless. Stupid. Warned her." The frog underlined the last part twice, then erased it all. "Would happen someday."

"How long were you, uh, making rain?"

The frog wrote, "Spring. Last year. Went away for summer."

"Why the hands?"

The frog wrote, "What you do. End all drought. No died 4 nothing."

"I don't understand," Kinsey said.

The frog wrote, "Big sacrifice, big rain. Her first time. Her death."

They looked at each other a few moments. The frog erased everything again with a foot and wrote, "Who serve?" He pointed the stick at her.

"I don't understand."

The frog wrote, "How gills?"

"I was born with them. Did you...become a Tlaloques?" She hoped she was saying it right. The frog bowed again.

"Can you undo it?"

The frog wrote, "Die."

"Is that why you want to die?"

The frog wrote, "Less rain, more need. Can't not. Two is too many."

"Jessica wasn't the first?"

The frog bowed.

"Who were you before? Do you have a name?"

The frog wrote, "Billy."

"Well, I can't arrest you. Can I come visit you?"

The frog pointed the stick downstream.

"Another bridge downstream?"

The frog held up two fingers.

"Great. I'll come by in a couple days, okay?" She started buttoning her shirt back up. The silk was ruined in the mud. She could live without it a few hours.

"Kinsey! What's wrong with your ribs." Kinsey turned and saw Saul stepping carefully down to the bank of the creek. She began trembling and tears welled up in her eyes. "What are you doing—My God, what the hell is that?"

Billy leaped into the water, just as Saul drew his pistol and fired.

"Saul, oh, no, Saul," she said. "Why did you come here?"

"Someone reported your car. What's happened to you. What was—"

"I'm sorry, Saul. I'm so sorry," she said, removing her shirt.

"Sorry? What's going on, Kinsey? What are you—"

She reached towards him and began to sing. Why couldn't they have sent Harvey? Or anyone else? At least she could finally give Saul what he wanted. He dropped his jaw, then his gun.

Afterwards, when she waded out of the creek, Billy was watching her. "We need to get out of here before they send someone else." Billy pointed downstream again. "Yes. Want to go together?" Billy bowed. "The voice doesn't work on you, does it?"

Billy shrugged. "But I don't need to sing for you, do I?" Kinsey asked.

The frog took a nervous step forward, then another, then leaped. They were together in the cold water, letting the slow current carry them down.

She walked back to her apartment, far off the side of the road. She cried a little, but when she heard the crack of thunder and felt the rain on her nakedness, she smiled and hummed a tune – a dangerous habit – then cried some more. She felt so full and content, more than she had in years. She tried to make it easy on Saul. She tried to make it last. She wanted him to be happy at the end.

But he was gone, and now she was looking forward to seeing Billy again. She would join him tomorrow.

She'd just collect a few things from her apartment. No one would be watching it this soon. McKinsey Swanson would disappear. It was a shame. It was her favorite name so far. Kinsey would become another victim of the Rag Creek Killer or whatever they ended up calling it. But she would be the last.

"Billy won't do anything like that again," she whispered. "Not when he has me."

# Mr. Guthrie's Familiar

## By: Glenn Dungan

It's wild, the things that come to you at night. Like memories almost forgotten and of no significance that bubble steadily, hidden in some forgotten pot. Only when you're older, do you realize the pot was a witches' brew and you're a frog at the bottom of the heating black cauldron.

It's these memories that arise during the hot and clammy moments in between fever dreams. And even though I'm dealing with a flu that my wife gave me, unintentionally, on my birthday, I can't help but become a little sentimental. I'm an accountant now, for a decent firm. It's boring work but it pays the bills and provides good insurance. I have a king-sized bed and the acne that once plagued my face has long since been defeated.

I stare in the darkened reflection of the turned off television in front of my bed, sweating and shivering at the same time, answering birthday calls and texts. I can't help but think, with a sudden clarity of the interlocking gears, how things really came to pass, or if it was a fever dream of a memory at all.

I don't know if the story of Mr. Guthrie's Familiar is true. If you look on any message board and crackpot website, they will tell you it is. I don't know what I believe. I do know some kids went missing and some grew up to be adults like me.

At sixteen, my dad told me to get a summer job, and while I wanted to play my Nintendo 64 all day, he took the liberty to apply on my behalf to all the "help wanted" signs not only in our town but the neighboring town. The only place to call me back was Comet Pizza, right at the end of Blueberry Street. Comet Pizza was in Cogs Hollow. A delivery boy only I needed a bike, which I had, and knowledge of the streets, which I also had.

I rolled my bike up and was introduced to Bart, Clyde, and Lionel. Bart was the head delivery boy, which I didn't know was a thing until that day. There were four of us. Each of us more pimple faced and greasy haired than the last.

Well, five. Sort of.

Her name was Maria, and at the time I thought she was the prettiest girl I'd ever seen. She was the bosses' daughter, and, like me, had been given a summer job. She was the counter girl, responsible for being the face of Comet Pizza, the empire she would no doubt inherit. She also took the calls, and I looked forward to hearing customers call in for a delivery so I could hear her voice.

I spent a large part of that first day sitting around and eating pizza, which was considered a tremendous perk at the time. The orientation was minimal; turns out, the training to be delivery boy meant being able to pedal fast. The three boys were on rotation, switching out every call. They told me stories. Bart once delivered pizza to a house and a naked woman answered the door. Lionel once delivered to the science-teacher who flunked him last year and, with a whisper, said that he made a point of licking each slice before handing it off. After about four hours of sitting in the back, reading magazines and failing to talk to Maria, I got the impression that I wasn't going to be making any deliveries at all.

"Not yet," said Bart, "there is a perfect house for you."

"You mean, it's close?" I asked, "I go to school in West Lake, but I know Cogs Hollow enough. And I've been studying a map for the past four hours."

Clyde shook his head, "Just wait, padawan."

I remember this clearly, too. I hadn't seen *The Phantom Menace* yet, but I was going to next week with my cousin. I remember being slightly offended after the fact.

Finally, a call came in and Maria's wonderful voice occupied the room. "One cheese pie for 451 Alberle Road."

Then the boys lit up, and I knew it was my time to shine.

"That's a good house," said Lionel, his face buried in a magazine.

"You know where that is?" asked Bart.

I nodded.

"You been there before?" Bart furthered.

I shook my head.

"Why don't one of us come with you?" Clyde said, suddenly standing. "Just in case you get lost."

"It's perfect first house," Lionel said, "it was my first house. I was fine."

"And Greg chose that as my first house when I started too," Bart said. Greg was the previous head delivery boy, who went off to college.

"I can do it," I said, wanting to impress these guys.

They weren't my friends, but I was used to not having many friends. I did, however, see a lot of commonalities between them and me. We were all physically misshapen in our own ways. Lionel was a little plump. Bart walked bowlegged. Clyde was tall and lanky. The way that the three of them interacted with Maria told me they don't talk to girls "in the real world" very much, and the number of books and magazines and comic books littered about the backroom told me they spent a lot of their time in between pages.

"He's fine," said Bart. Then he turned to me, "You got this. Your first house. Then tomorrow you'll come into the rotation with us and start making tips."

"Sure," I said, and received the pie from Maria, inhaled the fresh-baked aura, and put them in the warming container. My heart got a little fluttered.

She said, "Mr. Guthrie is kind of a weirdo. Just so you know. But if you can handle this one, the others will be easier. Trust me." And she winked at me.

Outside I got my bike out of its lock, fastened the container cradle onto the back, and latched the container. Clyde appeared next to me, curls of sweat matted underneath his cap. The ironed on Comet Pizza logo, with its lumpy asteroid made of melting cheese, made him look as if he had three eyes. The day had turned into swathes of tangerine and plum; twilight, but darkness by the time I'd get back.

"Hey," he said, "I just want you to know that Mr. Guthrie is sort of strange."

"That's what Maria said." I was happy to bring up her name. It felt empowering for reasons that I could only deduce now as the frightening thrill of puberty.

He shuffled on his feet, "Yeah, but I don't think you understand. His house is kind of a rite-of-passage. When I started, they made me deliver to him. And Greg made Bart do it too."

"Is Mr. Guthrie, like, a pedophile or something?"

"You haven't heard about Mr. Guthrie's Familiar?"

I took my bike and started to pedal down the path, past the beaten-up cars of the pizza makers, the dumpsters, the pizza trailing savory vespers behind me. "C'mon man."

"I'm not trying to scare you," he said. "It's just that if you get really weirded out, leave the pizzas on the porch. Knock if you feel like you have too. And then tail it out of there."

I slanted my eyes. "Is this a trick? Messing with the new guy? Someone will have to pay for the pizza."

"No," Clyde said, twisting his face, "I'll pay for it when you come back."

I took my bike to the road, waited for a car to pass by. The street was lined with thick elms. They looked like talons pointing towards the sky. Clyde followed.

"What's the deal?" I snapped.

"Look," he said, picking up his hat and readjusting his greasy hair before popping it back on. "It's just an urban myth."

Another car drove past. This was typically a busy street. If I had been alone, I would have weaved my bike past the cars. I sometimes rode my bike in Cogs Hollow afterschool, so I knew the avenues well enough. I could feel Mr. Guthrie's address like a beacon at the far end of the forest, nestled in the cul-de-sac that I could see in my mind's eye.

"What is it then? The myth?" I asked.. "What's the deal with his Familiar?"

Clyde chuckled, but it was a nervous chuckle. I would not realize until thirty years later how difficult this was for him. "The story goes that Mr. Guthrie used to be a really nice guy. He was a teacher, or a social worker, or something. A wife. Couple of kids. Then one day he must have accidentally purchased an antique or read a book backwards or played Ouija because *something* entered his house and never came out. Something horrible. Like a mega-demon or something."

"A mega-demon?" I asked. "You're making me late, you know."

Clyde shivered. Another car zoomed past. He continued, "it was around that time that Mr. Guthrie lost his job. Started talking about a voice in his noggin. Said that voices need to feed and in exchange it would give him eternal life. Then his wife and kids disappeared."

"No wonder." I looked down the road, found myself at the end of the collection of traffic. "He went bonkers. She probably took the kids."

I made to leave but Clyde grabbed me by the shoulders.

He said, "They say that whatever may or may not have happened, Mr. Guthrie entered into a sort of relationship with this force. But it wasn't an even trade off. And now the mega-demon is practically keeping the man hostage, said that if it doesn't feed, it'll feed on him."

"C'mon," I said, trying to shake Clyde away. He pulled tighter.

"He calls the shop every couple of weeks. Orders the same thing. A small cheese pie, with instructions to deliver personally. You know why he does that? Because delivery boys have a high turnover rate. And no one would miss us. Like Randall Fleck, that missing kid from the 80's? Yeah, he worked here for three days. Or what about Bobby Finch, you know, the same last name that's above the hardware store? That's his older brother. I'm telling you, Harold, just leave it on the porch."

"Okay," I said, realizing now that Clyde actually believed this. "How do you know all this?"

"You'll find that most towns have a myth or two."

"And you've done it, and Bart and Lionel," I said, "I'll be fine. I can outrun an old man."

"I did," Clyde said, and his eyes began to well up, which, to this day, makes me uncomfortable whenever anyone does that. "And I saw…I saw *something* in the window…and…and I just stayed too long. Look. I can't stop you, because I think I'm crazy too, but if you go, just leave it on the porch. If you come back and tell everyone you did it, I'll back you up. I'll tell them I tried to talk you out of it, but you were adamant."

I actually didn't know what the word *adamant* meant at the time, but that didn't stop me from pulling onto the road while Clyde kept yelling at me to *just put it on the porch!* I did my best to ignore his warnings, because I was too old to believe in that kind of stuff. It was this arrogance that armored me to Bart and Lionel's challenge, this silly delivery boy rite-of-passage. I so wanted them to like me, even though they hardly paid any attention to me.

Yet Clyde's fear was so genuine. I turned corners and made sharp turns down bike lanes, feeling as if I were slipping slowly into a quick sand of dread, especially knowing that Randall Fleck and Bobby Finch might have ridden these very paths. Because I knew those names. Everyone knew those names.

I don't recall Bobby Finch much, but his name sounded familiar because when Randall Fleck disappeared, they compared his absence to Bobby's. I was too young then, as I was at this moment of delivery, to really appreciate the pattern of how close I was to this cycle, this myth. That was before we grew up. That was before I developed my pimples and my long nose and my greasy hair.

I turned onto Aberle Road, and I recall very clearly being relieved to find the neighborhood exactly as boring as all neighborhoods should be, so unlike Clyde's tale. No ghosts, no hockey-masked men. Not even a pedophile van. I took my bike down the street, looking up at the ocean of stars above, a view that doesn't really exist anymore. Then I came to 451 and for a second I thought the guys were playing a joke on me.

The stupid run down house looked as if it had been set aflame and reduced to a charcoaled version of itself. The grass turned into crisp, nettle-esque blades. The car was stranded on the lawn, reclaimed nature hugging its corroded frame. The house sulked, the eaves of the single rancher like heavy, weary eye brows on windows so dusty as to be one-way, even in darkness. I actually rationalized that there was no way a married couple with two kids could fit comfortably in a house like that, so point against Clyde's validity. Still, there was something foreboding about the house. It stood like an animated corpse, washed up and chewed on like a sperm whale that lost a fight with a giant squid. Something happened here. One time my uncle's house had gone into foreclosure and when we came back it looked like Mr. Guthrie's. So maybe that was it.

Or perhaps it would have been, except for the faint flicker of a lightbulb that swung at the far end of the house, a pendulum akin to an uvula.

I parked my bike at the edge of the property. It felt rude to drive it across the lawn, not that I had any opportunities to do so. I put my hands in the container, felt the warmth from the pizza box. I looked around at the other houses. They seemed perfectly fine. Sleeping.

I remembered the operations. Knock on the door, wait a little bit, knock again, receive the cash, count it, make change, wait for the tip. The entire exchange should take no longer than it would take to reach the house.

To reach the house.

Maria said if I could do this, I could do anything.

With the pizza balanced on my forklift spread out hands, I advanced through the thicket of overgrowth, over the uneven cobblestones, the tangle of weeds, the smell of rotting vegetables. I could see the bent spokes of an abandoned bike consumed by the Jurassic grass. It was hard to think that kids once played on this lawn.

The porch was no more than a dais, unwalled, no handrail. It was like walking into the maw of a beast, or onto an altar. My footsteps echoed in the empty street. There was a spot that reminded me of Clyde's advice. A perfect square that I could drop the pie on and run. I could be back on my bike now. Although I knew that if I left, then I would have returned to Comet Pizza a liar. I did not want to have a secret with Clyde, one that would eventually reveal that I had failed the rite.

Balancing the pizza on my hip, I repositioned and rapped on the screen door. There was no doorbell. I waited, leaned to see if I could see inside. I knocked again. A silhouette passed in front of the bulb. What followed was the sound of unlatching several bolts, each metal unlocking sending a shiver down the frame of the rickety door. The door opened and Mr. Guthrie appeared.

I remember him not looking particularly abrasive. Not bird like, as Clyde had made him seem. He was also not quite a goblin, as I had begun to envision him; no lost eye nor a crooked nose nor an ugly scar. He looked more like a frail scarecrow, or a farmer from that famous painting. Lips receded with age, eyes hollow from gravity's curse, liver spots that could be countries on a map; Mr. Guthrie was just a lonely old man. Simple as that.

"Pizza delivery," I said, trying to sound cheery. In hindsight I realize how stupidly ingenuine I must have sounded. I repeated the order: "One small cheese pie."

Mr. Guthrie nodded. He grunted and pushed open the screen door with a skeletal hand and then it was just the two of us, himself in the threshold, a black infinity behind him, me with the jungle of his unkempt lawn behind me.

"One small cheese pie for Mr. Guthrie?" I said, repositioning myself so that I held the box before me, like a token.

Mr. Guthrie licked his lips to wet them before speaking. His voice sounded unused, out of tune, as if the internal wiring were rusty. He reached into his pocket and pulled out a money clip. Yellow, cracked thumbnails sifted through the bills. A light flickered behind him, right over his shoulder, at the edge of the darkness. With shaking hands, he offered what I had hoped was the correct amount on the first try. And it was at this precise moment I felt our interaction become a group. Felt that it was not just the two of us, that someone or something had joined. I felt like I was being watched, and a thought flashed within the undercurrent of my psyche that this was still one big joke by the delivery boys. That, at any moment, they would pop out of the brush with monster masks.

Mr. Guthrie handed me the bills. The cash was warm and damp. There were two twenties in there, which was more than enough for the pie. Horror swept me before I could understand why. I didn't have the balance to hold both the pizza and make change, and I didn't want to be there any longer than I had to. A second light had gone on behind him, two tiny lights as if at the end of a tunnel. A breeze swept by, moving the bent wheel of the broken bike entombed by Mr. Guthrie's unkempt lawn. The smell of pennies pierced the thick aroma of rotting vegetables. I got the sudden feeling of being on the precipice of some great void, as if the shoddy cement cube of a porch was miles above the lawn.

Mr. Guthrie stared at me, unblinking, as I tried to make change.

"Keep it," he said, "the change."

"Thank you," I said, and I felt something stir behind him, responding to my voice.

When I looked behind his bony shoulder I could make a faint outline of something. *Some Thing.* That was it. It was human but it wasn't. It was more like a painting, like something that mimicked human form, like a marble sculpture. The faraway lights turned into tiny jewels. I tried handing Mr. Guthrie the pizza but he did not budge.

"Would you like me to leave it on the porch?" I said, gesturing to a spot, thinking about Clyde.

*No!* something croaked, but it was underneath the passing rustle of trees and a bike chime somewhere in the distance.

Mr. Guthrie said, "No. Please."

"Okay," I said, and pushed it a little further into his trembling hands. The hands receded. In the corner of my eye something zipped around the corner. Like a black stray or something. "It's yours."

"I'm an old man," said Mr. Guthrie, his voice craggy. There was a certain surreal quality about him, as if space warped within the aura of his presence, or that whatever lay behind his back knew that it was only a flesh wall between itself and the outside. He continued, his jaw dropping slightly out of sync with his words. "I'm an old man. Can you help an old man. Please."

I didn't say anything. Clyde said to *put it on the porch*, and I already had the cash.

"Could you help an old man and come inside and put it on my kitchen table?" said Mr. Guthrie, his wiry frame twisting slightly, the creases of his splotchy, greasy shirt forming an obscure Rorschach simulacrum.

"Excuse me?"

"Please, I'm an old man. I can hardly lift the box," he said, a rustle in the wind sounded like *come inside* and then he said, his voice deeper, more coming from within his frail frame than from just his mouth. "Please."

A windchime startled me to action. Something moved with me. Another whistle said *come inside* again. I think.

"Others have," Mr. Guthrie said, "other boys."

I don't remember exactly when I dropped the pizza box, but I do remember, in hindsight, being unsettled. The world was suddenly very unsafe. There was a figure behind Mr. Guthrie, something vague and shapeless, too far for me to see, enveloped in the abyss of the house. The pungent smell of garlic breath from the black void behind Mr. Guthrie. When I put the boxes in the corner and stood, I saw, maybe, I don't know. I saw Mr. Guthrie floating several inches off the lip of his front door, his dirtied loafers dipping slightly to give the impression of a ballerina on their toes.

There was a loud noise, a honking of a car or some strong gust of wind, and I left Mr. Guthrie on the porch, walking backwards at first, tripping over the step and into the thicket, grabbing onto the overgrown bike and cutting my hands as I ran across his lawn and hopped onto my own bike. Before kicking off I looked over my shoulder and saw that lone bulb, swinging violently back and forth, like a wild pendulum. On the downswing of the light Mr. Guthrie's lanky figure appeared underneath it, shoulders hunched, arms as if guarding from something.

"I'm sorry," Mr. Guthrie croaked, but I was already speedily away so I couldn't be sure if it was for me or not.

I had no idea how out of sorts I was until I returned to the Comet Pizza. Grass stains on my knees, my new Comet Pizza shirt had been chewed by the derelict bike. I must have nicked my cheek too, for a small trail of blood now lined down my chin. I parked my bike, walked into the warm glow of the Comet Pizza.

The others looked up from their magazines. Clyde exhaled as if he had been holding his breath the entire time. Maria noticed my cut and she offered me a rag, and I hoped that interaction meant more to both of us.

"How was it?" asked Lionel, counting his tips, not really looking at me.

"You look like you got chewed on and spit out," Bart said.

"Yeah," I said, and sat down. Someone brought me a slice of pizza.

Clyde leaned over and whispered, "Did you leave it on the porch?"

I nodded, chewing a bite of pepperoni and mushroom. "He left a nice tip."

"He always does," Bart said, shaking his head.

"He'll call again in a couple of weeks?" I asked, wiping my mouth.

"Yeah," Lionel nodded. "Listen, I know Clyde tried talking you out of it. Glad that you went through. In the future though, just leave it on the porch and don't stay for chit-chat."

"Guy's got nothing to say anyway," Bart said, shrugging, "whatever, let's go home."

"You were waiting for me?" I asked.

"Don't all have to show up together, but we all have to leave together. Sort of a rule," Bart yawned.

On the way out the four of us said goodbye to Maria and went back to our bikes. I noticed a strange, almost black tar smudged on my seat, and Lionel pointed out that a similar smear was on my lower back too.

"Take a shower, new guy, and see you tomorrow," he said, kicking off his bike.

"Hey," Clyde said, suddenly near me, "did you really leave it on the porch like I asked?"

"Yeah." I nodded. "Not at first, but…yeah."."

This seemed to shake Clyde, who fell silent. "So, you met him. Did you…see it?"

"It?"

"Mr. Guthrie's Familiar. What did it look like?"

I shook my head. I wasn't trying to be coy but it was true. I couldn't quite place what I had seen on Mr. Guthrie's porch, I still wasn't sure if I saw anything at all. I shook my head and said, "Next time I'm really just going to leave it on the porch. Anyway thanks, Clyde. For the advice."

"Yeah, sure," he smiled, looking pleased to be validated. It was a feeling that I yearned for too. I felt his eyes trail me as I kicked my bike into gear, to follow the others down the road. And then it was the four of us riding home, each together, before going our separate ways until tomorrow.

I don't really remember Mr. Guthrie calling Comet Pizza much that summer, or at all. Most of the summer afterwards was in a haze, much in the way that all summers blend when you're young. Didn't lose my virginity, hardly had a summer fling. Us pizza delivery boys never hung out outside of the shop, and my only real interaction with Maria was when she handed me a pizza for delivery.

It was a dumb summer job, one that consisted of a bunch of teenagers who hardly knew themselves, buried themselves in magazines and yo-yos and the occasional cigarette to look cool. Mr. Guthrie himself was discovered half a year later in his house, his body reportedly looking like a dropped napkin in the middle of the floor, discovered after the neighbors complained of the rotting smell that had begun to invade the cul-de-sac. I remember people talking about this as they picked up a slice. It was old age, perhaps. Or cancer. And it was tragic that no one had come for him in his time of need. There were times when I wondered if Mr. Guthrie called for pizza to experience a glimpse of human companionment in an otherwise dark and lonely week, a pang of guilt that I perhaps had treated him poorly. But I remembered more clearly how terribly unsafe I felt, how disoriented. Like I had encountered the edge of a puma's den.

It's funny, how memories like this pop up in the middle of fever dreams, blossoming like stubborn flowers in the snow. Those two kids, Bobby Finch and Randall Fleck, were the only ones that had disappeared from Cogs Hollow, so hardly any excuse to fuel the urban legend. There were no calls after that day and all of us were too preoccupied with growing up to confirm any suspicions. Although one time I did circle back after work, staring at the edge of the Jurassic era lawn, trying to make sense of my experience. The house was as empty and dark as I left it, and a Comet Pizza box was on the porch, upturned as if dropped. Perhaps the birds or squirrels had gotten to its contents.

I guess I was the last. I don't know if Mr. Guthrie's Familiar was real. The memory feels on the precipice of reality, like how when you're young you climb because you don't realize how high you are, or the consequences of falling, and when you think back all you can remember is not how high you were, but how close to the edge you were. Mr. Guthrie was like that, for me, so inconsequential as to be buried in my mind, yet so significant for reasons that I could not, as of yet, determine.

# Saints and Monsters

By: Declan Finn

"**H**i. I'm Detective Thomas Nolan."

"You're the saint."

I blinked. I *hated* the name reporters had branded me with over two years ago.

*Although that was print media. I didn't think people his age* read *newspapers.*

I studied the young man in front of me. He was somewhere in his mid-twenties. He was 5'9", blond hair, blue eyes, and built more like a martial artist or a dancer than anything else. His eyes and his smile were stuck on "amused," as though there was some private joke he was in on. Like me, he wore a light t-shirt and shorts, perfect for the physically exhaustive day we had both expected when we arrived.

"No, I am not Simon Templar. I'm a cop," I corrected him.

He nodded slowly, his eyes scanning me. Though maybe I should say that he dissected me with his eyes.

"Marco Catalano," he finally told me.

We shook hands, then he stepped back. At first, I thought he was being standoffish. Then I realized that his position was more of a standoff. I half-expected to see guns at his hips, ready for a draw.

"We're both here for the Vatican ninja cross-training, right?" he asked.

I cocked my head and blinked. It was the first time I had heard the term used semi-seriously. "I suppose so. I was told they were SpecOps Swiss Guards that have dealt with supernatural threats from time to time."

Marco nodded, almost to himself. "As I said, Vatican Ninjas."

I rolled my eyes and looked around the gym. It was very simple, with minimal equipment. It seemed this place in particular was only for hand-to-hand combat, no melee weapons, which made a certain level of sense. We were within the Rome city limits, so there were only so many creative weapons that one could carry, legally or not.

Other training facilities would be differently armed.

"I was told that our hand-to-hand instructor was late today, so they're coming up with something else for us."

Marco shrugged casually. "I go hand-to-hand with *vampires*. I don't need more training."

"Really?"

Oh yes," he nodded. "Would you want to see?"

I frowned, studying him. I wanted a better handle on what I was dealing with. I had half a foot and probably a hundred pounds on him, give or take a few.

"Sure, why—"

He threw a wide haymaker at my head, mid-sentence. I twisted my upper body so my right forearm met his. His strike barely touched my block before he swung the other way, throwing his left fist. I twisted back, blocking his left while throwing a left hook of my own.

Marco dove under both of my arms and rolled to my right. Before I had a chance to chase after him, his right leg swept mine, hitting just below my knee. His left shin struck my ankle. Then he spun like he was wrapping spaghetti—my legs were the noodles, his legs were the fork tines.

I fell forward, landing on my forearms, not my face. I looked to Marco to see if he was trying to make me submit, or if he had some other goal.

His eyes were alive and bright with excitement. His smile grew as he pressed my calf along the back of my thigh.

I instantly recognized that there was something *wrong* with this boy.

Without thinking or asking for it, I bilocated. My second-self appeared only a few feet away from me. It was enough so that I could take three large steps and kick Marco right in the chest.

Marco's eyes went wide, then he blinked. The amused smirk vanished from his face.

Marco had just enough time to say "Aw crap," before throwing up his hands in a block. My kick knocked him aside, and I rolled away.

The body that Marco pinned vanished, which meant I was standing and ready to follow up. Now that I understood the rules Marco played by, I knew how to meet him.

His rules were the equivalent of a live-fire exercise.

I tried to kick Marco in the head, but he kept rolling. He kick-jumped to his feet like something out of pro-wrestling, then sidestepped in a leap, trying to get distance. I spun to track him.

To stop me, Marco threw a high-kick with his right leg. It was a surprise, since it was an MMA move, not something you wanted in a street fight. There were too many things that could go wrong. Ordinarily, it was a mistake.

I met it in a double-block, catching the kick on the flesh of my forearms. Then I caught his ankle. From here, I should have been able to end the fight easily. I twisted his ankle counter-clockwise, twisting the right foot to his right side.

I was right. It wasn't a mistake. It was a trap.

Marco went with the twist. His left foot left the mat to kick at the back of my head. I bent forward, taking the blow along my upper back.

Then I deliberately spun, hurling Marco away from me. He hit the mat rolling, then sprang to his feet. We were back to square one. He didn't seem tired, and I already felt bruises forming on my back.

At least he was breathing a little hard.

His right arm twitched, as though reaching, but checked himself. His eyes flicked over my body, looking for an angle of attack.

Marco relaxed, sliding from a fighting stance to a spine-straight position, almost like a ballroom dancer ready to begin a waltz.

"Bilocation, huh?" he panted. "That's a little cheaty."

I raised a brow and made sure to take deep breaths. "So's not explaining the rules of the game."

Marco shrugged. "I'm used to being underestimated by things a lot stronger and tougher than you. My default function is *kill*."

"Well, I'm used to playing underdog."

Pant. "I figured. Ever meet vampires?"

I shrugged. "A few. I've usually bled on them, and they turn to dust."

Marco's smile grew a little. "I'm told that saints and vampires don't mix. Your blood probably poisons them."

I nodded slowly, expecting him to come at me again. "Makes sense. And the term is wonder worker. Saints are dead."

"That part will happen soon enough," Marco said. "I'm certain. Given the crap we're fighting, the odds are against us from the start. One day, you have to figure the forces of darkness will conclude they should just put a hit on us and be done with us."

I chuckled. "Been there, done that, sent that guy to Hell."

"You too, huh?" Marco chuckled. "I know that feeling. Trust me, if I ever have to deal with a guy named Day ever again... ugh. Lousy Armani-wearing douchebag."

I blinked. *Mister Day?* I had dealt with a demon that called itself that once. It had been caught in a circle, so I didn't have to fight it. But it was mysteriously well-dressed for a fiend from the pit.

The door to the gym flew open before I could reply. It was a Swiss Guard in full regalia. With accented English, he said, "Come! We have a new task for you today. A mission in a controlled environment."

Marco and I said as one, "No such thing as a controlled environment."

We exchanged a glance.

Marco's smile expanded on both sides. "At least we have something in common."

Marco Catalano dressed on automatic pilot. While he wasn't an expert on getting guns through airport security, or acquiring them in Europe (and the Vatican Ninjas wouldn't give him any, the lousy bastards), he had less problem with collecting knives. Amanda had gotten him a set as an engagement present several years ago—though that had less to do with the engagement, and more to do with the wendigo that ate one of his patients.

The knives came in a set of eight. Each one had a sheath made of leather, worked and treated with holy oil. Six of them were Bowie knives, and they didn't get more American than that. Two were calf sheaths, two at his hips, and two were in shoulder holsters. The two throwing knives ran the length of Marco's inner forearm. The blades themselves were silver, which served to damage almost anything on this side of the pit.

Marco's experience taught him to wear as many of them as he could get away with. Since he was traveling with two law enforcement officers, he wore all eight. He fleetingly considered holding off wearing them at his hips… then he remembered this was a "controlled environment." That reassurance made certain that he carried those as well.

Marco topped off this ensemble with a leather jacket that was a little too long for him, but the length covered the knives at his hips. The leather served as a measure of extra defense—usually against knife attacks by humans. Between the leather and the lining of the jacket was a layer of Kevlar, soaked in a shear-thickening fluid colloquially known as liquid body armor. The physics meant that it was akin to slapping a body of water, only the impact caused the cloth to harden, not only diffusing the impact of the attack, but turning the kinetic energy of the strike against the attack. It wouldn't prevent Marco from feeling the impact of a vampire, but it would prevent his rib cage from caving in.

As Marco dressed, most of his thought process was turned on his sparring and training partner, Thomas Nolan.

Because Marco hated being wrong.

Thomas Nolan didn't seem like anything special. When he first heard the name, Marco looked him up. Nolan had taken on a serial killer. Who somehow inspired a prison riot in Rikers Island. After that, Nolan had earned the ire of a death cult, of which the serial killer was a member. Then there was how he had taken down New York's Mayor Hoynes, in a fracas the details of which were very vague.

Marco concluded that Nolan may have been a good detective and skilled in taking down human adversaries, but what did he know of fighting the supernatural? And Nolan had enough press to be drafted into this special course with the Vatican Ninjas.

*Oops. Those who assume … dammit.*

When Marco had been cured of lycanthropy, the lingering side effects left Marco's physical attributes on par with Olympic athletes. On days when he exercised every muscle, he had to eat like a pig just to keep his weight at 3% body fat. He was in his early twenties but could mimic Olympic gymnast routines and beat the time or distance of most other solo competitors.

Normally, that was barely enough for Marco to hold his own against any vampire who took him seriously.

And yet Nolan had forced Marco to play defense. Submission holds wouldn't work the moment bilocation was on the table.

Nolan was beatable, yes. Marco had the speed and endurance to outlast him. But he was one of the few humans that could make him work for it. Which was enough to make Marco respect him.

Also, Nolan had caught his number.

*Okay, maybe he wasn't chosen because of who he knew and his public image as super-Catholic?*

Marco glared hard at the locker. His smile had turned into a hard grimace. With a growl, he slammed the locker door. Then he punched the door, denting it.

He *hated* being wrong.

Both Marco and I had dressed in work clothes. The Swiss Guard who led us through the tunnels kept using terms on par with "milk run" and "isn't it easy?" and the longer he kept speaking, the more guns I wanted. But I wasn't allowed to bring my guns from home. Thankfully, I had a utility belt that was "Batman fighting the supernatural," filled with holy salt, vials of holy water, packets of holy oil, and my tactical baton.

Marco didn't quite clank as he walked, but I caught bulges at his calves, his forearms and under his jacket. I gave him a look, and his only answer was that permanent smile of his.

*I don't know what it is about this guy, but I want to punch him.*

Marco read my expression and rolled his eyes. He grabbed one lapel and opened his jacket enough to show me a brightly colored, blue squirt gun in a shoulder holster. I caught the hint of a knife pommel.

"I come prepared."

I pulled back my jacket to show him the belt. "We've both been around that same block."

Marco chuckled. "Yeah. I seem to recall it being paved with the skulls of corrupt bishops."

I blinked, then recalled he was stealing a line from Dante, and a few other saints.

We were passed off to another Swiss Guard, only he was dressed in basic black. Under his jacket, he had a simple sidearm.

"Today," the guard said as he led us down the street, "we're going into Christian catacombs. It's a supernatural tunnel of holiness."

Marco blinked. "How do you figure? You have one of those detectors out of *Ghostbusters?*"

The Guard shook his head as he came to an open gate. The gate was across a tunnel opening, with descending steps carved out of the rock.

The Guard stopped long enough to look back at Marco and smile. "I said they are Christian catacombs. Even the very dust is holy. Not even your vampire could survive."

Marco chuckled. "Don't bet on it. My wife goes to confession regularly, and her daily feeding is from the chalice."

I blinked and tried not to flinch. Marco's wife was a *vampire? What the Hell?*

Marco spared me a glance. His smile was intact. Either none of my shock registered on my face, or he wasn't offended by it. "You'd like her. She might give your prayer life a run for your money." The smile change from amused to wistful. "And damn is she the most beautiful woman on the planet."

*Well, at least I know he's human enough to love someone. Yay?*

"Where is she then?" I asked.

Marco blinked. "Amanda? She's getting some updates. She already went through a lot of the basics when she worked with the Vatican back in the … thirties? Forties? All of the above? It may have been from the twenties until the CIA was founded, to be honest. But she just needs a refresher course."

The Guard led us down the stairs, and into the catacombs.

If you're wondering what the catacombs looked like, imagine the crypt in *Indiana Jones and the Last Crusade* without the flooding, and you have the general idea. Except the walls were less stone and more… made of bone. And skulls. With every skull facing out, staring at passersby in a permanent *memento mori*.

*Like I need a reminder. I'm a homicide cop. On days they let me be a cop.*

The Guard wandered around for a while, leading us deeper and deeper into endless tunnels. The lecture was almost academic, but it was beyond tedious.

After thirty minutes of wandering, Marco sighed. "I passed bored about five minutes into this lecture. We've wandered through over a mile of tunnels, and all of the relevant information could have been covered on a three-by-five index card. What the heck is the point of all of this?"

The Guard looked to me. I put my hands in my pockets and stared right back at him. If he thought he was going to get any help from me against Marco, he was sadly mistaken.

The Guard muttered, "Hendershot was right about you." He sighed and opened his mouth to speak.

Before he could get a word out, he was interrupted by a loud *crack* from the floor.

All three of us looked down. The stone floor had split along the width of the tunnel. Another crack spread from that, going lengthwise.

Marco dove down the tunnel. I dove back the way we came.

It didn't matter. When we touched tunnel floor, the stone gave way. Our impact may have even hurried the collapse.

Marco calculated that it was not a straight drop. It may have been straight for a few feet. After that, the shaft became less of a drop, and more like a slide.

The end of the shaft caused Marco to spill out into another stone tunnel. He drew both of his squirt guns from his shoulder holsters. One of them was filled with holy water, the other was filled with acid. Even vampires had a problem with their face melting off.

Unfortunately, Marco's guns aimed down into pure darkness. There were no targets. There was nothing but endless, empty night. The hordes of Hell could have been an inch away from the muzzle of his squirt gun, and he wouldn't have known until they made a noise or struck out at him.

Marco stifled a curse and slid his guns away. He reached down to his back pocket and pulled out a red paisley bandanna. He wrapped it around his mouth and nose and tied it off before he resumed breathing normally. While the air in the catacombs above was tolerable and smelled of moisture, this smelled of death.

"Nolan? You here? Breathe through your nose and cover up if you can."

After a moment of movement in the dark, a light came on. It came off of the ring on Nolan's finger. It looked like a college ring, only with a diamond instead of a colored gem. The glow that came from it was bright and filled the corridor without blinding him.

Marco blinked. "You have a magic ring?"

"More useful than Sauron's, less useful than Green Lantern's," Nolan told him.

Marco glanced from the ring to Nolan's face. It was covered with a dark blue and gold Swiss Guard handkerchief. He blinked. "Where'd you get that?"

"The Vatican gift shop. Where else?"

Marco chuckled and looked around. These catacombs looked much like the ones above, only without any of the modern lighting systems. The shaft had dumped them into a T junction. "Why do you want the face masks?" Nolan asked.

Marco shrugged casually, still scanning the tunnels. "I'm less concerned about demons than I am about any molds, spores, and fungi lying around sealed catacombs. I know too much about how they kill archaeology teams.”

“You have a medical degree or something?”

“Better, I’m a Physician Assistant. I do the work doctors and nurses get the credit for.”

“Where—oh no.”

Marco glanced back and followed Nolan’s gaze. Huge blocks of stone work had fallen down with them. While both he and Nolan appeared miraculously unscathed, a pair of legs stuck out from under the stone.

Marco winced, then dismissed the dead Swiss Guard, turning back to the tunnel. Had he cared what Nolan thought, he might have explained that he didn’t want to waste time mourning the dead when the two of them were in enough trouble.

“Any chance they’ll send someone for us anytime soon?” Nolan asked.

“Not a chance. The Guard was a windbag who liked to hear himself talk. The catacombs above us went on for at least a mile. I wouldn’t bet on anyone looking for us until sundown.”

“Why sundown?”

“Because that’s when my wife will come for us. Assuming she doesn’t find a way to get here before then.”

There was a long moment of silence, longer than Marco was expecting. He glanced at Nolan. “Yes? Can I help you?”

“Your wife is a vampire who goes to confession and takes her blood from the chalice. I’m almost surprised she can’t move in daylight.”

“Oh, that. Point taken.” He turned back to the darkness around them. “All vampires are affected by all the secular weaknesses you find in Bram Stoker: silver, sunlight, fire, beheading, and a stake to the heart. Amanda wears a gold crucifix to bed.” Marco blinked as his mind drifted. “And sometimes, nothing else.” He blinked a few times and shook his head. “Anyway, we might be able to climb up the shaft.”

Nolan nodded. “I was thinking the same thing. I can probably levitate out, get help, come back with rope, and—”

There was another crack of stone. Nolan and Marco both leapt back from the shaft before it collapsed in upon itself. It came down in a crash of stone and dirt. Once everything had finished falling, it was clear that the passage was sealed solid.

Marco sighed. “Murphy strikes again. Typical.”

Nolan groaned and nodded. "No kidding. At least if we stay near the collapse, they'll find us. We just have to not move and wait—"

A long, wailing moan echoed down the hallways. It was followed by stone sliding on stone, like a sarcophagus or coffin sliding open.

"Or not," Nolan finished.

Marco and I closed, coming shoulder to shoulder. I brought up my left fist and shined the light of the Soul Ring down individual tunnels, searching for the threat. Then I pulled my tactical baton and flicked it open.

"You said that Ring was useful." Marco pulled out two massive Bowie knives from shoulder holsters. "How useful?"

"Good news," I told him over my shoulder, "it can probably hold off supernatural things in bulk. As long as there aren't too many. Bad news: it's not infinite. It stores energy, it doesn't create it. And I don't have a meter for what the charge is."

Marco grunted. "So you can't necessarily blast our way out." He shrugged. "Doesn't matter. I prefer action games to survival horror."

Something slid over stone down the center tunnel. I turned, flashing my ring down its length. Nothing moved..

Until it occurred to me that I was looking too far away.

The bodies on their stone slabs twitched. Fabric ripped as they pushed against their bindings. "Mummies?"

Marco's eyes narrowed. "These catacombs aren't Christian. It's something older and fouler in the deep places of the Earth."

I blinked. "You want to start quoting Tolkien, *now*?"

Marco gave a mirthless laugh. "Trust me, kill an elf, you start reading up on them."

I didn't even want to ask. I flashed my light down the hallway on the right.

Groans echoed down the hall as my light touched upon even more mummies. They were a ways down the tunnel, hundreds of yards away. They blocked the tunnel.

"Crap. Movement at three o'clock."

"Confirmed," Marco said. "Check nine."

I pivoted to shine the ring's light down the left tunnel. "Contact," I said. "Lots of contact."

I shone the light down the central tunnel. It was relatively clear for the moment.

"Straight up the middle it is," Marco said. "Moving."

Marco strode over to a mummy, still trying to fight free from its wrapping. He stabbed it in the head with the Bowie knife. The skin sizzled as the silver bit into flesh and bone. Unfortunately, the mummy didn't stop moving. Marco yanked out one Bowie and used the other to cut the mummy's head off.

The mummy continued to struggle.

Marco growled in frustration and stabbed the mummy again, this time in the heart. There was more sizzling, but the mummy continued to rip out of its confining rags.

I was tempted to offer Marco my lighter, but setting a fire in catacombs, sealed off by a cave-in, only added up to one bad idea. Mummies were bad enough without risking oxygen deprivation or suffocating on smoke.

With a quick movement, Marco pulled out a squirt gun and fired a burst of water onto a mummy's chest. The mummy shuddered once, then dropped, just as dead as it had been when we arrived.

Marco nodded, then slid away the squirt gun and pulled out the knife. "We kill them with holy. Good to know. Come on. If we're preserving the battery in your ring, light the passage ahead, I'll knock down anything in our way."

I looked down the tunnel ahead of us, trying to see what he saw. It took me only a beat, but I figured it out. I'd been calling it the center corridor, but it was wider than the side passages. It was a main trunk for the catacombs. Someone had put effort into making it taller and wider. In an age where most people were shorter than Marco, it made no sense for me to be able to stand straight with room to spare. Not unless there was something important about this hallway.

Marco and I moved forward.

The first wave of mummies were only a dozen strong. They moved like arthritic zombies.

Marco charged at them diagonally, kicking off of the wall and slamming into the nearest mummy with an elbow. His body weight concentrated at the narrow point of impact knocked the mummy back, smashing against the floor. It burst into parts and dust. Marco landed in a crouch. He twisted, slashing with both knives. With his left blade, the slash arced out and took the left leg of a mummy. Marco used his right blade to sever the right leg of the mummy directly in front of him.

I attacked the left end of the line with my tactical baton, dropping as much weight into the mummy's hip as possible. The hip shattered, and the mummy collapsed as it hit the ground. It didn't fall apart, but it would have to do. I twisted right with a backhand that slammed into the mummy at waist height. The mummy staggered but kept reaching for me. I sidestepped forward, smacking the arm to the outside. I wrapped my arm around the foul smelling creature, lifted it up and slammed it to the ground, making it shatter.

I started to reach toward my belt for holy water, but decided against it. I had a limited amount of holy gear. Better to see how far I could get without it.

Marco and I sprang forward, pushing into the center of the line. The mummies we had dealt with had been disabled, not destroyed. Even the shattered monsters had limbs twitching and moving, trying to head towards us.

We kicked the middle two mummies out of our way and kept running past them.

Marco was a sharp and pointy ping-pong ball. Every time we hit a group of mummies, he would leap from the floor, slash through some mummies, kick off the wall, and come down in a gymnastic spin, knives out. When he was done cutting through them, each mummy had only an arm and a leg. Few of them were utterly destroyed, but they were hobbled enough that they couldn't follow.

I was less elegant. I used my baton to smash into what few mummies were left in our way.

Marco slid to a stop. My heart pounded against my chest. I generally hated running for my cardio—at my height and weight, it just meant your knees and ankles hated you.

Then I saw why Marco had stopped. At the edge of the glow from my ring was a wall of mummies. They were out of their crypts, standing across the width of the tunnel like guardsmen holding the line. Their arms weren't out and reaching for us. They were silent and menacing.

We doubled back to one of the last turnoffs. Part of the tunnel wall had been carved out into a niche that had held a collection of mummies. I didn't know why, but I suspect it was a family crypt within the general catacombs.

Marco knelt, a distance runner straining to get off the leash. His eyes were locked ahead of us, darting to and fro, constantly scanning for the first motion of hell spawn. He pulled down his bandanna so he could take in larger gulps of breath.

His smile was almost a grin.

This wasn't the target of a demonic horde.

This was a hunter who had caught the scent of fresh prey.

Who was this guy, and what was his day job like?

"Etruscan mummies," Marco stated. "The catacombs were probably sealed off a while ago, as in Before Christ. The mummies are probably animated by old ancestral spirits—look like angels, are like demons."

I raised a brow and spared him a glance. "How can you possibly know this?"

Marco didn't even look my way. "I make it a practice to study up on the demonic fauna of any given area. Trust me, when a Wendigo eats one of your patients, you don't make that mistake again."

I blinked. "A wendigo? What? Did it get out of its lair or something?"

"No. It was a marital dispute." He shrugged, again, not looking my way. "Someone decided a wendigo was a better investment than a divorce lawyer."

"Great. Tell me about these spirits. Etruscan, you said?"

Marco nodded. "Etruscans were basically Italians seven hundred years before Caesar. Maybe nine hundred. Their culture was a little Greek, a little Italian. They were absorbed into the Roman Empire. And yes, they had mummies. Apparently, lots of mummies. As for ancestral spirits, they're the sort of thing that will usually wreak havoc and vengeance on enemies of the family."

I nodded slowly, absorbing his data. "You say the spirits aren't angels. But if they do favors, what do they get in return?"

Marco paused, thinking. "I honestly don't know offhand. But let's face it, they probably get to own your soul, and that of everyone in the family—especially if you utilize them."

I frowned. "Probably right."

Without a segue, or even a flicker on his face, he said, "You know, it occurs to me that you could bi-locate yourself out of this. You *can* get away, can't you?"

I scoffed. "Of course. But I'm not *leaving you* down here. That would be insane."

Marco glanced away from the tunnel and leveled his focus on me. He blinked at me as though I was a species he couldn't classify. His smile turned to a slight, thoughtful frown, then turned back to the tunnels. "How about bi-locating to send help to the outside world?"

"I've been trying. It's a gift, not a superpower. Also? We've been busy."

"Point taken."

"Give me a—"

"—moment," I finished, standing in the middle an office of marble. I glanced around, surprised to find myself there. I hadn't even been trying to bi-locate at the time. "Huh."

The only people in the room was a Persian man I hadn't seen before, wearing a black tactical outfit, and a beautiful woman with long, red-gold hair. I usually didn't notice women other than my wife, which probably meant she was five kinds of stunning—just enough for me to notice.

"Quick, send help to the catacombs."

Both of them looked confused. She asked, "What catacombs?"

"The ones that Marco and I are trapped in."

In the blink of an eye, she had gone from the chair to grabbing my lapels. She yanked me in close like I weighed nothing.

"Marco is trapped?" she demanded.

With strength like that, I could only conclude who this was. "You must be Amanda. Yes, Marco and I are stuck in some Etruscan catacombs. We fell through the floor of the Christian catacombs and into undiscovered tunnels. They have mummies. Lots of mummies. I feel like I'm in a Brendan Fraser movie."

Amanda looked over to the man in tactical garb. "Bram, is that possible?"

He shrugged. "Maybe. Rome is basically one big archaeological tell. There are so many layers to the city, any local with a basic knowledge of history calls it *The Lasagna*."

Amanda looked back to me. Her eyes were amber gold, the color of Frangelico. "How is Marco?"

"Having the time of his life, to be honest."

"That's my man." Amanda laughed. "Try not to do anything rash. We are coming."

"We're stymied by a wall of mummies that seem to be guarding something. I don't think we can move any farther."

"That won't stop Marco."

Nolan stopped in the middle of his sentence. Marco hoped that either he was caught by a useful thought or was bi-locating at that moment. He'd take either.

Marco turned back to the tunnels. He was slightly more comfortable with focusing on the mummies. Nolan was interesting, but Marco didn't know many people like him. The simple, straightforward way he'd said "But I'm not *leaving you* down here. That would be insane" was … incredulous. He said it as though Nolan couldn't even believe Marco had considered being left behind.

*Maybe it's time for me to not automatically assume that everyone is a craven idiot until proven otherwise.*

Either way, Nolan was definitely someone to keep an eye on, especially if they both lived in New York City.

Nolan blinked a few times, then looked around. "Amanda knows we're in trouble. So does someone named Bram."

Marco nodded. "Yeah, we're friends."

"You have friends?"

Marco chuckled. "After a fashion." He nodded towards the direction of the mummy horde. "So, are we going to hit them or not?"

Nolan raised a brow. "I should mention that Amanda said not to do anything rash."

Marco laughed. "This isn't rash. This is taking out the garbage." His mirth faded a little. "Besides, we've managed to keep ahead of the main body of mummies for a while now. But I have to figure they're converging on our position. The ones over there are obviously protecting something. If we can punch through these guys and get to the source, we can avoid dealing with *every* mummy in the catacombs at the same time."

Nolan frowned, thinking it over. "Holy salt," he muttered.

Marco blinked. "Yes, Robin, holy salt would be useful."

Nolan glanced at Marco like he was crazy… or craz*ier*. After a moment, he reached back into his belt and pulled off a leather pouch the size of a Ziploc sandwich bag. "Holy salt. We enter the hallway with the guardian mummies, then use a line of this to cut off the hallway behind us. With luck, that will at least cover our backs while we deal with the mummies."

Marco nodded. "Sound plan. We're probably going to want to hit them hard and fast. Think your ring is up for that?"

"Maybe." Nolan took a breath. "Did you hear about the problems in New England last week?"

Marco blinked. "New England? Try half the Eastern Seaboard. Why?"

"Part of the problems there drained my ring. I'm not even sure that this is back up to full power."

Marco shook his head. "I know what you mean, but I don't think we can afford to go melee through the mummy royal guard. I'm good for the first dozen, easy, but my guess is there's at least sixty in there. I didn't see how deep that tunnel goes. There could be double that, if not triple."

Nolan took a deep breath and let it out slowly. "Understood." He handed Marco the bag. "You pour, I'll blast."

Marco grabbed the bag. "Sure thing, Detective."

"People who fight the forces of darkness next to me can call me Tommy."

Marco immediately went to work pouring salt as Nolan stepped towards the barricade of mummies. He brought his fist up to waist height and aimed the Soul Ring. It projected a beam of light as thin as a wire. It punched a hole through the first mummy in the line. The rags and wrappings around it turned bright orange, as though they were going to ignite. The mummy shuddered, like it had been shot in the stomach, and staggered. It raised its arms and stepped forward, about to do battle.

The other mummies standing guard also raised their hands and stepped forward, about to come for Marco and Nolan.

The beam of light punched through the other side of the mummy and into the next. It slid through each mummy in turn, like a needle through cloth. When it stopped at metal doors at the end of the tunnel, Nolan slashed through the line of mummies, cutting them in half at the waist.

All of them, as one, burst into ash.

Marco smiled as he placed the last of the salt. Nolan was right. The salt was enough to reach from one end of the tunnel mouth to the other.

The shuffling reached his ears a split-second later.

Marco looked up. The tunnel intersection had five branches off it, including the corridor leading to the primary objective. Unfortunately, all four of the others were filled with mummies.

Marco took a step back and drew his knives. "Contact!" he called over his shoulder. "Lots of contact!"

Nolan approached, his fist raised and ready to blast away until they ran out of mummies, or the Soul Ring ran out of charge.

The first mummy to cross over the line disintegrated without a sound. It vanished in mid-step, starting from when its fingers crossed the line, to when it passed through.

Marco laughed and pumped his fist. "The salt acts as a barrier. Nicely done, man."

Nolan nodded, then blinked. He sniffed the air. First, he turned his head behind them to sniff, and then leaned forward, towards the mummies.

Marco arched a brow. "What gives?"

Nolan frowned in thought. He casually reached back into his utility belt and came out with several packets of holy oil. He handed it off to Marco without a word. Marco slipped them into his pocket and followed as Nolan went towards the massive metal doors the mummies had protected.

"Whatever the cause is, it's over here. I smell evil."

Marco blinked at him. "What do you mean, you smell evil *now*? We've been fighting mummies this entire time, and you're *just* picking up on it?" He blinked again. As he'd learned long ago, the most difficult clue was noticing the *lack* of something. "Wait. If you didn't smell evil the moment we dropped into the catacombs…"

Nolan frowned, nodding slowly. He glanced at Marco, his eyes intense and angry. His face had tightened. His mouth was in a solid line, and his eyes had hardened. "You were right. We're fighting Etruscan guardian spirits."

Marco's eyes narrowed as he thought through the implications. "And the mummies *aren't* evil?"

"No." Nolan stepped forward towards the chamber door. "The mummies are the victims."

Nolan raised a knee and kicked out at the door. It didn't budge. Without a word, he lifted the fist with the ring and fired a blast of lightning into the doors, blowing them off the hinges.

The next room was more like a cavern. The high ceilings were thirty feet above their heads. The room itself was circular, with columns every few feet. The statues between the columns were ancient and crumbling, to the point where Marco couldn't even figure out if they were originally supposed to be human. Even the basic forms had been worn away by time.

Nolan stepped forward. He wasn't worried. He wasn't cautious. He didn't hesitate.

With a roar, Nolan bellowed, "Come out and face me you cowardly sons of bitches!"

Marco blinked. *I didn't think this guy could get angry. Huh.*

Marco stayed at Nolan's back, looking at the other end of the chamber. Each statue began to glow slightly. The balls of white light grew out of the statues, stepping forward into the chamber two paces each. They coalesced into glowing forms of white energy, with wings of light.

"Ancestral spirits," Marco said, almost to himself. "Look like angels, are like demons."

"Remember Saint Paul saying that if a being of light spoke contrary to what he taught, they're not from Heaven?" Nolan said to Marco. "I think he meant these guys."

Under his breath, Marco asked, "How many do you think there are? Two dozen?"

"Thereabout." Nolan stepped towards the center of the chamber. He looked from each ancestral spirit to another. "The jig is up. It's time for your racket to end. You protect families in exchange for souls of whoever makes the deal."

Light airy music sang in the air as disembodied voices, acting as one, almost sang, "And the souls of those who call upon us."

Marco scoffed. "Please. That's irrelevant. There haven't been Etruscans for two thousand years. You're out of date."

"No," they corrected. "We are called upon daily."

Marco blinked, then looked to Nolan. "What the Hell are they talking about?"

Nolan's face didn't shift from its enraged state, but he tried to sound calm as he said, "In Italy, there are ten thousand cases a year that require an exorcist. Hundreds of those cases are curses, from one person onto another."

Marco glanced around at the spirits. "The curses call on these guys," he concluded.

Nolan looked around at the glowing, ethereal figures. "I'm giving you—all of you—one chance. Just one. Release all of the souls in your possession. Every soul of every member of every family. Let them go right now, or else."

There were a series of light and bubbly musical notes that Marco could only interpret as laughter. The disembodied voice answered, "But their suffering is so tasty. Especially that of the children."

"I said *one* chance," Nolan thundered. "And you're wasting that."

The music returned. "How will you do that, thaumaturge? Your ring does not have enough power to defeat us all."

Nolan's face broke into a little smile that unnerved Marco. *I wonder if that's what people see on my face.* "Who said *anything* about using the ring?"

A *thump* crashed outside. It was followed by another and another. Marco glanced outside the chamber. The line of salt was now broken by multiple stones thrown at it. The mummies stepped over the stones, all of them moving for the chamber.

"You think you can defeat us?" the spirits asked. "We have an army of monsters, and you have only one ally!"

Marco grinned. "You have that wrong, sonny. You have an army of targets. *I'm* the monster."

Marco charged towards one of the spirits heading for Nolan's back. It stood there, haughty and seemingly untouchable.

Then Marco rammed his Bowie knife into its guts.

Finally, eyes and mouths opened on the featureless head. It let out a scream that was a cross between the screams of terrified horses and nails on a blackboard.

Marco grinned into its face as it wailed in death. "Tell them Marco sends his regards."

The spirit burst apart, like a light bulb that gave up the ghost.

Nolan brought up the fist with the ring, calling up a shield the size and shape of a concave manhole cover, as the spirits roared and threw beams of light at both of them.

"Keep them off me," Nolan told Marco as he leaned into the blasts from the spirits.

Marco looked at the mummies staggering through the gap. He grinned. "It'll be a pleasure."

"God of Heaven and Earth," Nolan started, "God of the angels and archangels, God of the prophets and apostles, God of the martyrs and virgins, God who has power to bestow life after death and rest after toil; for there is no other God than you, nor can there be another true God beside you, the Creator of Heaven and Earth, who are truly a King, whose kingdom is without end; I humbly entreat your glorious majesty to deliver these servants of yours from the unclean spirits; through Christ our Lord. Amen."

The spirits hesitated as the mummies rushed Nolan's back. Marco burst forward, coming in low. He slashed at the mummy's hip. The oil that Nolan gave him bit into the desiccated corpse, severing the mummy's connection to the spirits. It collapsed.

The next one rushed Marco directly. Marco stabbed up with his Bowie knife. He kicked it aside and stood back.

Nolan looked at the spirits, barking through gritted teeth, "Therefore, I adjure you every unclean spirit. Every specter from hell. Every satanic power, in the name of Jesus Christ of Nazareth, who was led into the desert to vanquish you in your citadel, to cease your assaults against Man."

A mummy rushed Marco, and he sidestepped, ramming his knife into its chest. Another one charged, and he dropped, sweeping its legs out from under it. He spun in a crouch and stabbed it in the chest.

"*Yield to God*," Nolan roared, "who by His servant, Moses, cast you and your malice, in the person of Pharaoh and his army, into the depths of the sea."

Marco burst to his feet and slammed into the next mummy before it could close with them, slashing the arms away. It dropped immediately.

"*Yield to God,*" Nolan barked, "who, by the singing of holy canticles on the part of David, His faithful servant, banished you from the heart of King Saul."

The next mummies came in a group of three. Marco slashed his right blade at the mummy in front of him, catching it in the face. He used a left backhand slash to catch the one on his left at the hand. He used a right backhand to get the mummy on the right. He followed the spin to the right, sweeping all of them off of their feet so they didn't fall onto Marco.

Nolan staggered back as the spirits continued their onslaught. He tracked Marco with his peripheral vision, trying to cover Marco from the blasts even as they knocked him around. "*Yield to God*, who condemned you in the person of Judas Iscariot, the traitor. For He now flails you with His divine scourges."

Marco made as if to throw his Bowie knife across the room at another spirit. Another five mummies spilled into the room, coming at him in a rush.

*I guess they shook the dust from their joints*, Marco thought with a smile. He leapt into the air, drove both feet into the central mummy, crushing its chest. Marco hit the floor, then kicked to his feet, driving his knives into the skulls of the mummies on either side of him. The two remaining mummies closed with him, one on either side. Marco burst forward, spinning towards them, so they were both on one side.

Nolan put himself between the spirits and Marco. "Now He drives you back into the everlasting fire. For you, O evil one, and for your followers there will be worms that never die."

Marco dove and rolled between the two remaining mummies, slashing at their legs as he went by. Both of them dropped. He bounded to his feet and whirled, only to see two more mummies going for Nolan's back.

"An unquenchable *fire* stands ready for you and for your minions, you prince of accursed murderers, father of lechery, instigator of sacrileges, model of vileness, promoter of heresies, inventor of every obscenity."

Marco raised both Bowie knives above his head and threw them at the mummies. They both landed with a solid *thunk*. He stopped being fancy and drew his squirt gun, blasting holy water at all of the mummies coming into the room. The desiccated bastards were all making for Tommy.

Marco realized that they were going for Nolan the entire time. He had just been an obstacle in their way.

"*Depart*, then, impious one. *Depart*, accursed one. *Depart* with all your deceits, for God has willed that man should be His temple."

Marco ran up to Nolan's back and clapped him on the shoulder to let him know where he was. Marco opened fire with his squirt gun. And hoped that he had enough water.

"Why do you still linger here?" Nolan asked. "Give honor to God the Father almighty, before whom every knee must bow. Give place to the Lord Jesus Christ, who shed His most precious blood for man. *Begone*, now! *Begone*, seducer! Your place is in solitude; your abode is in the nest of serpents; get down and crawl with them."

The spirits roared now. It was a sound of pain and anger … and fear.

"You might delude man, but God you cannot mock."

The spirits shook, practically vibrating. Their blasts went astray, falling around Marco and Tommy rather than at them. One was doubled over in pain, a wild dog thrashing at the air.

"It is He who casts you out, from Whose Sight nothing is hidden. It is He who repels you, to Whose Might all things are subject."

The spirits stopped shaking, and clamped their hands over their heads, as though that would serve to block out the sound of Tommy's voice. They writhed in pain, and their music turned into discordant wails.

"It is *He* who expels you! *He* who has prepared everlasting hellfire for you and your angels, from whose mouth shall come a sharp sword, who is coming to judge both the living and the dead and the world by fire."

With a final scream, the spirits exploded in balls of flame and electricity that crackled and filled the room. The wave slammed into Tommy, and threw him and Marco out of the chamber. The concussion wave broke the walls and shattered the statutes that lined the room. The columns also broke, removing all support for the chamber ceiling. With a shudder, the ceiling collapsed. Everything above the chamber, an entire building of white marble, also came down, shaking the catacombs with the impact. Dust and debris shot out and turned the air gray and white.

The now-inanimate mummies provided a soft landing for Marco and Tommy in the outer hallway.

The two of them lay there for a moment. Their eyes closed.after a minute or two, Marco said, "You alive, Tommy?"

"So far. Give me a minute. That may change."

Marco let out a deep sigh. Then he chuckled. "You know," he panted, "in New York, we usually just say, 'The power of Christ compels you, you son of a bitch.' "

Nolan smiled. "Well, we're not in New York anymore."

Marco laughed. "Pity. I could go for a real slice right about now."

Nolan coughed. "Yeah. I've had the pizza here. Yikes."

Marco nodded. "Yikes is a good word for it." He tried to sit up. "Ugh. I don't want to move."

Tommy opened his eyes. Dust and dirt had accumulated on the shield. He peeked out under the shield and saw the chamber replaced with a building that had fallen into the pit.

"I don't think we have to. We sent up a big enough flare." He closed his eyes and using both arms to push away the debris that had accumulated on his shield. It slid off onto the tunnel floor.

Then the shield flicked out of existence.

Tommy sighed. "My Ring's out of charge."

Marco laughed. "Now *that's* timing. A few seconds' more bombardment, we'd probably be toast."

Then there was a solid thump of feet landing on the floor of the catacombs.

"Aw Hell," Marco muttered. He tried sitting up, but his back hurt like hell. *If this isn't a rescue party, we're dead.*

Hands gripped Marco's arms. He tensed, ready to go out with his teeth in someone's throat.

Then he was pulled up, his head pressed into warm, soft skin he knew rather well at this point.

"Amanda. What took you so long?"

Between Amanda dragging both Marco and Tommy like they were mannequins, and the Swiss Guards at the top helping them, they were in fresh air in relative short order. Amanda had come to get them wearing a thick cloak and hood that covered her entire body. She looked like something out of *Lord of the Rings*, but it kept her from being cooked by the sun.

The emergency services had their hands full. The building that crashed had been a repulsive white marble building raised by Victor Emanuelle, often called by the locals "the wedding cake." Meant as his palace, it had been mostly a big white elephant for years.

The only comments Marco heard on the way amounted to "Good riddance."

Tommy, Marco and Amanda were all loaded into the back of an ambulance. Amanda pulled back her hood. She smiled at the two men, then reached forward and pulled down their masks. Then she patted down their chests, creating small clouds of dust.

"So, Marco," she said in her light Russian accent, amused, "did you have fun playing in the dirt with your new friend?"

Marco sagged against the ambulance wall. "Honestly? I've had worse outings."

Nolan chuckled. "So have I."

Marco weakly raised a fist. Nolan bumped it.

They were asleep before they arrived at the Vatican.

The next morning, Marco didn't seem phased by yesterday's venture except for a little stiffness. We quietly stretched in the gym set aside for our hand-to-hand combat training.

This time, our instructor arrived.

The doors flung open. In came a short man, around 5'6", with black hair and bright, blazing electric-blue eyes. He was tan from time in the sun. His step was jaunty, almost bouncy. With a big grin he clapped his hands.

"Hello, guys! I'm the hand-to-hand combat instructor. I'm to evaluate your abilities and give you some pointers before the Swiss come to add their own twist. You can call me Sean. Or Mister Ryan, if you insist."

I smiled. "I'm Tommy Nolan."

Marco chuckled and added, "He's the saint."

# Dark Tooth

## By: Josh VanZile

She had never heard a noise like that before, a bawling yawp that cut through the night and straight down her spine. Tilly Mae shot up from her seat, her curly locks bouncing about her shoulders. She hustled from the kitchen table, scraping the chair across the floor with a grating squeak. Tilly Mae pressed her face into the window over the sink and peered into the charcoal darkness.

"What is it mom?" Ira asked.

Tilly Mae glanced back at her son, Ira, and held out a hand in reassurance. "Just a moment, baby. Let me look and you just finish your dinner."

She waited until his fork hit the plate and filled with macaroni before she turned back to the window. Stark darkness greeted Tilly Mae. Across the long yard strewn with Ira's playground equipment and the road out ahead, she saw the beaming lights of Mr. Warren's estate shining brightly like always through the gloom. The jungle gym swing swayed gently in the breeze, a slight familiar squeal ringing out of the partially rusted over chains.

There was a patter of feet and the flicker of a shadow around the kitchen porch corner. Tilly Mae drew a long breath. "Ira, stay here," she ordered.

"What is it mom?" Ira asked without looking up, playing about in his macaroni.

"I think Mr. Warren's dog is loose again." She crossed over into the living room. There was a sharp crack and a skitter as her foot collided with playing blocks. Tilly Mae drew a long breath as she collected herself and rubbed at her toe, wishing Ira would remember to put his toys away. It wasn't the first time. She would have to remind Ira to pick up after himself, again.

She opened the door and stepped onto their porch that stretched the length of the front of the house from end to end. Boxes and pails filled with all manner of gardening implements, rope, and other various supplies were pushed to the far ends of timber planks. Tilly Mae shivered in the cool night breeze, chillier than she expected. She drew her patterned flannel shirt a bit more tightly around her shoulders and strode to the porch end where the shadow had disappeared. She stretched out over the white painted porch railing, her eyes still adjusting to the darkness.

"Bear?" she called the dog's name. Silence. "Bear?" she called again a bit more loudly. There was a skitter of commotion on the end of her property. Something shot through the tall grass out into the woods at high speed, the parting of leaves and brush giving it away. It was then she noticed the quiet surrounding her. The chirp of crickets, hoots of owls, all the accompanying sounds of night were gone, an apparition swallowed in the night air.

Tilly Mae instinctively drew her shirt a bit tighter inward. She slowly turned and made her way back down the porch. Planks squeaked as she padded along, barefoot, quite unprepared for her unexpected evening stroll. Tilly Mae paused at her entrance door and glanced over her shoulder. A cricket chirped. Then another. She stood there as the sounds of the night returned one by one, easing her nerves. Drawing a deep breath, Tilly Mae closed the front door tight behind her.

Exhausted, Tilly Mae plopped back into her kitchen chair limp as one of Ira's stuffed animals. Ira's plate was nearly clean, his macaroni tower nothing but a smear of yellow across the plate. Laying her head into her hands, Tilly Mae placed her elbows on the table and let loose a great yawn.

There was a discordant clatter as Ira's fork struck the table then the floor in turn. Tilly Mae's head shot up. Ira was quivering, his right side shaking uncontrollably. Eyes wide, his hand wobbled and his foot tapped repeatedly, thumping into the chair leg. His mouth moved like he was trying to speak but only a gasp passed trembling lips.

Tilly Mae drew a deep breath and forced herself to remain calm. "Your spray, the nasal spray. Do you have it, baby?"

Ira slowly but surely nodded through the twitching and trembles. Struggling, he twisted about and gave a shrug with his shoulder to the kitchen counter. There on the egg shell and silver marble, a small white bottle of nasal spray right next to the refrigerator.

Tilly Mae nodded, quickly retrieving the spray and bringing it over to Ira. She titled his head back and gave two squirts, one in each nostril, a wisp of fine vapor trailing as she removed the nozzle from his nose. She held Ira's head to her chest and smoothed his blonde hair as he slowly stilled into deep steady breaths.

"Have to keep this on you for your seizures," Tilly Mae said, placing the nasal spray on the table. "We talked about this, remember?"

"Yes mam." Ira responded, his head hung low.

She continued to smooth his hair. "Think you can get upstairs and take your bath?"

"Yes mam." Ira said a bit, perking up.

"Go on then. I'll clean up here."

Ira pushed his chair out and tentatively began to walk away.

"Ira." Tilly Mae said sharply to get her son's attention.

Standing tall, Ira planted his hands on his hips.

"You forgetting something?" Tilly Mae asked, dipping her head at the bottle of nasal spray still on the kitchen table.

Ira gave a sheepish grin and retrieved the bottle; stuffing it in his pocket before bounding up the stairs, his youthful energy returning.

Grinning, Tilly Mae drew a deep breath. She cleaned the kitchen as she always did, hung the dishes to dry, wiped her hands on her pants and trudged into the living room. Her foot struck something hard that shot across the floor. She didn't even bother to look down.

"Gotta remind Ira to pick up," she mumbled under her breath as she crashed on the couch, hoping that Ira would remember to keep his spray with him from here on out. Shaking the sleep from her foggy brain, she forced herself upright. Tilly Mae trudged to the stairs, intent on finding her way to her bed.

A sharp knock at the door roused her from a deep slumber. She stumbled out of her bedroom, stopped at the end of the stairs and as she had so many times before peered into Ira's bedroom. Tilly Mae's son was sound asleep, lightly snoring. A second jarring knock inspired her feet to move again and she was down the stairs in a flash. In her haste, Tilly Mae's foot caught the tail end of a toy helicopter that rolled her ankle, only catching herself from falling by grasping the stair railing. The metal of the toy's propeller was sharp enough to scratch her ankle as it spun, end over end, before crashing into the door, its steel propellers left spinning from the tumble.

"Dang it," Tilly Mae rubbed her reddened ankle.

A quick peek through the eyehole revealed a grizzled old man clothed in a white shirt covered with blue jean overalls. Tilly Mae sucked in a long breath and opened her front door.

"Good morning, Mr. Warren," she said politely, the early morning sun streaming through the doorway.

"Just Bob, Tilly Mae." Mr. Warren shook his head, hair so gray it was nearly white tossing about as he did. "No need for the mister business."

Tilly Mae nodded, although she had no intention of calling the man Bob. He was more her parent's friend than hers, not that she had anything against him. She had known the man since she was a child, living across from him all these years, the same as when her parents lived in the house, and he had always been kind to her. Mr. Warren was in his sixties when she was a kid, so she knew he had to be at least…

"Got something you should see," Mr. Warren interrupted her thoughts. "Out by the road." He stuck a thumb over his shoulder.

Tilly Mae glanced back up the stairs toward Ira's room.

"Leave him be," Mr. Warren said like he was reading her thoughts. "We won't be but a minute."

She followed alongside the grizzled old timer, his heels clacking hard against flopping sandals as he navigated the junk strewn front lawn. Tilly Mae marveled at the ease Mr. Warren was able to compared to her own father. When her pops was Mr. Warren's age, he was nearly bed ridden with Tilly Mae caring for him day and night. If it weren't for the deeply woven trench-like wrinkles across his hands and face she may have mistaken Mr. Warren for a man thirty years younger.

"I think I saw Bear running about my kitchen porch last night," Tilly Mae offered tentatively. "I tried to follow him around but he took off out in the woods."

Mr. Warren cocked a weathered eye at her and slowed his pace. "Oh? Huh."

Tilly Mae stopped short as they reached the road, throwing her a hand over her mouth as she stifled a gasp.

"Yup," Mr. Warren drawled as he stopped alongside her. "I just about had the same reaction."

Tilly Mae lowered her hand from her face and drew closer to the carcass lying roadside, beside Mr. Warren's mailbox. It was a white check marked goat, stiff, eyes sunk in unnaturally, two large gouges in the neck like an ice pick bored a hole right into it. Flies buzzed about the empty holes, pushing each other out of the way struggling for position in the empty wound.

Tilly Mae cleared her throat. "One of the Patterson's?"

"I reckon so, yeah." Mr. Warren scratched his beard. "You notice what's not here though?"

Tilly Mae scrunched her brow and shrugged.

"Blood. There ain't no blood." Mr. Warren continued scratching his beard. "I poked my finger in those holes and ain't no blood anywhere, but that goat sure is dead."

Tilly Mae squinted with concern as she eyed the fly filled holes in the goat's neck then the fingers that stroked Mr. Warren's twisted white beard. She smacked her lips in disgust.

"What do you think did this?" Tilly Mae asked. She breathed a quiet sigh of relief when Mr. Warren dropped his goat stained hands from his beard.

"Don't know. Never seen nothing quite like it." He shook his head. "Wolf, dog, coyote?" He clapped his wrinkled hands together. "Well, just thought you should know. I'll go on to the Patterson's place and give them the bad news."

Tilly Mae nodded. "Thank you, Mr. Warren. I appreciate it."

The old man nodded. "Yup. And just Bob, Tilly Mae. No need for the Mr. Warren business."

Tilly Mae smiled and nodded politely.

"Oh. And uh, Bear was inside with me all night. He didn't go out till first thing in the morning, although he whined so much and scratched at the door last night, I nearly put him out." Mr. Warren paused for a moment in thought before shrugging. The old man then turned on down the road, leaving Tilly Mae to stew in her thoughts as she chewed on her lip.

Tilly Mae found Ira on the swing as she approached her ranch house. He waved at her as she slipped behind him and gave a push, sending him higher on the swing, the chain giving its customary rusty squeal.

"How about breakfast?" she asked.

"Already made toast. Left you some on the counter," Ira answered with earnest pleasure.

"Oh, you made me breakfast? Well thank you," she said with a smile.

She gave him a few more cheerful pushes before her mind wandered. Tilly Mae wondered what she had heard or seen the night before if it could not have been Mr. Warren's hound, Bear, as the man himself asserted. She supposed it could have been wild hogs, it wasn't unusual for boars to be about these parts, but the image of the bloodless dead goat was stuck in her head. She suddenly wanted her son inside.

Tilly Mae tapped a slender finger on Ira's head. "You need to pick up your toys in the living room. I nearly cut my ankle open on that sharp helicopter of yours. Or would you like me to throw it away?"

Ira popped off the swing, his blonde hair bouncing. "No. No, I will pick them up." He raced for the front door.

"You have your nasal spray?" Tilly Mae shouted after him.

"Yes mam!"

Tilly Mae took another wary glance about the brown, dried grass yard, before slipping inside and closing the door behind her.

"King me," Ira boasted, placing his checker piece on the back end of the board.

Tilly Mae smiled ruefully. She obliged and placed a black checker piece on top of Ira's. "I think you are going to win."

There was a sharp knock at the door. Tilly Mae looked at the door, then back to Ira. Another knock, louder than before. She drew in a long breath, then carefully made her way through the toys strewn about the floor, somehow all over the place again even though Ira had put them away earlier. She resolved to remind Ira to pick up every single time.

She peeked through the eyehole to see Mr. Warren ambling about the porch, the flooring creaking softly under his weight. There was a man in a dusty khaki uniform behind him, the sheriff. They were both pacing, hands behind their backs. Mr. Warren reached out to knock again. Tilly Mae opened the door before his knuckles hit the wood.

"Afternoon. Sorry to keep you waiting." Tilly Mae smiled.

The sheriff tipped his wide brim cord wrapped hat. "Tilly Mae, good to see you."

"Likewise, Sheriff Brodie. What's this about?"

Sheriff Brodie cocked an eye at Mr. Warren, encouraging him to speak. Tilly Mae wasn't surprised. The sheriff was not usually interested in explaining himself.

"The Patterson's were gone when I went to their house to tell them about their goat. Front door was open, looked like it had been pried apart…"

"Ahem." The sheriff cleared his throat.

Mr. Warren frowned as he glanced sideways at Sheriff Brodie. "Well, the door was open, so I went on in and no one was there. It looked suspicious so I called the sheriff."

"The two of them are prone to run off hunting. It's not a stretch to think they left the door open." Sheriff Brodie shrugged. "I'm not saying you didn't do the right thing, Mr. Warren, but it's probably not cause for alarm."

"Yeah…" Mr. Warren stretched the word out. "Well, all the goats in the pen are gone too. I found just one of them wandering over by David and, uh…"

"Ann?" Tilly Mae offered.

"David and Ann's place, yeah." Mr. Warren nodded. "I talked with them two and they said they heard some strange noises last night, then I remembered you heard or saw something too."

"Anything you can tell us about it?" Sheriff Brodie asked a bit loudly. He was fidgety, anxious.

Tilly Mae drew a deep breath. "Well I didn't see anything, really. Just heard. Thought it might be a dog, coyote maybe?"

Sheriff Brodie rubbed his hands together. "Alright well, I'll be back in the morning. If the Patterson's aren't back, I'll arrange a search for them. Really not much we can do otherwise, they haven't even been gone twenty-four hours."

"So we think," Mr. Warren interjected.

The sheriff glared at Mr. Warren. "Anyway, I'll check on you folks tomorrow as well. Good afternoon to ya." Sheriff Brodie tipped his hat and shuffled off the porch and down the driveway to his patrol car at the road's edge. He peeled out, riding off in a trail of dust.

Mr. Warren watched the sheriff closely until the car was out of view. "David and, uh…"

"Ann," Tilly Mae gently offered.

"Dang it, why can't I remember that." Mr. Warren shook his head, jostling his shaggy beard. "They said the noises they heard were like loud yelps or growls."

Tilly Mae sucked in a deep breath. "Yeah, that may be what I heard too."

Mr. Warren wasn't looking at her. He was looking over her shoulder into the house. Tilly Mae turned to find Ira on the couch, his right arm trembling and his head listing to the side. He was blinking rapidly, his breathing shallow and quick. His right foot, pressed to the table where they had been playing checkers, began to shake the table hard enough to topple some of the game pieces, clicking to the floor.

Tilly Mae forced herself to remain calm. "Ira, your spray. Do you have it?"

Slowly, Ira's left hand moved to his pants pocket. With effort, he retrieved a small white bottle and brought it to his nose. After a moment of great effort, he found a nostril and released the spray in a short spritz. He sprayed again, then let his hand fall limply to the couch cushion, the bottle still in hand. Slowly but surely, his quivering right side quelled, his blinking slowed and returned to normal.

"Can I…can I get a snack?" Ira asked, unsteadily rising to his feet.

Tilly Mae nodded. "Just take your time baby."

Ira nodded, tip-toeing over his own mess of toys to the kitchen.

"He's getting better." Mr. Warren remarked.

"Hmmm, yeah. His seizures used to be worse. The spray helps. I want him to learn and be able to do it on his own. I can't always be there." Tilly Mae said a bit more freely than she intended. She sighed, cleared her throat and tossed her curly locks off her shoulder. "I hope he grows out of the seizures, but if he doesn't…"

Mr. Warren nodded patiently. He glanced off over the porch in the direction of the Patterson's place. "Look, I know what the sheriff said, but it sure looked like the Patterson's door had been pried open, maybe even torn open." He stroked his beard thoughtfully. "You have guns in the house?" He asked in his gruff voice.

Tilly Mae shook her head, tugging at the ends of her flannel shirt nervously. "No. After dad passed, I just couldn't. I had to get rid of them."

Mr. Warren nodded. "Well, keep the door locked up tight. And uh, you know, I'm just across the road if you need something."

"Thank you, Mr. Warren."

"Just Bob is good." Mr. Warren waved as he strode off the porch on his way home.

Ira fumbled with the knife, the implement not quite doing his bidding and succeeding in only mashing his pork chop into an indiscernible mess. Tilly Mae reached over the table, stuck her fork into the chop, then slid her knife along the very edge of the fork through the chop until a neatly portioned chunk of the meat slid off.

"Like that," she said, letting Ira take over again.

Squinting his eyes, Ira followed suit and went back to work at the chop. He was better, not good, but better, and managed a bit of meat off that found its way to his eager lips. He lumped it in and chewed it in one corner of his mouth, the skin pushing out on that cheek.

Already finished with her meal, Tilly Mae collected her plate and began washing it in the sink. She could not resist peering into the darkness beyond her porch. The stars were out, shining brightly under a cloudless sky. She could just make out Mr. Warren's porchlight across the road, twinkling through the darkness, a bit dimmer than usual.

A shadow streaked near the corner of her vision, startling her enough to drop the plate into the sink. It fell with a clunk against the stainless steel, cracking but not breaking.

"Mom?"

"It's alright Ira, just finish your dinner." Tilly Mae huffed through a sigh.

She grabbed the plate, her hand shaking as she tossed it aside to the counter. Another shadow trailed into her vision, moving slow this time and accompanied by a soft bleat.

"Ira, stay at the table and finish your meal," she said as she reached for the front door.

She tentatively stuck a foot out onto the wood porch, the wood creaking under her weight. Tilly Mae winced, frowning at the revealing noise of her footsteps. Placing both hands on the smooth wood railing, she leaned out into the darkness, not a cricket chirping or trilling in the stark quiet..

The chains on the swing rattled. Tilly Mae jerked to the outline of the playground, a bit lighter than the surrounding blot of inkiness. She heard the bleat again, soft and subdued. A dark shape by the jungle gym moved towards her. She gripped the rail hard, her knuckles white; fingertips aching with the pressure.

A small white furred goat ambled into view and Tilly Mae breathed a sigh of relief. It cried at her loudly, the scruff of its neck shook along with its head.

"Come here," Tilly Mae said beckoning.

She rummaged through the boxes and pails along her porch until she found a length of rope. The nearly all white furred goat was on the porch steps now, one hoof tapping the stoop in agitation.

"You're one of the Patterson's herd, aren't you?" she whispered as she looped the rope around its neck and tied it to the porch frame near the steps. She scratched it under the chin. It was surprisingly placid to her touch. "You stay here. I'll see about taking you back in the morning." With a parting glance at the goat, Tilly Mae entered her house and closed the front door behind her.

She was astounded to see Ira had already cleared the table, rinsed the dishes off, and had them drying on the rack. He was in the living room playing with his toys. She watched as he flew his metal helicopter over some army men, making fake engine noises with his mouth. Tilly Mae smiled as she walked past the stairs and the under-stair closet to the back bathroom. She washed her face with sudsy soap and steaming hot water that saturated the mirror with a murky mist. When she had cleaned up to her satisfaction, she wiped the mirror with a hand towel, drew a long breath, and stared at her reflection.

The goat let loose a shrill bleat. Something collided into the porch with a bang. Nervously peeking down the hall, Tilly Mae glanced at the front door. Sucking in a deep ragged breath, she tossed the hand towel to the side. Leaving the bathroom, she navigated her way through the expanding litany of toys spread from the living room to the kitchen precipice to the golden hickory front door.

Tilly Mae fiddled with the door handle, nervously glancing at Ira, who was quietly playing by himself as if he hadn't heard a sound. Thinking better of it, Tilly Mae took her hand off the door knob and pressed her face to the eyehole.

The white goat was gone. She peered to the left then right as far as the eyehole would allow, seeing almost the entire expanse of the porch. A flicker of white fur just below the edge of the porch somewhat obscured by the four porch steps shimmied in and out of sight. The rope, still tied to the porch rail flexed, went taut, then relaxed. Tilly Mae, worried the goat had fallen and hurt itself, unlocked the front door and flung it open.

She rushed to the end of the porch with an outstretched hand, the boards creaking under her feet. She stopped short as she reached the stairs and gasped. The little goat was twitching in the shadow of the porch, two large puncture holes in its neck. The white hair stained dark around the neck, liquid oozing from the wounds.

Tilly Mae's mind went blank. She stood there, feet rooted to the porch, one hand over her mouth. Blinking hard, her thoughts slowly came to her.

She placed one hand on the porch railing, steadying herself. She looked out over her yard, past the playground equipment toward the road where she and Mr. Warren had stood over the dead, blood drained goat only that morning. The goat gasped at her feet, a gurgle of blood on its lips as it slowly succumbed to its wound and stilled.

The chains of the rusty swing set rustled and squealed. Tilly Mae's eyes snapped to the playground and found an unwavering green eye-shine staring back at her. The inky outline of a canine stood behind the ominous shine, shrouded in the black of night just beyond the light spilling from the open door of Tilly Mae's ranch house. Her body went rigid. Her face flushed white hot. A pit opened up in her stomach, sinking into her pelvis with nausea inducing authority.

The gloom shadowed eyes did not move, staring unblinkingly in her direction.

Tilly Mae took a tentative step backwards, the floor creaking as she did. She winced at her footfalls, terrified each sound would set the creature off. There was a low growl. She felt it as much as she heard it, like it vibrated through her skin and sunk into her bones. Nearly to the door, she extended her hand behind her, feeling for the door knob blindly with numb fingers.

The green eye shine burst into motion, the shadow a flurry behind it. Tilly Mae whirled about, flinging herself through the door and slamming it shut hard behind her. The door shook as the beast crashed into it, the shock reverberating through wood, door handle and into Tilly Mae's arm.

"Mom?" Ira stood near the stairs.

"Upstairs, Ira, quickly!" Tilly Mae waved her hand.

Eyes wide, Ira did not hesitate. He bounded up the steps, two at a time. Tilly Mae rushed to the kitchen and retrieved a knife. She danced around Ira's loose toys flooding the living room and frantically rushed up the stairs, her arms waving wildly with each pounding step.

"Mom," Ira whispered from his room.

Tilly Mae slipped into Ira's room and closed the door, not quite all the way, leaving just a sliver of a crack to peek through. She knelt next to the door frame, one arm around Ira, clutching him to her side, the other gripping the knife so tightly her fingers ached. Peering through the door crack, Tilly Mae peeked down the stairs to the bit of front door she was able to make out from her angle.

Tilly Mae's anxious breaths came ragged. Realizing how loud she was breathing, she swallowed hard, steadying herself until her chest rose and fell in a steady rhythm. She peeked at Ira, hoping he hadn't noticed her fear.

Just outside Ira's window, below on the porch, the boards creaked. The decking groaned, old rusted nails squealing as something wandered about in the dark. Heavy distinct thumps followed, seemingly getting louder with each passing moment. Something sniffed the air like the snuffle of a wild pig, thick and coarse with a hesitance like the airways were blocked. The snort cut through the silence, welling a lump in Tilly Mae's throat.

She felt Ira tremble under her arm. She tipped her chin over his head ready to soothe him, assure him all would be well. Her face fell. Ira's right arm and leg shook. The right side of his face was stuck in a grimace and his eyes shuttered open and closed rapidly.

In a panic, Tilly Mae ran her hands over Ira's pockets. "Ira, your spray?" she whispered, daring not to raise her voice over a squeak.

"Kit…kit…kit…" he stammered. Her stomach sank into her feet. Tilly Mae did not need her son to finish. It was in the kitchen.

"Stay here. Stay here my brave boy." She smoothed his hair back and laid him quivering on his side, so as not to swallow his own tongue. "I will be right back." She placed her hand on the doorknob and drew in a deep breath. She exhaled slowly, releasing the air as she slid out into the hallway and quietly shut the bedroom door behind her.

She gripped the stairwell banister tightly with a sweaty palm. Brandishing the knife in her other, Tilly Mae descended the stairwell, eyes fixed on the front door. The squeak of loose, tired porch decking grew louder and louder as she neared. Tilly Mae padded softly in her bare feet off the stairs, through Ira's playthings, and into the kitchen.

Ducking low under the kitchen sink window, she scanned the room for the little white bottle. There it was, on the counter just beside the fridge. Breathing a sigh of relief, Tilly Mae crawled, hand over knee as quickly as she safely dared. Creaking wood and a loud huff near the kitchen window stopped her in her tracks. She gasped, throwing a hand over her mouth to stifle the abrupt squeak. There was a long pause. It felt like an eternity. Her arms began to shake. Her knees were sore and Tilly Mae could not remember the last breath she had taken.

Groaning wood and the soft pad of feet broke the stillness. Whatever was out on the porch walked away from the window, the squeaking of boards growing distant as it wandered away. Still shaking, Tilly Mae allowed herself to inhale, finally drawing a breath she didn't realize how desperately she needed.

Springing to her feet, Tilly Mae snatched Ira's nasal spray from the counter and raced through the living room, past the front door, back to the stairs. Crack! She heard it skittering across the floor and crashing into the wall before she felt the pain in her foot. In her hectic haste she had inadvertently booted one of Ira's toys clear across the room. She cursed under her breath at her foolishness.

There was a sharp bang as something crashed into the front door, splintering the wood near the frame. Guttural growls emanated from the porch, deep and disturbing. A grotesque paw shot through the quickly widening gap between frame and the fracturing front door. Claws tore at the wood, shredding it like it was little more than paper and pulling chunks with each grasping snatch.

A horrified Tilly Mae retreated a few steps, stumbling over something sharp. She awkwardly fell to the floor, pain shooting up from her rear and up her spine in a great jolt. The knife fell from her grasp, clattering to the floor. Not even bothering to search for the knife, her eyes were transfixed on the front door, the only thing between her, Ira, and whatever was on her porch, tearing that last protective barrier to shreds.

A cold sweat broke across her body. She opened her mouth to scream but nothing came out. The door was nearly pried apart.

On hands and knees, Tilly Mae scrambled to the hallway closet. She pushed her way past a pile of Ira's toys and pressed to the back wall. Still clutching Ira's spray to her chest, she began to swing the closet door shut.

There was a booming crack and the front door burst open. Tilly Mae halted closing the door just as the creature stalked into her living room, leaving a sliver of an opening just large enough to peep through. The beast was canine, hairless with an almost reptilian, scaly head. Rigid spines ran down the length of its back to a scraggly, thin tail.

Stifling a gasp, Tilly Mae made herself as small as possible as the beast licked its lips, gray tongue lingering over a protruding dark tooth. Shaking, Tilly Mae wrapped her arms around her legs and pulled them close to her chest, the pounding of her heart evident on her thighs. Through the closet door gap, she watched as the beast put its talons into her hardwood living room floor and pulled, scraping splinters and shavings up like it was digging a hole. Its unnatural snout lifted into the air and sniffed with loud gusty puffs that rankled her nerves. It stopped mid sniff and cocked a golden bloodshot eye right at the closet door. Right at her.

A knocking from the floor above stilled Tilly Mae's heart. A tapping, a repeated thump, soft but definitive from Ira's room. His seizure was still going, his repeated uncontrolled tapping giving his position away. She glanced at the spray in her hand. Tears welled in her eyes. Ira couldn't help himself.

The canine beast cocked its ears at the disturbance, the pointed lobes twitching at each tap. It moved to the stairs and looked up, droplets of drool oozing from its maw, lips pulled back in a hungry sneer.

Tilly Mae made her decision in an instant. Grinding her teeth until they grit like sandpaper, she kicked the closet door open, sprinting for the front door, determined to get the beast to chase her and as far away from Ira as she could.

The beast lunged at her in an instant. The creature snatched her by the ankle, its dark tooth sinking deep into her flesh through muscle and sinew. White hot pain shot up Tilly Mae's leg. She kicked as hard as she was able, her bare feet aching as they struck cold leathery skin. The creature did not relent; it pawed at her jeans and flannel, shredding them and pulling her closer to the snapping maw. Tilly Mae pictured the goats, their throats punctured and lifeless.

Tilly Mae flung a free hand behind her, over her head, searching with panicked desperation. Her fingers skidded across the floor, fumbling through a myriad of Ira's toys that just eluded her faltering grasp. She kicked again, hard, striking the snarling creature with enough force to get a bit of separation, a precious few inches, moments of time.

In her blind search, her hand struck something sharp. Tilly Mae clutched at the object, fumbled with it. Pawing across her jeans and flannel, tearing holes in the clothing and gouges in her skin that welled with blood, the beast gathered nearer her face. A dark tooth snapped a hair's breadth from her neck.

With a primal shout, Tilly Mae swung with all her might and thrust the toy helicopter propeller into the side of the creature's snout. The beast yelped, one clawed paw slapping frantically at the toy protruding from its face as it retreated a few paces. The body of the helicopter flopped wildly back and forth under the embedded propeller, blood spitting from the whirling toy. The beast pawed frantically, throwing its head about fiercely to shake the object loose.

Tilly Mae scrambled to her feet, limping from her wounds, her blood laden flannel stuck to her heaving chest. She readied to spring around the creature and race up the stairs to Ira when she heard the porch creak behind her. She spun around in abject fright, wide-eyed and her pulse racing.

Mr. Warren, his shaggy white beard flying in all directions filled the broken front door frame. "Get down girl!" Mr. Warren leveled a double barrel shotgun just beneath his chin.

Tilly Mae spun out of the way and hit the ground, facing the thrashing beast. The toy helicopter broke free from the creature's mouth and struck the wood floor with a metallic clang just as the shotgun blast cut through the night.

Mr. Warren's aim was true, striking the thing in the exposed neck. A spatter of the canine's blood struck the stairs as the snarling creature reeled back, head listing to the side. Mr. Warren confidently stepped into the living room, cocking the shotgun with an audible click. He pressed the butt of the gun into his beard-covered shoulder and sprayed another booming blast that set Tilly Mae's ears ringing.

Side and neck splattered with blood and shot, the beast collapsed on its side, legs twitching. Its mouth closed slightly, gums pulled back revealing the single dark tooth all the way to the root. It sucked in a short-ragged breath, then became still.

"You alright there?" Mr. Warren didn't look at her. He slowly edged closer to the carcass, one step at a time. A large floppy eared bloodhound followed him, his dog Bear. The dog growled softly, nostrils flaring as he sniffed at the dead thing on Tilly Mae's floor. "You alright?" Mr. Warren repeated.

"Yeah, yes," Tilly Mae stammered as she gingerly rose to her feet, the pain in her ankle throbbing the more weight she put on it. "Ira!" she gasped, vainly attempting to wipe the blood from her shirt as she hobbled to the stairs.

"Mom?" The voice at the top of the stairs stopped her short. Ira calmly stood with one hand on the stair rail, a bit unsteady but no longer shaking.

Tilly Mae's heart warmed at the sight of her son. She allowed herself to slump down on the bottom step, a smile gracing her lips.

"What is that…what is that thing?" Ira asked.

"Goatsucker." Mr. Warren answered gruffly.

He kicked the gray lifeless carcass a few times with a sandaled toe to ensure it was dead. Lowering his gun, Bear ceased his growling and took a seat at Mr. Warren's feet.

"An actual Chupacabra." the old man mused as he shook his head. "Eighty-two years in this world and I thought I had seen everything."

Tilly Mae stroked Ira's back in the rear of the paramedic van. Her ankle was wrapped, a large bandage strapped around her chest to help close up the ghastly gash she had suffered across her ribs along with numerous other scrapes and cuts. The pain medication helped but it all still hurt. Tilly Mae had no doubt there would be some well earned scars.

Glancing at Ira, she found him far better off than her. She stroked his back in an effort to soothe him, but the truth was he didn't need it, Tilly Mae was only soothing herself. Still harried by the dire road the night could have taken, Tilly Mae drew a deep breath.

Sheriff Brodie was there, taking statements and photos for his official records as the patrol car's blue and red lights smothered her lawn in an ethereal glow. The sheriff blustered about, staking his authority over the scene like a child would claim a spot on the playground. He bickered with the Wildlife Control personnel, the man's official uniform even whiter than his truck.

An argument broke out between Mr. Warren, the sheriff and officer, the ensuing insults loud enough for Tilly Mae to put her hands over Ira's ears. Mr. Warren waved his hand dismissively at the sheriff, storming off, the shotgun still dangling from his hand like a just baked loaf of bread. Mr. Warren's beard shook as he approached, the scruffy white strands jostling in all directions. Bear bounded behind him, tongue wagging happily out of his head.

Mr. Warren stuck a thumb back behind him toward Sheriff Brodie and the Wildlife Control officer. "A dog! A dog with a skin disease and parasites. That's what they say it is." He shook his head as he leaned on the paramedic van next to Tilly Mae. "Can you believe that?"

Tilly Mae glanced back at her ravaged front door then her bandaged body. "Wasn't no dog," she whispered just loudly enough for Mr. Warren to hear.

Mr. Warren shook his head vigorously. "Nah, weren't no dog." He waved his hand dismissively towards the sheriff. "Fools just want the easiest answer, so they can fill out their paperwork and be done with it."

"What about the Pattersons?" Tilly Mae asked.

"Yeah, no sign of them." Mr. Warren's face darkened. "They'll send out a search party in the morning, but…" He trailed off, shook his head and shrugged.

Tilly Mae swallowed hard and stroked Ira's back a bit harder.

"Well, best I get Bear to bed. He's getting a bit long in the tooth for all this action." Mr. Warren grinned and patted his dog on the head. He turned and ambled toward his house, sandals clacking.

"Mr. Warren." Tilly Mae said, holding out a hand to stop him.

She scooted a bit out of the paramedic van to get closer, though the slash across her rips and tight bandage kept her from moving too quickly. She sighed, taking the time to choose her words carefully as she looked over Mr. Warren's hulking frame and white beard in a different light than she had in all her years.

Mr. Warren eyed her expectantly, his bright eyes flickering.

"Bob." Tilly Mae corrected herself, choosing to honor the man with his first name as he always insisted. "Thank you, Bob."

Bob Warren grinned, barely visible under the bushy hair covering his lips and chin. "Good night, neighbor."

END

# Last Bus to Travina

By: James Donzella

Nathan Kent reviewed his notes in the dim light of the old bus as it vaulted over large potholes that peppered the road between the villages of Prad and Travina in the Carpathian Mountains of Southern Romania. His month-long research project, collecting and analyzing verities of native plants and their medicinal properties. Nathan looked past his reflection in the bus window, focusing on the large yellow moon as it began to rise, changing day into night. It was the first full moon in January.

As he gazed, lost in thoughts of what it must have been like centuries ago, it began to rain, unusual for this time of year. In the distance he noticed flashes on movement between trees along the road. Howl of a wolf cut through the hum of the bus engine. Nathan perked up.

"Children of the night," a woman's voice said.

Nathan snickered. He twisted himself in his seat. His left arm draped over the back of the bench. In the seat behind him sat a woman about sixty, wrapped up to the neck in a cloth overcoat. A moth-eaten scarf covered her throat. Kerchief tied tightly over her head. Her face baring the deep lines of a hard life. The quintessential peasant woman of the Carpathian's.

"Pardon me for laughin'. I mean *children of the night*? Dracula's pet wolves? It's so cliché."

Another howl. The old woman clutched her scarf with weathered arthritic hand.

"The moon," she said bending forward close to Nathan.

He held his breath for a moment, mesmerized by her dark eyes.

"It is time of year."

"Time of year?" Nathan said.

"A time for worry. Time of wolf moon."

"I've heard tales," Nathan said. "But seriously—"

"We start late. Danger is on this road in darkness," she said as she turned to the window across the aisle.

A loud, piercing howl cut through the night.

"They search for victim," she said as she pointed a bony finger toward a thicket of trees.

"Are you jokin' me?"

"See! There!" she said.

Nathan caught a glimpse of shadows darting between the pines. A chill race through his body as the shadowy figures ran parallel to the bus.

"English?" she said.

"English?" he said trancelike.

Suddenly her question brought him out of his spell.

"What?" he said. "I'm sorry."

"You are English?"

"American. I'm here doin' research on the medicinal uses of the wood-soral. Oxalis acetosella."

She looked at him like he'd grown an extra head. He cleared his throat.

"You are liking this country?"

"Yes. Fascinating."

"Where is it you go?"

"Vrance."

The woman's face went white.

"No!" she exclaimed making the sign of the cross. "Not good. You must go to Travina, For your safety."

Another howl. The old woman turned to the window.

"They," she said. "Children of Vrance!"

"That's ridiculous," Nathan said. "We have coyote's where I come from. During the winter months food becomes scarce. Wolves hunt at night. They're more aggressive. It's science. Totally normal."

He watched as she blessed herself again, removed a silver amulet from around her neck, cupping it between the palms of her hands.

"It will keep you safe," she said offering the silver medal.

Nathan stared at the amulet in her palm.

"Thanks, but that's not—"

"Please!" she said, her face registered a deep fear. Her hand shook as she offered the talisman.

"Please, sir. I beg of you!"

The old woman took hold of Nathan's wrist. Her hand felt cold. The texture of sandpaper. She pressed the amulet into his palm. Closed his fingers around it. Nathan saw the fear in her eyes. She leaned forward.

Gently kissed his curled fingers. Then released her grip. He pulled his hand back. The chain of the medal dangled from his closed palm.

"Thank you," he said hesitantly.

She sat back in her seat. Tightened the collar of you coat around her neck as though she had caught a chill. Nathan turned away from her, sunk into his seat as the bus jostled him left then right as it raced along the road dodging potholes. He opened his fist. Held the amulet up to the window. As the bus passed through a clearing. Light from the full moon illuminated the interior enough that he could inspect the object. A round piece of metal. Appeared to be hammered copper. A blood red stone in its center. Nathan guessed it to be a chip of ruby. From left to right around its outer ridge an inscription. Nathan didn't recognize the language. *Tatra Gatva Niguhatam* it read. At the bottom of the charm a raised cross. The cross appeared to be worn down from years of once young hands rubbing the object for luck.

"Children of the night," Nathan muttered. "Come to Carpathian Mountains where the locals will scare the crap out of you. Ridiculous!"

Nathan hung the chain on the window latch.


Nathan rode along in silence. Lost in thoughts of the classic Hammer horror films. Snow began to fall as the bus bounced along the country road. Nathan wrapped his jacket tight around him. Closed his eyes for a moment when the bus suddenly screeched to a halt.

"*Vrance!*" shouted the bus driver. "Your destination meester."

"Yeah, thanks," Nathan said as he gathered his backpack and walked to the front of the vehicle.

"Falkon Inn?" Nathan said.

"Walk to next street— turn to right. I must go—late."

"Yeah, thanks," Nathan said as he turned to the rear of the vehicle.

The old woman stared out of the window.

Nathan stepped off the bus. The driver put the bus in gear. Pulled away with a lurch. As the vehicle passed Nathan its rear wheels dropped into a pothole splashing a deluge of mud on Nathan's pants and coat, causing him to jump out of the way and into an icy puddle. Cold water filled his left shoe.

"Goddammit!" he said. "Hey! Wait a minute. My medallion!"

He started to run after the bus but he could only watch its red taillights disappear around a bend. Snow stopped falling. Nathan began the quarter mile journey to the inn. The hunting wolves must have cornered its prey as the howling increased and echoed through the tiny village. As he trudged along the muddy path the howling stopped. He could hear the rustling of leaves and branches on either side of the narrow path. He picked up his pace. A feeling crept into his bones. He caught of glimpse of moving shadows. He moved quickly along the cottage-lined lane. Shadows darted between the trees. Stalking him. He could see smoke from the chimneys of the little village, but the doors and windows. All shut tighter than two coats of paint.

Nathan nearly walked past the Falkon Inn. It appeared shut down for the season. Not a ray of light visible from its interior. No smoke rose from its chimney. He pounded a fist on the door.

"We are closed," a woman's voice said from behind the door.

"My name is Kent. I have reserved a room."

There was no response from the interior of the inn.

"Hello!" Nathan said.

The lock clicked behind the door and it slowly opened, an eye peered through the sliver of an opening.

"In! Quickly!" she said.

Nathan squeezed by the half-opened door.

"It is dark. No one come after dark."

"Bus left late. You have a room for me?"

"Come," she said.

He followed the woman to the second floor. Room was small—bed comfortable.

"You must be hungry," she said.

"I am a bit, but I hate to put you out."

"I bring food," she said.

The women proprietor brought Nathan a bottle of beer, cheese and some rye bread.

"After dark, windows must stay locked," the woman said as she retired for the night.

The room was oppressively warm. Coal burning stoves in every room—stoked to capacity. Besides the heat, an unpleasant musty odor of mold and mildew permeated the room. Nathan went to the windows that opened onto a small balcony. Sliding back the curtains, he attempted to open the window but wound tightly across the two latches handles a rosary. Nathan removed the rosary and swung the windows wide, letting in fresh air and yellow moonlight. Nathan crawled into bed and quickly drifted off to sleep.

A sound—Nathan half-opened one eye, peered through his lashes. Framed in the balcony widow stood a woman, moonlight behind her gave a glowing effect—an aura of light that made her appear suspended in air. A blink and she was inside the room. She moved closer to him—observed him for some time. The moonlight filling the room revealed her complexion. Clear and white as fresh fallen snow. High regal cheekbones, thin pointed nose, piercing eyes, like sapphires illuminated from within. Wavy mass of golden hair hung down to her shoulders.

She smiled—white teeth like polished pearls blazed brightly against the contrast of her voluptuous ruby red lips. Nathan's heart quickened. A yearning came over him. Desiring she'd come closer to him.

He held his breath, to what seemed an eternity—hoping she would kiss him. He longed to feel her warm exquisite lips pressed against his. He watched her through his squinted lids, as she stood motionless. It was pure torture in a delightful way. She advanced quietly, gliding towards him like a skater on ice.

She bent down over him. He could feel her breath on his eyelids. Her breath, sweet smelling but acidic at the same time, was familiar to him. Nathan tried to open his eyes but he couldn't. She dropper to her knees, her head arched over him. Her lips so close to his forehead he imagined for an instant their touch. He watched through squinted eyes as her tongue lapped across her lips, the glistening moisture reflected in the moonlight.

She moved lower, hovered above his mouth—then lower just above his chin. Down her head moved until it was above his throat. Nathan heard a gurgling sound as she raked her tongue across those brilliant white teeth and red lips. His skin tingled as her hot breath swept across his neck.

The nerves in his body came alive.

Her lips caressed his neck—so gently.

It was pure ecstasy. Nathan's heart pounded. He felt a sting. At first, it was just a nip, then sharp teeth plunging deep into his flesh—ripping—gashing.

Sweet acidic smell of blood. It was blood!

Her golden hair covered his face as he struggled. He felt his life drain from his body. A high-pitched screeching sound pierced his ears followed by a sharp pain on the right side of his head.

"*Vrance!*" shouted the bus driver.

The bus bounced to a stop. Nathan tried to shake the sleep from his brain.

"Stopping for you meester!" the driver said. "You get off now."

"Yeah," Nathan said still a little groggy from his nightmare.

He stood up pulled his backpack from the upper rack.

"It was nice talking to you," he said to the old woman sitting behind him.

She blessed herself, mumbling a short prayer. Nathan moved to the front of the vehicle.

"Falkon Inn?" Nathan said as he stepped off the bus.

"Walk to next street. Turn to right. I must go—late."

Nathan stepped off the bus. The driver put the bus in gear. Pulled away with a lurch. As the vehicle passed Nathan its rear wheels dropped into a pothole splashing a deluge of mud on Nathan's pants a coat, causing him to jump out of the way and into an icy puddle. Cold water filled his left shoe.

"Goddammit!" he said. "Hey! Wait a minute. My medallion!"

He started to run after the bus but he could only watch its red taillights disappear around a bend. Nathan looked down at his mud-splashed coat. Wolves howled in the distance. As the bus lumbered along the rough road, the old woman worriedly gazed out her window, silently praying. Her prayer interrupted by a tapping sound. Her eyes followed the sound. The amulet, hanging from the latch, knocked against the window. She turned— catching a glimpse of Nathan standing by the side of the road. She blessed herself.

END

# Composite

By: Sarah Doebereiner

"Islands in the Aleutian chain are beautiful, charming, and quaint."

Ryan yawned intentionally towards the screen in front of him and thought, *like every other 'road to nowhere' tourist destination.*

"Many consider this frontier to be the last remaining wilderness because of its isolation from the mainland. In such small communities, there is very little crime or disturbances other than native wildlife and the occasional weather related incursion."

*Sure, there is no crime. Also, no entertainment, no box stores, no proper hospital, and milk is like $20 because everything is "imported,"* Ryan added.

"However, many people don't realize that the islands have a history of strategic positioning in war time. In fact, you can still find military memorabilia if you dig in remote areas."

The woman on the pulldown screen faded away to reveal vintage photos of the property in its heyday. They swiped left and right onto the screen and settled into a collage style. The work was amateur even for a video tour. It looked like the city paid their cousin a barrel of live bait to make the film. It was one of the most boring presentations Ryan Montane had seen. He set his notebook into his lap and sighed.

Ryan interned at a newspaper on the mainland, and while he fancied himself to be the best intern in webzine's history, *no one* who mattered came to a place like this. Even though he was unpaid, he devoted himself completely to his assignments in the hopes of impressing Irene, his mentor. This, like all the other tasks they had given him, turned out to be little more than fact checking and fluff gathering. He could have *literally* done this on the internet back home. That's where the real news happened. Internet journalism was growing by the minute and was more sustainable than paper print anyway. Really, he was an environmental *warrior* or whatever. All the information in the whole world was just a google click away.

Irene's words echoed through his mind, creating an argument in his thoughts to hold off the monotony. "We have to find the subtle nuances. Each story needs a personal touch or the reader won't be able to connect with it. If you surf the internet all day, then you'll only see what's already been done, what people want you to see."

When Ryan's internship first started, Irene often went into long-winded rants to get him fired up. During those soap box tirades, she would always smile sideways so that only the right side of her mouth ascended. Ryan wasn't stupid enough to argue. He was supposed to be learning the trade from her. If he was ever going to become her, then he would have to accept everything she told him, eat her words of wisdom, and gain her knowledge.

That said, he often spent large portions of their conversations tracing the lines on her forty-something face and wondering if he really wanted to end up like her. Even now, Ryan couldn't help but think that he was sitting here, listening to this drivel, because she was too tired bother with a ferry ride. He tried to feign the look of a captive audience.

Ryan refocused enough to draw circles near the bottom of his notebook. The short, skeletal woman in charge of the welcome center trained her eyes at the screen. She sat uncomfortably straight. The rigidness in her position made Ryan feel like he should appear even more studious. He watched the woman out of the corner of his eye. *Blonde-petite-fragile-militant-strict.* Ryan jotted down a few notes about the woman. She seemed unusually focused for a civilian volunteer.

Since Ryan wasn't really invested in coming here, he hadn't paid too much attention to the two-page dossier that Irene attached to his itinerary. If he remembered correctly, his host's name was Jessica. Her husband worked in the facility behind the welcome center that they currently sat in. She was a homemaker, a nobody. He might have just added that last part himself, but it could easily have been true.

"We are developing methods of recycling composite substances into commercially valuable materials. These techniques will not only reduce pollution, but they will also help eliminate waste and increase the long-term sustainability of the human race," the screen said.

Jessica nodded her head along with the voice. Ryan counted the seconds between her blinks. His own eyes burned at 'seven.' He made a short coughing noise into a loosely closed fist.

Jessica definitely heard him. Her shoulders crept up for an instant, and she smiled, but didn't turn. He dug the tip of the pen into his palm until it stung. The pain momentarily distracted from his boredom. A little dot of ink spread into his skin. He set the pen horizontally on the paper so that it nestled perfectly between two empty script lines.

*I wonder if the people who move to deserted islands are all a bit weird or if their weirdness is born later from living on a deserted island*, Ryan wondered. He ran the tip of his index finger along the metal spirals of his notebook. Thunk, thunk, thunk. That would make a more interesting story than advances in waste management technology. Irene probably would have agreed, but they would never get permission to run a story like that: 'Weirdos in the Wild.'

But no. People didn't like to be told their way of life was emotionally damaging. A widely publicized criticism of their home and their lives under the pretense of a recycling feature would be unwelcome and unethical.

Ryan tapped his foot. He watched the muscles in Jessica's neck tense. Her fragile collarbone pressed against the thin layer of skin on her chest. Ryan stared at her ear. Surely, it was more polite than unethical to record information about their daily routines.

Ryan leaned toward Jessica. "How long have you lived here?"

Jessica turned and whispered a two-word response, "five years," before snapping her head forwards again. The movie played in the background.

Ryan glanced around the room. A handful of empty chairs haunted the perimeter. Light streamed in through cracks in the blinds behind the chairs. If he focused, Ryan could peer out into the empty lot besides the building. One of Ryan's eyebrows edged upwards. There was no one to be *disturbed* by their conversation.

"Do you use the recycled materials in your town?" Ryan questioned.

"Yea," Jessica responded. There was an edge to her voice that made the word buzz.

"My mentor said that your husband works at the plant. What does he do there?" Ryan continued.

The woman shifted her focus briefly from the screen to his face as he spoke. Her eyes settled near his chin before returning to the screen. "All sorts of things," she responded.

Jessica pointed a finger back towards the screen. Then, she folded her hands together in her lap.

"Did he make this video?" Ryan wondered aloud.

Jessica smiled briefly without taking her attention from the screen. Anger bubbled in Ryan's belly. For an instant, he fantasized about jamming the pen into her hand instead of his own. Then, she'd be *forced* to give him her full attention.

The voice on the screen segwayed into the use of organic compounds in the recycling process. At first, Ryan likened the speech to composting, and the use of detrital material to grow crops or feed livestock. In reality, they folded recycled organics into the construction of other non-organic materials. Ryan looked at the side of Jessica's head again. The hair pulled over her ear flopped a bit when she breathed.

"Wait, does that mean—like grinding up bone to use as chalk, or tanning leather to make shoes?" Ryan guessed.

Jessica uncrossed her legs and recrossed them with the opposite leg on top. "Listen," she suggested.

Ryan pulled his eyebrows into a scowl and listened, but the video was glossing over the interesting parts, or rather the more controversial parts. If this turned out to be some a little more fanatical, a zero-waste initiative with an ugly manufacturing process, that was a story he could sell. If it was all horse feet and baby chick beaks, then human interest could easily tip to human outrage. All it would take was a little – nudge.

A loud sound filled the air between them. Ryan jumped. His heart bumped a few extra beats. Jessica looked around the room with her hand on her chest. She rose and crossed to a desk in the corner of the room. She paused the film with the use of a beat-up, outdated PC.

"Give me one moment please," Jessica requested. She shuffled herself through a door into an adjoining office without waiting for his reply.

Ryan leaned back in his seat. The noise repeated again. Ryan tried to make notes. It sounded like a boom-whack-thud. He trained his ears towards the window. It was loud enough to be a car crash, except that the noise lacked the clinks of metal. No, he thought it sounded like a deeper, almost groaning, sort of noise. *Concrete? Maybe a problem at the plant*, Ryan hoped. He moved to the window. *That would be nice.*

Ryan stood. He tossed the paper and pen onto the plastic seat of the chair before stretching. A bone in his shoulder popped. He slid in-between the chairs near the window and parted the crooked blinds with his fingers to make a wider gap. This side of the building faced the East. It was early enough in the day that sunlight assaulted his eyes, and it took a moment to adjust his gaze from the dimness of the room. The plant stood on the southern part of the island. It was within walking distance, but he couldn't see it from this vantage point. He didn't have clearance to wander around unescorted, but if he could find a way to sneak out without Jessica stopping him, then he could say he was worried about the noise and went to find out what was happening. He could try to incapacitate her, but it would have to be in such a way that she wouldn't be able to have him arrested.

Jessica's voice leaked through the office door. She spoke too quickly for Ryan to make out her conversation, but he didn't put much effort into deciphering her speech. The woman only knew what she was told. She worked, no she volunteered, in the visitor center of an island with zero tourism. Even if something was amiss, Ryan doubted that her husband would be able to tell her much about it. As long as she focused her attention on the phone, there was opportunity for escape.

A blur of motion crossed his vision. A small, dark bag floated like a tumbleweed past the window. It blew with the wind, tossing and turning, end over end, as it went. Ryan let out a short chuckle at how inexplicably jumpy he suddenly felt.

Sirens rattled the air. They began as a whisper and roared - louder and louder - until Ryan covered his ears to block out some of the sound. The alert system must have been on top of the visitor's center.

*So, that phone call was to set off the sirens.* Ryan guessed. He listened for Jessica's voice. The sunbeams mocked the siren. There was no rain or storm activity to warrant a weather alert. Ryan shifted his weight.

Jessica popped her head through the threshold of the office door. She smiled—too big. Smiling didn't come naturally to such a difficult woman.

Ryan grunted. *Here is the part where she tries to reassure me*, he mused. Only she was too horrible, too abrasive, for that.

"Stay put, just testing the system," Jessica promised.

"That sound-"

"Don't worry," Jessica answered.

Ryan squinted in her direction. She *looked* worried. The moment she started to turn away from him, her smile dropped.

Ryan grinned. He believed that she didn't know what was happening, but not that everything was business as usual. Ryan circled the room. He snatched the pad of paper from the chair and took it to the window. The hole he made in the blinds remained. The thin vinyl strips were more askew now, but Ryan didn't have time to worry about damaging private property.

He flipped through the notes he made before his arrival and underlined the chemicals used at the plant. Then, he transferred them to a crisp, empty sheet of paper. What could go wrong in the process? The village was set apart from the visitor's center and the plant. The people should be relatively safe, nothing ever happens in a place like this. He tucked the paper into his pocket so that he could type a quick message to Irene on his cell phone. After the message sent, he switched the phone to camera mode. The button at the bottom toggled between video and picture.

Ryan tugged on the long, flat handle of the window. After a moment of strain, the lever gave and the window cracked outwards. It wasn't wide enough to stick his head out. Ryan pushed his arm up to the shoulder through the hole. He angled his camera towards the South and snapped a few pictures. Weight against the metal framing pressed into his armpit. A line of dust marred his light blue button up. Still, Ryan snapped photos until hand felt tingly from the lack of blood supply. Numbness forced him to withdraw rather than risk losing hold on his phone. He snapped the window closed and latched it again. The blinds settled - more or less - into place with a loud rustling.

The black plastic bag had caught on a patch of grass on the lawn outside the window. Ryan wondered if perhaps a shipment container had been damaged. Maybe they used vacuum sealing for shipment: Ryan guessed an explosion could create a sound like that.

The environmental implications of a spill would make a perfect headline. Ryan scrolled through the pictures. His camera automatically tried to focus on facial features. When there were none, it took longer to focus. The images were blurred. He could make out dark spots on the ground. He looked at the plastic bag. It moved with the wind like a kite. The downdraft pulled it closer to the building. Ryan angled his camera for a close-up and hoped they weren't biodegradable. The cleanup effort would be a lot more extreme if the plastic was damaging to the local environment. Alaska law on conservation of wildlife and endangered species was incredibly strict.

"I wonder if they have eagles here," Ryan spoke in hushed tones. Many of the islands did have endangered populations. He had been warned not to touch or interact with them other than snapping pictures. Apparently, eagles were a lot larger than people thought, and *mean* when the fishing was bad.

Wind currents on the island made trees all but nonexistent. The only brush was near the edges of buildings where they were sheltered from the force of the wind. Ryan figured he would have to look harder to find evidence of distress in the wildlife.

The camera on his phone zoomed in and out. A bright green box appeared in the center of the bag. Its handles flared out towards the ground. The top billowed out until it looked momentarily like a mushroom. Ryan hit the button a few times in hopes of getting an in-focus close-up. He noticed two bluish dots in the center of the bag. The green box centered them. Click, click, click.

"What are you doing?" Jessica asked in a loud voice.

Ryan withdrew from the window. He pushed his phone into his pocket without locking the screen. The siren wailed above them. He retrieved his paper and pen from his pocket. "Did something happen?"

"I couldn't get through, but I'm sure everything is fine," Jessica reassured him. "Why don't we finish the movie?

"Why did you turn on the siren if you don't know what's happening?"

Jessica smashed her lips together and rubbed them back and forth. The siren ebbed. Both glanced towards the ceiling as the sound faded. "I didn't. It's an automated system."

"At least we can hear again," Ryan joked.

Jessica frowned. "What were you doing?"

"I was taking a picture of the plastic bags out the window," Ryan said.

He created a large space in the blinds again. Jessica walked over and looked out. The edge of her shoulder brushed against him. He could feel her tiny body breathing in and out as she stood. Short, quick breaths puffed out of her petite frame. *What a trite, horrible woman*, Ryan thought, like a little bird. He probably could have snapped her in half like a toothpick if he really wanted to, but he didn't dare imagine the headlines.

"Our grocery bags are usually brown," she commented nonchalantly.

"I think there might be flecks of metal in it. When I took a picture, it caught the light."

"Not metal. It's a composite material, but using something metallic would be counterproductive. A composite like that wouldn't be compatible. Recycling is all about separating out like components that could be used well together. Metal and plastic would be opposite sides of that spectrum," Jessica responded.

For one moment his hatred waned. Ryan wrote 'never plastic/metal' across the margin of the paper and circled it. He had evidence to the contrary, or at least he thought he did. Titles flashed through his mind. *Bad batch spells bad news for local wildlife. Composite recycling, helping or hurting. The little town that couldn't do anything right.*

They watched the bag roll across the ground. A few more scraps of plastic wafted into view. They floated to and fro on the breeze before settling to the ground. Jessica moved to the far edge of the window. She pressed her cheek against the glass and tried to look behind the building. A snort forced through her nostrils. The way they flared made a cloud of condensation on the window that blocked her vision.

"I know I'm a stranger, but everything is <u>not</u> fine. The materials you use aren't toxic, right?"

"No," Jessica confirmed.

"So, there is no need to worry. Let's walk up to the plant and you can see what's going on," Ryan suggested.

"We are supposed to stay inside. The siren means stay inside."

"I hear that, but we are so close. We could pop over and check on your husband, and be back before anyone noticed," Ryan prodded her obvious devotion to her spouse. If she wouldn't let people talk through his stupid movie, then she would never be comfortable until she knew he was safe.

Jessica rung her hands together in front of her. Ryan could feel her settling into the idea.

Then, a shout broke the silence between them. Ryan practically ripped the blinds down to look out the window again. Several of the aging, plastic slats snapped in the middle. They would never close properly again, but he didn't care. His journalistic instincts were taking over.

What Ryan had first registered as one shout, was actually the combined voices of three people dashing forward in the empty grass outside the window. Ryan kept his eyes trained on them. His hands moved on their own, unseen, scribbling words that slanted down the paper like a waterfall.

"2 women / 1 man. No trauma. All sprinting - woman #1 fastest."

The first woman moved away from the open grass and pressed tightly to the edge of the building. She gestured for the others to join her, but they were too preoccupied with their own progress to heed her advice. The other man a woman, perhaps a couple, ran together hand-in-hand. The man was faster, so he yanked her arm forwards like a child.

Ryan blinked. It wouldn't help her run faster, it would only slow him down.

"What in heavens name-" Jessica started, but Ryan tuned her out.

The people outside couldn't hear her voice through the glass. They moved at a frenzied pace. The wind picked up the bag closest to the building and propelled it towards the couple. As soon as it detached from the earth, the wind filled the bag. The straps of the sack fell down below it. They had ripped and splintered from being caught in the brush. The hanging tendrils from the rounded top reminded Ryan of a jellyfish.

"They are headed for the door. Let's go and meet them," Jessica suggested.

"Wait," Ryan ordered. "Just wait a minute."

"For what?!"

"I don't know," he admitted.

His stomach rolled. He felt an instinctual urge to stay inside. Something about the situation repulsed him, but at the same time, he couldn't look away. The bag sent nervous chills along the edge of his thoughts. He hated touching garbage, and this whole trip had been garbage up until this point.

The trash wafted in the wind randomly. There should have been nothing malicious about it to make him feel so ill at ease.

The lone woman froze on the opposite side of Ryan's window. She shouted at the couple. The bag blew into the woman's leg. She fell to the ground and screamed. Her body spasmed. The man reached down and pulled on the bag. Instead of tearing or detaching, the material stuck to his hands. He dropped to his knees and wailed. More bags floated into view. They converged on the couple as if caught in a dust tornado. They circled closer and closer before settling on the bodies of the people.

Ryan leaned in. His face hit the window with a thud, leaving an oily spot from his nose and forehead.

The lone woman heard the noise and pressed her finger against the glass. "Open the window! Let me in!" She shouted. As she spoke, she looked over her shoulder to see if the bags had noticed her. The people on the ground were covered in a layer of plastic. The plastic moved and shook as the bodies underneath it struggled. Ryan watched the spastic movement under the plastic grow weaker.

"It doesn't open that far. Come around!" Jessica instructed.

She bolted towards the door. The woman outside pressed her body against the brick and slid away from Ryan. He ignored her progress. His eyes remained fixed to the couple under the floating sheets of plastic.

He slapped his cheeks with his hand to sharpen his focus and punish himself for being so stupid. *Get your phone, start recording. You're missing it.*

He let the pad of paper fall to the floor. He withdrew the device from his pocket and angled it at the spectacle. Several of the bags rustled against each other. The force of their movement dislodged some of the thinner bags from the ground. They rose into the air and floated away. Part of the fallen couples arm was momentarily visible as the plastic ascended. The skin was bright red and bulbous. It looked blistered. Blood oozed out of deep tracts in the flesh were the plastic had wrapped tighter around the skin. The couple remained silent and still. Ryan fought to keep his emotions in check somewhere between fearful and excited.

*Keep breathing*, Ryan ordered himself. He looked away from the fallen couple, but the image of their bodies under the plastic danced through his memory.

He was torn between taking notes and continuing to film and photograph as Jessica and the woman entered the room. The new visitor was heavier than Jessica and more muscular. The name tag dangling from her right breast pocket said Rose Cala-something. Ryan shorthanded the new women to 'Rose' in his mental landscape of notes.

Rose dropped to the floor and panted. Jessica sat so she could encircle the woman in her arms.

*They must know each other*, Ryan thought. It made sense, since there were only about a thousand people on the island.

Ryan snapped a candid picture.

"We need to block the doors," Rose spoke. Her voice only had enough air behind it to slither out as a whisper.

Ryan looked down at the two women. A small smile spread across his face before he could stop it. He covered his mouth with his hand to hide the inappropriate gesture.

"It's a bag," Jessica said. "They were bags weren't they? Why are they so toxic? There is nothing in the refining process that should cause acidity in the final products."

"I think we are okay. They would never be able to push open doors," Ryan commented. He forced his excitement down. His phone had one shaky bar. It wasn't enough for a call, but he could text Irene. A landline would be better. It was a lot to explain in writing. He tried to send the pictures first.

"I didn't say barricade the doors, I said block them. They are thinner than a piece of paper. They drift through impossibly small spaces, anywhere a draft could. That's how they got out of the warehouse." Rose added.

"Are they *alive*?" Ryan asked.

"No," Jessica answered. "Just toxic, right Rose?"

Rose pulled her knees to her chest. "I don't know. They move with a kind of sinister intelligence, but they are just plastic—just thin sheets of composite material. We were trying to find a biomaterial that could be used in medical transport."

Ryan noticed a band of red splotches on her arm. "Did you touch one?"

He moved towards the women and touched Rose's arm. She squirmed away from the touch. Her voice edged upwards and she squeaked in pain. Jessica reached out with her hand and pushed him backwards.

"It looks really inflamed," Jessica commented. "We should wash it."

"Do you have any vinegar?" Ryan asked.

"Why would we have vinegar in an office?"

"I think they look like jellyfish. The chemical burns could be stings. You don't have jellyfish in cold climates like this, but the recycling plant uses tissue and materials from all over the place in your research. That's what the video said, isn't it Jessica?" Ryan looked at his hand. It hummed where he had touched Rose's skin. He worried for a moment he might have picked up a few stray stingers.

"If the composite material had a dead jellyfish as the base, maybe some of the spores are still in the mesh. All we have to do is not touch them, or burn them," Jessica suggested.

"Not fire. We tried placing them in the incinerator. The plastic melted together, and we just made bigger ones. The hide is rough," Rose explained.

"Like an octopus?" Ryan questioned. People loved octopi. They were clever and crafty. They could squeeze into small places and hunt with camouflage.

"I don't know what composites were in this batch. They are plastic. They shouldn't have properties of anything, octopuses or otherwise!" Rose shouted.

"Octopi," Ryan corrected.

"They couldn't be alive. They are just bags, they can't eat or breath or anything," Jessica reminded him.

Ryan stood. He went to the window and looked out. The bodies in the clearing were free from the plastic cocoon. Their flesh was pulpy and discolored, but nothing seemed to be missing. Ryan focused on their chests. Their mouths hung open in one last, frozen scream.

They were dead. They had to be dead. At least, he hoped they were. A creature that hunted but could never satisfy its urge to eat. Mindless, lifeless, flesh driven by instinct. Ryan remembered the blue flashes in the picture. They could have been eyes. More headlines flashed through his thoughts. *When trash attacks. Nature fights back. Playing God to save the world.*

"Okay. Okay," Ryan said. "Let me think."

He didn't know enough about it. Math and science were low on the list for English/Journalism majors. No, understanding it didn't matter. There would be someone else to theorize, investigate, and explain it. That wasn't what a journalist was. They record and catalogue; they listen and observe.

Ryan steadied his breath. All they had to do was survive. This story would go viral. It would trend for months. Zombified bags made out of jellyfish. Ryan kept working on a title for his masterpiece. *Recompiled life? Resurrected trash? Population pollutant?* He checked his phone for any sign that Irene had received his messages.

"We need to think small," Ryan decided. "We have to focus on our immediate problems so we can keep ourselves safe."

"What about-," Jessica began.

Ryan cut her off again, "Shush and let me think."

"We aren't in the least bit capable of handling this. So, we should stay put and wait for people who actually know what's going on to formulate a solution," Jessica said.

Ryan didn't bother to argue as Jessica puffed herself up like a spoiled child. From the very beginning, he could tell that she would be a combative and unwilling witness. At first, it had vexed him.

*Too bad that ship has sailed*, he thought. In fact, <u>he</u> was the perfect person to handle this, to tell this story. Ryan was part of it now, so he really didn't have to pretend to care about her opinion anymore. He knew what needed to happen next. The first voice to reach the shore would own the story. The island would be quarantined. They had to get out before that happened, or he'd get scooped.

"We should try to get to the ferry and evacuate before those things get to the water; or worse before they blow all the way to the mainland. We have to warn everyone."

"Who the hell are you? You've never even been to this island before. You don't know anything about anything. They are bags of acidic plastic caught in the wind," Jessica argued.

"God knows you won't leave without out finishing the movie first, Jessica!" Ryan shouted at the woman's face.

"At least I'm not happy people are hurt. I'm not hopping around with my hands in the air like a frat boy just because I am seeing something culturally relevant for the first time," the woman retorted.

Ryan winced. The smile fell off of his face and on to the floor. She was a horrible, boring, hostile woman. He was likely to get stuck with her for a hundred news interviews when they got back to the mainland. His story would always have her in it- the overpaid, welcome wagon lady with the bean pole frame.

Ryan watched Rose crouch in front of the door and wedge paper from a bulletin board underneath the door. "Fighting won't solve anything."

Just then a crackling, crunching sound hit the window. One of the bags had blown into the glass and stuck suspended there by the force of the wind. Ryan heart jumped the moment he saw the dark color invade their space.

Jessica's attention focused on Rose. The two women spoke in quietly reassuring tones while they combined their efforts to seal the door off. Ryan frowned. The only way to decide if they were alive was to capture one.

Ryan's eyes moved along the window. If the glass wasn't there, the air current would push the creature towards the center of the room, away from him. With any luck it might land on Jessica's face and quiet her insults. No one would know. They said themselves that the particles of the bags could fit through impossibly small spaces. Who's to say it didn't wriggle through a crack, the gutter, or the vents. Ryan's smile returned. The harrowing tale of survival, the helplessness to stop the tragedy, the prime-time specials with his name on them.

"There is packing tape over here. Let's tape over the cracks," Rose coordinated with Jessica.

"That's a great idea! I'll put some tape backwards on this yard stick. The bags should stick to it, and it's long enough that it shouldn't touch our skin," Jessica added.

"We could even build netting and section off a smaller area of the room," Rode offered.

The women hugged seconds before Ryan opened a gap in the window. As soon as they felt the wind, the women shouted in surprise. It was too late. The black bag funneled into the room. Ryan stepped to the side to watch the progress of his plan. He grabbed a book to throw on top of the plastic to keep it weighted down until he could retrieve the tape. A tendril of plastic reached out and looped around the broken blinds. Though the air forced its body to billow outward, a pair of blue dots rested on the warmth of the body closest to itself. Before Ryan realized what was happening, the window inched closed so that the opening was narrower. The bag wafted onto his arm. The fabric of his shirt absorbed the initial sting. The bag wrapped a handle around his throat and rolled onto his face.

Ryan tried to scream. The plastic burned and tore at his flesh. His mind raced. He couldn't breathe. People survived jellyfish stings, didn't they? *But I'm suffocating! How can I fight it? How can I survive it? This is MY story of beating the odds.*

A sticky yard stick came down on his temple. The women shouted in victory as the bag anchored to the adhesive. Their makeshift weapon worked like a charm.

"Is he breathing?" Rose asked. She hovered a safe distance from Ryan without touching him.

Jessica kept her eyes focused on the slender piece of wood and the trapped animal. "I think the spores, or stingers, or whatever got down his throat when he screamed. There is nothing we can do. At least the fall knocked him out."

Rose chewed the bottom of her lip. "That or the shot to the head."

"I told him not to go for the ferry. How did he think he was going to fit out that window anyway?" Jessica asked. "Look at it. They are definitely alive. He was right about that much at least."

The bag writhed and squirmed in attempt to detach itself from the end of the stick. The girls stuck the end out the window and slammed the metal frame hard enough to break off the end of the yard stick. The bag rolled away, weighted somewhat by the wood tip of the yard stick. The girls taped over the windows before abandoning Ryan and falling back to the interior office.

"I feel sorta bad that I don't feel worse for him. I didn't know him or anything," Rose admitted.

"Honestly, he was kind of a prick, anyway. I think you get a pass."

The end

# Homunculus

By Steven Streeter

“**B**ullshit.”

Okay, that was probably not the nicest thing to say to a child-hood friend who had just told me his plans, but that was what I thought and there was no way I was going to let him think I was in favor of him wasting his life on something futile.

Yet again.

His response was what I expected. A smirk, a raised eyebrow, and a shake of the head; some things never changed. When he was determined and I called him crazy, that was the reply I. No words, just a look so condescending it infuriated me all the more.

And, again, through years of dealing with him, I knew what I had to do. I calmed myself and shook my head as well, then said, “I don’t believe you.”

“Why not?” A simple question, throwing it all back on me. Another tactic I had grown used to.

“Because magic does not exist,” I stated firmly, not letting my eyes drop. That smirk was irritating as ever.

He shrugged and then nodded. “You’re right,” he agreed. “Magic is bullshit. But this is not magic.”

“Creating life from nothing is not magic?” I laughed. “Sure sounds like it to me.”

“So cloning is magic?” he countered.

“Cloning involves an ovum and cells. There is a starting point. Not magic potions and bullshit.” I poked a finger at him. “They are living things. You’re starting with nothing but liquids. What do you have?”

“My sperm.”

That stopped me. I had to really force myself to retain my calm exterior. “Your what?” I asked. I knew I’d heard him correctly, but just had to make sure.

“My sperm,” he repeated. He said it so simply, as if it was obvious.

“Do I want to know?” I asked.

He stared at me and that little grin re-appeared.

"Man, you are fucked," I growled. I shook my head and turned away. "Call me when you're sober."

"See you round," he said with too much cheer. I didn't turn back. Look, this was not the first time he had hit me with some grand plan – though not as insane as this – and so I thought that, like every other time, he'd come to his senses like and, in a month or so, I'd get an invitation to go have a drink or something. It was what he had been doing since we were teenagers, in high school together. That was what happened after he decided to become a professional wrestler when we were twenty, and what had happened when he had decided to have a go at car racing a few years after that, and even when he decided to have a go at writing the "next great novel" a week after his thirtieth birthday, as well as all those other times.

But this time, it would be over a year before I heard from Luke Thompson again, and even then, at first, it was indirectly.

I'd known Sallyanne for a long time. She was a friend of my sister through netball. Overweight, with unfashionably long hair and shy as all out, I found her sitting alone at one of my sister's parties when I was sixteen, and she was eighteen. She was still there half an hour later, being ignored by everyone else. I admit it, I felt sorry for her, so I sat down. We got to talking, and by the end of the netball season we had become friends. We never dated. I did ask her out when I was maybe nineteen, but she said it would ruin the friendship, and she was probably right. He did date Luke at one stage before dumping him. Said he creeped her out. I assured her I didn't care, and we remained friends.

But as people get older, they fall out of contact. It's just one of those things that happens sometimes. She got married when I was twenty-three or twenty-four, and that was what did it for us. I later heard, through my sister – who was her friend on Facebook or something – that they were divorced, but that was about it. I was not on social media myself, so I never connected with her that way. I did occasionally think about her, but I was in my early thirties by this time and she was a part of my past.

But, quite out of the blue, one night after I'd finished work, I was sitting at home watching Netflix when my phone rang. I looked at the screen. There was no name and I did not recognize the number, so I simply answered with my usual, "Ay-yuh." It annoyed people – my grandma said I sounded like my long-dead grandpa – but it was standard.

"Is that Sean Walker?" came a nervous female voice.

I was instantly wary. "I'm Sean," I replied slowly. That tone of voice always indicated something bad.

"This is Sallyanne," said the woman. "Sallyanne Barker… uhh, Sallyanne Hogan."

"Sallyanne?" Old memories ran through my head in a torrent, rendering me incapable of speech.

"I hope you don't mind," she went on, the strange uneasy quality of her voice not leaving. "Katrina gave me your number."

My sister; made sense. She knew this history between the two of us and the fact we had drifted apart not through any bad blood. "That's fine," I said. "What's up?"

"I… Look, I'm not sure, but… I mean… I don't know…" She was almost scared. I was used to her being shy, but this was beyond that, even for Sallyanne.

"Relax. Just…" I started, but she interrupted before I could get anything more out.

"Can I see you? Please? Tonight?" The words came out like a river, desperation about her tone.

I was taken aback for a few moments. "Sure," I responded, knowing I sounded as unsure as she did.

"I know a decent pub where we can probably be alone and…"

"No," I said. "Would you like to come here?"

"That'd be good." The relief was so sudden in her tone I knew I'd said the right thing.

"Okay. Good." I gave her my address, she wouldn't answer any questions and said she'd see me in half an hour or so.

In fact, it was only twenty minutes later when she turned up. I recognized her straight away. She was the same girl I remembered. No bigger or smaller than before, hair even longer, although her thick brown tresses were streaked with a little grey now, and dressed in the same clothes I remembered from the 1990s. Sallyanne had not changed at all. She greeted me with a brief hug and I led her into my house for one.

She looked around nervously. "Katrina doesn't talk about you online," she said. "I thought for sure you'd be married."

"Engaged twice." I smiled sadly and guided her to the kitchen table. "After the second one, decided I didn't need the headache." I laughed at myself. "Flying solo, I guess."

"I know the feeling," she muttered.

"Tea? Coffee?" I asked, changing the subject. She stared at me and a look of indecision crossed her face. "Scotch?" I added.

She half-smiled. "Got any Coke?"

"Sure." Minutes later, we were holding glasses that were too big containing too much Scotch and not enough Coke. We tapped them together, then sipped.

"It's been a while," I said, trying to start a conversation.

"Too long," she muttered. "I should have stayed in touch, but Doug didn't want me to and after we split, I felt embarrassed and... yeah."

"I'm glad you rang, though," I said, reaching across to touch the back of her hand. "I have missed having you to talk to."

She moved her hand to grasp my fingers. I left my hand in hers. "I've missed you, too," she mumbled.

The atmosphere became uncomfortable. "So, why did you want to see me?"

Her grip on me tightened a little. "What's Luke doing nowadays?"

I recoiled as if slapped, something she noticed straight away, moving her grip on me to take my whole hand. The problem was, hearing his name reminded me I had not seen or heard from him in a very long time. "I have no idea," I admitted, sounding sad even to my own ears. It wasn't how I felt – I was more stunned than anything else – but that was how it came out. She stared at our entwined hands. "I saw him two nights ago," she muttered. "He was in my house."

"What?" I hissed.

She held my hand even tighter. "This is going to sound crazy, but..." She closed her eyes. "Remember Denise Williams?"

I winced. "Oh yeah," I said. After Sallyanne had dumped Luke, the two of them had got together and had stayed together for over two years before it fell apart. He said she was too clingy; Katrina told me he was acting too possessive of her. Whatever it was, it ended pretty badly.

Sallyanne let go of my hand and pulled her phone out. She tapped the screen and then held it up. *Car Crash Claims Local Artist*, the headline read. The photo showed an older woman than I remembered, but it was still Denise. I read the first few paragraphs. Witnesses said she suddenly seemed to lose control of her car on a suburban road and slammed into a tree at speed.

Before I could say anything, she asked, "who was Greg McCabe?"

"School bully. Really had it in for our group. He stopped when I beat the living shit out of him one lunch-time," I replied. Then a memory hit me. "Luke and him had a fight a few months after school ended. Luke had his arse handed to him. But after the police got involved, I'm pretty sure…"

"He mentioned him to me once," she muttered. "That's why when I saw…" *House fire claims one*, the next headline said. Gregory McCabe was alone in the house when it happened. Investigators believed a faulty gas stove was to blame. I just stared at her as she flicked through the phone again, then asked, "Ingrid Bowman?"

"His boss at… Shit." *Woman 'ran in front of car' say witnesses.* She seemed to be fleeing something that no-one else could see. No drugs were in her system beyond a benzodiazepine derivative.

"There's four more," she said, putting the phone down. "All have something to do with Luke." She paused. "And now I've seen him."

"Call the police. tell them. This is crazy…" I started, but she lifted her head and I saw the tears streaming down her face. "What is it?"

"They won't believe me," she whispered.

"Why not?"

"Because the Luke I saw was only three inches tall."

No, I didn't believe her. But I also saw that she was pretty adamant about it. She must have seen the expression on my face because she insisted, then she broke down in a mess of tears. I went across and held her, offered her the spare room, and saw her to bed. Then I spent an hour or so drinking a bit more of the Scotch and looking through my phone. Luke's number was right there; old messages I hadn't deleted were there for me to read; a few photos of the two of us doing stupid things were decent reminders of some good times.

A year. I could not believe it had been a year.

Sleep felt like something I didn't want to do, so I made sure Sallyanne's door was closed, turned the TV on at a low volume and set myself to watch whatever I could find on Netflix. I guessed I would eventually drift off, but I don't even remember seeing past the opening scene of a film I'd watched a few times before. Instead, I felt myself jerked awake sometime later as Sallyanne snuggled in next to me. I didn't think, and simply placed my arm around her.

She kissed my cheek. I kissed her on the mouth..

We woke up together in the bed I'd given her.

She went home to get ready for work before breakfast, and I went to work as though all of this was normal. She turned up at my place that evening with a small bag. I didn't even comment.

Without so much as a word about it, we fell quickly into the life of a couple, so much so that I forgot about trying to reconnect with Luke. For her part, Sallyanne did not mention him or the little version of him she claimed to have seen either.

The following Sunday, Sallyanne returned to her own house. She had another week of work ahead of her and wanted to get clothes and things ready. It felt odd seeing her go; I liked the pattern we had so easily fallen into.

One o'clock in the morning and the phone jolted me out of my sleep. I looked at the screen and saw Sallyanne's name. "What's up?" was the first thing I said.

"He's here," she whispered, her voice hoarse and trembling.

I was about to ask what she was talking about, but I didn't have to. I knew. "I'll be there as soon as I can."

"Thank-you."

Less than twenty minutes later I was being let inside her house, a place I had yet to see. It looked like my grandmother's home before she died — once belonging to a couple, but now covered by the collections of a single person with only one picture of her wedding anywhere to be seen. The unicorns she had liked when she was younger dominated everything. Maybe there were other ways she had not changed as well, or maybe retreating to her childhood was her coping mechanism after the divorce. And maybe I should not analyze the people I care about.

"This way," she said, taking my hand, bringing me back to reality. She led me down the hall to what was clearly the master bedroom, large but sparsely furnished, the bed and a single bedside table the only things I could see apart from the built-in wardrobes. She pointed at the window. "There," she whispered. "That's where it went."

"Where did you first see it?"

She grabbed the long braid that hung down lower than the tops of her legs. "It was climbing up this, like a rope. I screamed. It fell off. It went that way, up the curtain, and out .." She couldn't finish, clutching her hair to her chest, tears dropping down her cheeks.

All I could see on her face was pure panic. Nothing else. I moved away from her; she only reluctantly let me go, staying at the door. I moved across the carpet slowly. One last look back at her, and then I shifted the curtains.

The window sill was white, glowing in the light from a street-lamp one door down.

The brown, muddy marks were obvious. A line of them, from the corner of the flyscreen, which had been bent inwards to the end where the curtain cord hung to the floor. The tracks of a mouse, that was all, and yet I peered at them closer.

"Shit."

The word came out before I realised I was talking out loud. There was no denying what I was seeing. Those marks were not the signs of a rodent, they were human footprints. Tiny human footprints, but footprints just the same. I got on my hands and knees and soon found the trail on the floor, but before it reached the bed, the prints had gone; I assumed the dirt had been rubbed off by the floor covering. No; that was impossible. I must have been putting images onto what I was seeing. Pareidolia or something.

Then I saw the hand-prints. Two of them. So very small, on the sheet, half-way up.

I knelt up and leant on the edge of the bed. I felt cold, despite the warmth of the summer night.

"Well?" Sallyanne whispered.

"There is nothing here now that I can see," I replied carefully.

"Now?"

I nodded slowly.

"So, I'm not going crazy?"

I shook my head. No, she was not going crazy.

Unfortunately.

I left Sallyanne asleep in my bed. She had already decided to take the day off work, but I didn't feel I could do that. Still, her relaxing at my place was probably for the best — it was away from her home and she could just chill out without stress, where no-one knew she was.

Especially not Luke and whatever the hell it was Sallyanne had seen.

Why did I believe her? It was insane, and those tiny footprints and handprints could have been just something we both made up in our heads, seeing, as I had first assumed, mouse paw-prints or the like and reading into it what we wanted to. But… Look, I can understand why Sallyanne thought that after the experiences and the fact she had already seen the little man, which had led her to contacting me in the first place. But why would I? She hadn't really told me much about her experience beyond waking up and finding the small man climbing her long plait — she explained she tended to sleep at the edge of the bed with a leg hanging out, and her hair often also hung down to the floor — which could well have been the last vestiges of a dream. In fact, I felt I was more humoring her than anything else, and yet I was sure of what I had seen as well.

So, I ask again: why?

It's because that last conversation Luke and I had had a year earlier. Him doing another thing that he would fail at and then leave behind and come back to our friendship with his tail between his legs. He was going to try "ancient alchemy". He was going to create that "homunculus."

I even knew what that meant.

Sallyanne had no idea about his plans, and yet she had seen what could well have been one. And the fact that he had not come back like he had every other time now rang strange. It would not be embarrassment — nothing could beat his attempts at becoming a professional wrestler when he came back on crutches, with two black eyes and a photograph of him in Speedos that made his manhood look smaller than he would have liked — and it was not that he had killed or seriously injured himself, or else his brother would have got in touch with me.

That told me the one thing I did not want to think about — he, at least in his own mind, had somehow managed to succeed. Why would he not get in touch to gloat? The same reason I would never see him while he was trying everything else: he would become so caught up in what he was doing that nothing else would matter. Even work went by the way-side; I wondered how on Earth he was supporting himself, and for a year as well. Surely, he had not had that sort of money saved up.

The homunculus conversation and the lack of contact had me at least worried. So, was that why I was seeing the same things Sallyanne was? I had to consider the possibility.

I was distracted at work. My supervisor asked me what my problem was, I told him I didn't know, but me not having my mind on the job was probably dangerous. There were trucks and palettes and crates and boxes, so I went into a corner, stuck my fingers down my throat, and then made sure I made a lot of noise as I threw up into one of the drains dotted along the wall.

That was good enough – I was sent home to go to the doctor and told to have the next 'few days' off. I had enough sick leave built up and I was a good enough worker, so it was nothing major. I claimed I must have eaten something that didn't agree with me and I'd be back the next day, but I was told to have the time off. Just shows that it's always good to not make waves at work and do your job well.

I sat in the car for a few minutes, debating what I should do next. That ended up being a smart move; the boss himself came out to check on me, asking me if I was okay to drive I told him I just needed a few minutes to calm myself. He nodded and asked if I wanted a taxi. I told him I'd be fine. He nodded sagely, and I saw him watching me from his office before I eventually drove off, slowly, cautiously.

I went to a pub first, but did not leave the car.

I had to be completely in control, not even a little off. So, then I went to a deli and bought a lemonade. That helped wipe out the taste of vomit still in my mouth. That was when I stopped thinking about what I should do and simply drove to Luke's place.

The first thing I noted was the new garden that had been planted around every single wall of the place. I am not much of a gardener, but even I knew the plants he had decided to surround his house with were all lavender. It was even more obvious when I stepped out of my car – the smell hung in the air like a cloud. It had gone beyond a pleasant aroma to an almost overpowering stench.

That set an alarm bell off in the back of my head. Not the garden – he grew pot back in the day quite successfully, and his herb garden was not too shabby – but the fact there was so much of the one plant to the point of nausea.

Bees buzzed around, but there was so much for them I was left alone as I climbed the stairs to the front porch. I paused and had to gather myself.

I did not think just doing this simple action would be so difficult. I clenched my teeth and pressed the door-bell.

After a few minutes I pressed it again. I waited even longer, before I stepped back to take in the window beside the door, then turned to walk away.

"Sean? Is that you?"

I turned with a start. Truth be told, it took me a few moments to realize the man beaming at me was Luke. His face was lined, his hair thinning and grey, his beard unkempt and wild. But those eyes were Luke's, and they were as bright as I had ever seen them. I plastered a smile onto my face. "Hey, mate," I said with false cheer that was undoubtedly noticeable. "Been a while."

"It has," he agreed. The silence was almost instantaneous and I felt if I didn't say something, it was all going to come to a crashing halt.

"I got a day off work, been thinking about you, and so…" I shrugged. "How are you, mate?"

His smile widened a fraction. "Come in," he said suddenly. "It has been way too long."

"Thanks." I followed him inside.

The odor hit me straight away. Whereas the lavender was overpowering and cloying, in here whatever I smelled was underneath everything else, it stung my nose and was quite putrid. It was like something rotted was in the refrigerator, but the fridge was closed, so it was just that hint that could be detected. Still, I had to pretend everything was normal and so I just nodded as I took in the decorations that had appeared over the twelve months since I had last been here. Ancient maps, constellation star maps, charts featuring arcane symbols, the periodic table, things written in languages I could only guess at – the sorts of things you would see in the store of a very dedicated medium.

"Like it?" Luke asked, and yet again I jumped at the sound of his voice.

"What is it?" I asked.

He slapped my shoulder. "It's my life. And it is incredible."

I just stared at him blankly.

He laughed. "Come with me," he said. We went into what I remember was the large back-room, where he had set up an impressive personal gym. As soon as he opened the door, the stench struck me and I hesitated a fraction. "You get used to it," was all Luke said. At least that explained the lavender. If the neighbors could smell this, the police would be here in a heart-beat.

The room was no longer a home gym. It was now filled with workbenches and what looked like everything from a high school science laboratory. The windows were all blacked out by what looked like a thick coating of some poly-plastic. Not a hint of light could get in from outside. Even the door that should have led to the rear patio was sealed shut. "What do you think?" Luke asked.

"This is incredible," I muttered. And I was not lying. The place looked incredible. Everything from crystal balls and braziers to centrifuges and incubators was set up amongst a myriad of chemistry glass-ware. The same sorts of posters that decorated the living room were also present here, but there were more of them, and a lot of smaller things pinned up all over the place, many with pencil, pen and charcoal markings on them. And jars of things – animals preserved, plants, creatures that could still have been alive – along with the skeletons of a human skeleton and a large snake that did not look like they were made of plastic were set out in one corner. "What is this?" I finally asked.

"I told you what I was going to do," he replied.

"Make little men?" My voice was cautious and nervous.

He laughed again. "That's right – that was the argument we had. Well, not really. But maybe sort of?" He looked at me and his laughter grew louder. "No. This is alchemy. Alchemy in all its forms," he whispered suddenly. "I've had failures, and it takes its toll on you" – he indicated his aged face – "but when it works…"

"Works?"

He nodded and went across to one of the many wooden cupboards along one wall. He pulled the doors apart, revealing a few shelves with more beakers and test-tubes. He pulled this aside, the glass items staying attached to the wood, uncovering an old-fashioned safe. He rotated the dial left, right, left, right, left again, then opened it and reached in.

"Shit a brick," I managed. What he held was a hunk of gold about the size of a fist. "Is that pyrite?" I suggested.

He shook his head. "It works," he whispered. "I've made gold from lead. It's how I support myself." He threw it at me. I caught it. I wouldn't have known a gold nugget from a piece of gold-painted marble, but it felt heavy and was solid. I walked across and handed it back to him. He put it back in the safe and replaced everything.

"What else have you done?" I found myself asking.

He nodded and went to one of the incubators, then carefully pulled out something which he held in front of me. It was a snake, a small snake, but the thing that got me was the two wings coming from its back. I just stared at it. It wriggled a little and he returned it to the machine. "I've done many things," he said, his eyes twinkling.

"But no homunculus men, right?" I asked before I really thought about what I was saying.

He stopped short and stared at me. I felt uncomfortable under his intense gaze. Then he asked, "Why did you come here?"

I shrugged. "My sister asked about you." I dropped my eyes. "It made me realize it's been a year. We just... shit, mate, I'm sorry. I guess I thought you'd... I'm sorry."

He nodded. "Like everything else, you thought I'd bomb out, right?"

I couldn't look at him. "Sorry," I repeated.

He was nodding and the grin had returned. "That's okay. You're being honest." The grin became the same sort of smirk I knew, with the raised eyebrow and shake of his head. Then: "Want to see the homunculus?"

My mouth fell open and he laughed, then grabbed my elbow and guided me across to another wardrobe. He opened the door and I looked in. The front was shielded by mesh netting. It was set up like a huge doll's house, and there, on a small bed, was a creature that looked like a thin, younger version of Luke. I was about to ask if it was real when it moved underneath the covering and rolled over. "Shit..." I hissed.

He closed the door. "I managed to do it," he said.

"I'm... I'm stunned." I looked at him. "And very bloody impressed."

That smile was so damn wide. "I did it," he repeated.

"So... what does it do?"

He hesitated, then said, "Sleeps. I tried to do things with it, but I have to be asleep, and my consciousness goes into it, so I control it. It's hard, and I can feel what it feels, so I just let it sleep. The fact is, I did it. That's all that matters." There was a hint of suspicion in his tone, a wariness that had not been there, even when he had shown me the gold.

He was suddenly a little tense, so I did not press it. I had the confirmation I needed. But I could not just leave it there. That would look even more suspicious, and it was already bad enough. He had shown me his little man, probably only because of the old bond we shared; maybe he had even been waiting for some-one to come along that he could tell what he had been doing. He was so keen to talk about his failures, which was how we knew what had happened to him so often, so why not this one success? But that feeling I had was that he suddenly regretted his decision. I had to make sure he felt comfortable.

"All right, it's a robot or something, isn't it," I said.

"No, it's real." That suspicion was still there, but now it was tempered by a sense of indignation.

"How?" I shook my head. "Look, it's very impressive, but it can't be real."

He smirked, raised that eyebrow, shook his head, even cocked his head to one side. "Come here," he said.

He took me to a book that looked like it was incredibly old. He placed white gloves on his hands and carefully opened the front cover. He went to a leather bookmark and very tentatively opened the pages to it. He tapped it. I put my hands behind my back and looked at the words on the page.

"Sorry," I said. "I gave up ancient languages in high school."

"That's right. Latin and Enochian. Sorry." He actually sounded like he meant it, too. He opened a drawer, fiddled about, and then pulled out a hand-written page which he placed on top of the book, so I could still see the diagrams of tubes and flasks and little men.

It was a recipe. I don't remember all of it, but it involved putting sperm into a glass container that was sealed completely with fresh beeswax. This was buried in horse dung for forty days and forty nights, then a burst of electricity or "lightning" was put through it while it was in a circle of magnets. Then, for the next forty days, human blood and pus, beside which word Luke had written "plasma" in brackets, was given to it regularly, giving it nourishment. If it came from the same person, then it would take on that person's appearance; if a mixture of people, it would not look like anyone.

"This works?" I asked, but there was no doubt in my voice, just awe.

"You've seen it." I looked past him at the cupboard. "It's alive. These things work."

"It's real?"

"Alchemy is real." He took in the whole room with a sad smile. "This is my life now."

"So, you couldn't come to the pub for lunch?" I asked.

His grin was what I had hoped for. "Of course," he said. "It has been too long."

At lunch he told me what he hoped to do next, with his "studies" – looking into the past, to see the truth of certain events – and me asking questions and giving away very little of myself, except to say my life never changed. He asked me if I'd heard from anyone else; I told him that my sister kept me in the loop when she remembered, but not really.

He then actually mentioned Denise Williams, that she was dead. I did not have to act shocked; it was at the fact he had brought her up, but he did not know that. And I think my surprised, wordless response that made him think I knew nothing about what he was doing, because after that he seemed to relax a little more. It was a good afternoon, I guess. I could have done without the knowledge I now had, but to catch up with Luke was really good.

Why didn't I tell him about the strange and sudden coupling Sallyanne and I now shared? I really can't say, but seeing that homunculus told me everything, foremost being that she had not been imagining things, and I felt that it would put me in danger. If he knew I knew something was amiss… well, the list of those already harmed that Sallyanne had shown me was on my mind. Did I trust Luke? No. Was I glad to see him again? Yes.

However, I didn't know what to say to Sallyanne, so I didn't tell her anything about my day.

She stayed with me for a few more days. We fell into a very comfortable living arrangement. I was happy to not be alone and I think she was happy to be with some-one she felt could protect her. But there was a part of me that felt it was only a matter of time before Luke decided to find out what was going on with her, why she wasn't at home. I was at a loss what to do, but I knew we had to do something.

That Friday, it came to a head before I was really ready.

I was finishing up at work when my phone rang. It was Sallyanne's name on the screen. "Hiya," I greeted. "What's up?"

"He's here," she hissed.

"Where?"

"At work!" My heart froze. There was only one thing that could mean – Luke had grown tired of waiting for her to come home and so had gone after her at the next best place. My mind clicked into gear. I had to think of something right now…

"Catch a taxi home," I said.

"But my car…"

"Please," I said. My thought was it would be waiting in her car, maybe to cause an accident or something, and she had to get away without it seeing her. The plan in my head was crude, but it was something. "I'll meet you at your place."

She paused. "I'm trusting you," she whispered.

"I know." My next problem was how I was going to get there. I needed my car because if this went the way I prayed it was going to go, then I would be seeing Luke before the night was through, but I did not want that homunculus thing to have any idea I was there. There was a connection to Luke – he had said as much – and my presence and knowledge could prove dangerous, I was sure. I had until I arrived at Sallyanne's place to work it out. .

"What do you think he's trying to do?" Sallyanne asked.

"Well, I think he was trying to drive you to do something stupid, like run into traffic or something like that," I explained. "Maybe even have an accident in the house. But you coming to stay with me threw his plans out of whack, and so I think he was trying to do the same thing to you at work. In fact, I reckon the thing was hiding in your car, and you could have had a sudden accident – foot on the gas instead of the brake, maybe – on your way home."

She nodded. She now understood why I had asked her to come home by taxi. "But does that mean it's here?" she asked.

I shook my head. "Not yet. But it will come. Tonight, I reckon. It's just got to get here from your work and it's small."

My ideas were not fully formed yet and I was still trying to work out what I was going to do when she said suddenly, "I went to the hairdresser this morning."

"Oh?" That came out of the blue.

"I was going to get all my hair cut off," she went on. "The thought of that thing climbing up me gave me nightmares." She snorted a laugh. "I've always had long hair, and I couldn't do it. I could not do it. So, I had my usual trim and felt like a coward." She let go of me and draped the long tresses over one shoulder. Sitting down, even after a slight cut, it still pooled in her lap.

The idea in my head started to firm up.

"Maybe I should…" she whispered. "You could…" She looked at me and I saw the tears had already welled in her eyes.

"No. I think I know…" Slowly, more clearly, I could see what I had to do.

"Know what?"

"It's going to be a little uncomfortable for us, but I think I have a, well, a plan."

She leant forward. "What is it?' she whispered.

I stroked that long, thick hair. This could work.

I stayed under the bed. That way I was close by, but when the little thing looked inside, it wouldn't see me; all it would see would be Sallyanne asleep like normal. She braided her hair as she always did at night, but I made sure she finished the plait with six inches or so of hair untied.

She put herself to bed and let the ponytail hang down. It touched the floor easily. I made sure she was comfortable, in a position that would be normal for her, and then used the unbound hair to cover a mousetrap. Sallyanne knew she could not move, so she was frozen in position and I was on my stomach, hidden by shadows and the bedclothes, an additional pile of clothes hiding my face. Maybe what I should have done was gone home, got my GoPro, hooked that up, and watched on my tablet from the next room, but these are the things we think about afterwards.

Look, the plan was rushed and very simple, but this thing had shown a degree of patterned behavior, designed, I think, to drive Sallyanne to something dangerous. Maybe the goal wasn't to hurt her like the others, only to torment her; I mean, we didn't know if that had happened to anyone else. All we had were a list of deaths. That actually seemed to make some degree of sense, but still the idea she had been harassed at work meant that maybe he was upping the ante because she had managed to elude him so effectively.

We waited.

Sallyanne later told me she was not letting herself go to sleep, making sure she did not move, just lying there with a sense of nervous tension. I was in the same boat, but I did find myself starting to drift off more than once.

The noise was so slight I almost missed it; Sallyanne later said she didn't hear a thing. It was a scrape on the glass, something that could have been nothing more than a moth or the like. I strained to listen. A twang; metal moving? Then nothing. I waited.

The curtains moved just a fraction. No more than a hint. Could have been a very slight breeze,, some sort of a bug. So subtle. And I would have ignored it except, from my angle, peering through the clothing, I saw the shadow.

It was about the length of my hand and climbing down the curtain's draw-cord. And it was human. Seeing it apparently asleep in a cupboard surrounded by the ephemera of a pseudo-scientist was one thing; watching it enter my girlfriend's bedroom with the skill of a miniature James Bond was something else. It dropped to the carpet and waited. Sallyanne moved a fraction above me so the bed squeaked a little and the sound of bedclothes shifting reached came out.

That made the little creature drop to a crouch. Then, with a sudden burst of speed, it ran across the carpet and leapt in order to grab the plaited section of hair. I stifled a groan; it had avoided the trap. Did that mean I would have to catch it and give myself away completely? Yes, I was worried about that connection with Luke and hence him finding out I knew more than I let on. I couldn't help it.

The little hands missed the hair-tie and the plait. Sallyanne let out a little squeak. It tried to grab hold of the smooth tresses, but it was as though it was not quite in a good position and it slid down.

The snap was loud; the cry high-pitched and brief.

Sallyanne sat up before I could grab the thing and disappeared. Her own cries and sobs came to me as I wormed my way out from under the bed.

By the time I found her in the bathroom, she was sitting in a corner, crying, a pair of scissors in her hand.

The mousetrap, holding the remains of the little Luke and a chunk of her hair, was sitting in the middle of the floor. I grabbed a towel and wrapped the whole thing up, then went across to her. She grabbed me and held me and sobbed.

It was over.

Unless, of course, he made another one.

My initial plan had been to confront Luke as soon as we had caught the creature. I had parked in a hotel car-park a couple of kilometers away to hide myself from the prying eyes of a tiny homunculus, but sitting there, holding Sallyanne, going to take his creation back to Luke was the last thing I felt like I could do.

I managed to get her to come with me to the living room, and I kissed her and held her, and she kissed me back and would not let go of me. Then, quite out of the blue, she let her hair out of its braid and gave the scissors she had brought with her from the bathroom. "Can you make it even?" she asked. "Make it like this didn't happen?"

I did as she asked. She'd lost maybe eight inches by the time I finished trying to even it up, its length finishing just above the top of her panties. Long, but after her being able to sit on it, noticeably shorter. She then lifted it so it hung only to the center of her back. "Maybe shorter still?" she asked.

"Why?" I stroked it.

She faced me. She was finally smiling. "You like it this long?" she asked.

"I love it long," I replied. She let go so that it fell over my arm. I ran my hands over it.

"Love my hair?" she asked. "Just my hair?"

I kissed her softly. "Not just your hair," I murmured. "All of you. You." I don't know where that had come from, but there it was.

"Me, too," she whispered. "You. Just you." That strange conversation was all it took. Even after everything that had happened on this night — and maybe because of it all — this was the best night we had spent together so far.

That put me in a strange mood as I drove to Luke's house the next morning, Saturday. My anger at what had happened was dissipated somewhat, but I still had to confront him. All of my thoughts of not letting him know that I knew what he was up to went out the window after Sallyanne and I spent the night in her living room doing what we did. We had spent two weeks together, but that felt like we connected on a deeper level than just the physical, and I could tell that Sallyanne could feel it, too. We had been too young when we had first been friends; now it felt like the natural progression and I was not unhappy at the prospect of being with her at all.

How could I be completely mad at Luke when he had brought the two of us together? Our friendship should never have been allowed to fade like it had. Coming together now felt very comfortable and instantly perfect.

I think all that I really wanted to do was warn him away.

I drove Sallyanne to her work, so she could get her car, then headed straight for Luke's place, the towel wrapped around the dead being sitting in the boot where neither of us could see it. It was there and that was bad enough.

I parked, grabbed my cargo from the rear and walked through that lavender cloud to the front door. I pressed the doorbell, waited, then pressed it again. This time there was no response at all. I think he knew it was me; maybe he even guessed what I was doing there, holding that towel in my hands. If he had been connected, maybe he would have seen it. But the thing was surely dead by then. Nope, didn't care. I just had to give it to him and tell him to back off.

I hammered a fist against the door and then pressed my face to the glass beside it. The sound of a car pulling to a halt close by did not even disturb me as I tried to see in through the curtains covering the inside of the front windows. Not until a pair of arms wrapped around my waist and a kiss was placed on my neck did I realize it was Sallyanne.

"Not home, huh?" she asked.

"He's home." I turned in her grip and kissed the tip of her nose. I couldn't help myself.

"He's just not answering." "Go around the back," she suggested.

"He's sealed off the door to the back room."

"And the laundry?"

I shrugged in response and led the way through the side gate to the back yard. The lavender back here was even thicker, the smell genuinely sickening. We both covered our faces as we made our way to the rear patio. I banged my palm against the blacked-out windows of the rear room, but I felt like I was shouting into the wind. Sallyanne tried the laundry door, but it was locked. However, the small window beside it was slightly ajar. She pulled at it and it screeched as it came out and away from the wall. She looked at me in panic and I shrugged. She smiled and reached an arm in. She fiddled for a few moments, then I heard a click and the wooden door swung inwards. She then worked on the screen door lock and stepped back so that could open as well. She stepped aside.

"Nervous?" I asked.

Sallyanne nodded. I offered her a hand. She took it. Holding her made me feel better as well, to be honest. We walked in and I slowly guided her towards that back room and his alchemical set-up. She was stunned enough when she saw the mystical decorations of the living room, but she baulked at entering the rear room with its putrid odor and collection of oddities.

"Come on," I urged.

"It stinks and…" She could not finish. I knew what she was worried about. What if that little man was not the only one? It wasn't Luke that had her scared, it was what he could have hidden in here.

"We'll be right," I whispered. Her grip on my hand tightened and she pushed her whole body against my arm. We walked in and both of us looked around.

I felt her body tense up beside me as she took in the set-up of the room, much as I had when I had first come here. The glassware, the writings and posters on the walls, the skeletons, the jarred things, all of it. It was like something out of a 50s movie. That thought hitting me was when I realised that there was no computer in here; this was all done the really old-fashioned way, incubator notwithstanding. "There," Sallyanne whispered, her voice breaking my train of thought.

Luke was lying on his back on a mattress on the floor in front of the cupboard that had housed the small creature.

Blood leaked from his mouth and nose, his eyes wide open. I set the towel on the floor and uncovered the mousetrap and its contents. This was the first time I had looked at the homunculus properly since we had captured it. The small being was naked and the mouse-trap had almost snapped him in half. I opened the trap and dropped the little body beside Luke, then quickly wrapped the towel up again, covering the hunk of Sallyanne's hair; there was no way I was going to let that be found with any of this.

Sallyanne let go of me and crouched down beside Luke, looking at his face for a few long moments before touching his neck, her hand shaking.

"He's dead," she managed, I think both of us had known or at least suspected that already.

I swallowed hard and lifted Luke's shirt..

His entire midsection was caved in, as if crushed by the bar of a huge mouse-trap.

# The Wine King

## By S.A. Barton

By the time the metal blade found my side I had forgotten myself. In that moment I realized I didn't know who, what, or even *that* I was. For the first moments I was sensation and only sensation. The ringing slash across my immobile ribs was a streak of sudden pain, the searing light of spring sun through the grass was pain as well, and I could not close my eyes or wriggle away from what had struck me. A motionless spasm of hunger gnawed at my gut. I had forgotten it too, when I was nothing.

This experience seemed entirely new, but I quickly realized it was not the first time that something had changed enough to bring my focus back to existing. I had long been locked under the earth, bound in olive roots that had grown and rotted away and regrown many times now. I had been disturbed by the rumble of an earthquake, or by the cold of water flooding the soil, or even by a bull itching its heavy flank on the gnarled olive trunk above me. That had happened before, I was almost certain. My memory was a fuzzy, chaotic thing, but I could feel sense trying to coalesce in it.

Somehow, the long ages had not buried me too deeply.

The world above ground was a wheeling confusion; I had forgotten what it looked like. My unearthing took time and more rasps of iron pain on my strange unyielding skin, the blade of a tool eating the dirt from around me.

It was cold and I could not shiver, could not move in the slightest as if I'd frozen solid as a mountain glacier.

My rescuer freed me from the dirt; the world spun as he turned me over in his hands, chuckling and talking. The words were a familiar seeming jumble of sound; my mind would not parse them. I wondered if I was dreaming but it all seemed too sharp, the sights and sensations too vivid and multiplicitous.

He brought me up a little hill and passed a weather-grayed fence lined with a mesh of fine wire, into a cozy little home where he washed the dirt off me in a bucket of water. The stiff bristles of the brush tingled and he brushed every inch of me, body and face. I couldn't see much of myself but the tip of the beak; it was yellow and crystalline. I was stone; I had been a stone buried in the earth for ages. I could remember that much.

I was placed on a broad mantle over the hearth I'd been washed beside. And there I stayed in the crackle and gentle smoke of the always burning fire for years, watching the farmer and his wife and their four little ones grow and age. As the little ones learned to talk, my own command of language returned in fits and starts, season by season, with a slowness that was nearly as frustrating as my immobility. The order of language brought some sense back to the chaos my mind had become while I was buried in the maddening dark. I could think again.

The little ones touched and moved me with care sometimes, played games around and about me. They showed me to their friends; their many hands polished my features; they began to call me the little king of wine for the purple grapes the inert sculpture of me apparently rested upon. I began to fear one of them would carry me out to show me off and lose me beside an olive stump, perhaps the same one I had been interred by, and I would return to my long dark hades.

And once they did carry me out. They placed me on an olive stump near a little pond to let the sun show off my colors. Pleasure at the warmth of it and the beauty of the pastoral landscape warred with my petrified fear. But of course I could do nothing about either.

Look, they said, the deep purples of the bunch little basilikos perches upon. The smoky translucence of the scaly little dragon body with its long tail and neatly folded neck, the amberlike yellows of its rooster feet and beak, the rich bright garnet of his comb and wattles, the perfect detail of the obsidian pupil within the gold iris within the milky pearl of the eye. Imagine the sculptor—they must have been famous! My mind strained—not a sculpture I thought, but famous. I could almost remember my origins but that long hallucinatory sojourn underground stood in my way. My mind slid off the broad chaotic darkness between me and then.

Motionless, I quaked on that stump. Eventually the sun dipped beneath the trees of the windbreak across the fields and they brought me back, and were mildly punished for my absence. I stayed home on that mantle unmoved for a couple more years, until the war.

The radio gave slim warning of a coming attack and I was forgotten on the mantle as the grand-family fled. I might have been a minor family treasure but even a statue of stone the size of a rooster is heavy, and food and clothes and the smallest most meaningful keepsakes are most precious to those who must flee for their lives.

There was a days-long racket of arms and detonations far beyond what the javelins and siege engines of my past ever brought, or so it seemed in my misty memories; the front wall eventually crumbled in the assault to show me chickens fleeing wild through the skewed and torn fence, some of them smoldering. Others lay torn and bloody among the flinders of the chicken coop.

I wondered if Zeus had gotten around even more than usual during my long dirt dream as a stone imprisoned in roots; that's how I remembered Zeus although I'd never seen him.

Who, in fact, had I seen? I wondered a moment, but then there were soldiers derailing my thoughts with the sharp edged grins of victors sacking, speaking a tongue I did not recognize, bearing unfamiliar arms and emblems of lightning and broken crosses. I was lifted down cavalierly by one and stuffed into a small metal chest through a thick layer of newsprint. The chest smelled of oil and sulfur and I could hear through its thin walls easily—voices and the mechanical racket of a conveyance that jostled rapidly as it traveled, and then for a time the sounds of passage over the sea. If I cursed the dark blindness of the box that contained me, I was grateful for the voices of people and seagulls even if I understood neither.

And then another racketing conveyance, and casual inscrutable conversation while my box was briskly carried and shelved or stacked with a dull thud of metal on wood, and then quiet.

Time passed and nightmares of timeless olive roots came to me. How to count years in dark and silence with no way to keep time, not even breathing lungs or a beating heart? I feared the smeary floating of madness; my mind grasped desperately at the sometimes sounds of footfalls, distant voices, the scrabbling of rats passing by, a storm beating on a metal roof.

Finally, after what I soon understood to be some two decades, my case was transported again and opened.

Opened by a young bookish man in spectacles who spoke to me in his language reminiscent of the soldiers' tongue but with fewer hard edges.

He knew what to call me: basilikos; cockatrice; little king; little death. It was impossible to learn much of his language from monologue, but his intentions were clear. I took up a portion of a wide and broad work table; day by day he gloved himself, cleaned and polished me in meticulous detail with the softest leathers and cloths, used the finest picks of metal and wood to clear my every crevice. I was photographed many times along the way—I understood the roots of the word but how a box and a flare of brightness would write anything about me in light, I could not quite understand until he brought back some of the images and set them on the table in my sight for a while before he archived them.

I was on the bench with many other figures of statuary and pottery for a couple of weeks; the young man listened to the radio as he worked and I began to pick up more of his barbarian language. Eventually he turned me over while holding me in a large clean sheet of chamois and I felt the cool tackiness of paint against my hind left foot—no doubt the same word or numbers he recorded in a heavy catalog that lived on a book stand among the many shelves beyond the room I was in.

And then one early morning I was moved to a gallery; there were two windows facing east and though they showed me nothing but the tops of trees and sky I could see the faint glimmer of gloaming among the early clouds. I knew where I was by then: a museum in a city with the alien name of London, in a place for the study of antiquities. I was certainly an antiquity and I was more than they knew. But mute and motionless I could only wait and watch.

From atop a pedestal and inside a cubic box of preternaturally clear and thick glass, I watched hundreds upon hundreds of people wander past, curious and conversing softly in many languages—mostly English. I was obviously labeled "Basilisk perched upon a bunch of grapes, unknown artist, circa 3000 BC". I heard many patrons mumble it to themselves as they showed me their bald spots.

Unknown artist. I could still not recall how I had come to be in my state—were all statues of sufficient artistry imbued with mind, cursed to a paralyzed hell? It seemed unlikely.

And in this gallery, too, the scent of the people concentrated in a subtle way; if a stone stomach could growl mine would have. Where does hunger originate but from life? I was not a mere figurine; once I had lived. I believed that.

I was grateful for the visitors of the gallery and even the endless gnawing hunger they sparked. Their presence pushed away the fear of the olive stump and the dark box.

Thirty years passed in that gallery; toward the latter part many of the patrons greeted me as a familiar, with casual hellos and remember-you-from-childhoods. But eventually one night after the museum closed it was out of the glass box and back to the bench where I had been polished upon my arrival. It looked the same. The fear rose again as if no time had passed at all: I was to vanish into the silence of the dark again, helpless, shelved. I might molder in the storehouse of such a great collection of antiquities for centuries, I thought.

But instead the one who came to deal with me was my first admirer. I had seen him frequently, watched him grow slightly stouter and much grayer as the many seasons passed. He came to the work table late in the night when all was still; in the indistinct periphery of my vision I saw him put some other artifact in the open cubicle apparently prepared for me, and he took me home in the bottom of his leather shoulder bag under a cardigan and beside a clear little box containing a half-eaten chicken sandwich.

Perhaps he would find a way to release me, or at least come to suspect such a thing was necessary at all? I knew it was a deranged and unlikely hope born of my many centuries of mute and immobile captivity.

So imagine my fear and disappointment when, in a rumpled and half empty little home, I was placed upon and wrapped in a soft little blanket and nailed into a snug box of wood to wait, jostle, wait, jostle, and wait some more.

But I was not shelved or forgotten again. The nails and wood were pried back open in mere days. I emerged by his hands into something of a cozy library room evidently still being arranged—a new household, likely a place of retirement for my gray admirer.

I was placed high up behind the glass door of a wine cabinet—made of olive wood, I noted with an internal shudder.

The bottles were fragrant behind me; ahead and to my left a window overlooked great buildings so tall I could not see their tops or the streets below but only occasionally hear the sounds of them.

My benefactor spent a few days tidying the new home, and then there were visitors: a younger couple of whom the woman was his daughter, and three teen boys straining towards adulthood.

Even through the glass I could smell them all, vibrant and spicy and delicious. My hope deepened, though I had no reason to be optimistic.

In the wee hours of that night, with a full moon peering through the window, they came. The three callow boy-men, redolent of cannabis, giggling and whispering among themselves. One produced a key and, with the other two slapping his back and pawing at his shoulders, he unlocked the wine cabinet door. Jostled by his compatriots, he fumbled a magnum loose from a shelf above me and it dropped from his fingers. The heavy glass fell on the inviolate stone of me and shattered, soaking me in rich red wine, knocking me to the heavily carpeted floor.

The boy muttered an oath; the other two gasped and swiveled their heads to the library door as if punishment would arrive immediately.

The one who had dropped the wine knelt and grasped me carelessly in my nest of glass; the shards opened his fingers and added his blood to the mess of wine that coated me.

Blood of man plus ichor of the gods and vines was apparently the key; for the first time in millennia breath flowed into me. My wings stirred and I did not hesitate at my chance: I struck the boy's palm with my beak before he could withdraw.

He gasped, gripped his glass and beak torn hand, tried to stand, then stumbled and fell prostrate before me like a worshiper as the gangrene I had sparked raced up his arm. The poisons of it flowed through his veins and his eyes fluttered, rolling to show the whites.

His friends turned away from the door to face him and I cunningly froze in place; he whimpered for help and they grasped his shoulders trying to help him up. Seeing my chance I spread my wings and fluttered to perch between his rot-softening shoulder blades, and struck swiftly to the right and left. Both of the boys fell writhing as the swift gangrene I had wrought poured poison into their veins.

Once they all quieted I began to move the "grapes" into the rotting mass of them. Not grapes, but eggs. The restoration of life had restored a memory: the Gorgon had caught me on my brooding clutch and stopped me cold the night before hatching-time, saving old Athens from the wrath of me and mine. But this Manhattan would do; it seemed far more grand a feeding ground.

My eggs safe in the softening mound of food for my hatchlings, I nosed the library door open enough to pass and listen for the sleeping breath of my rescuer and his guests. The doors of this place were made of wood, and wood would rot as easily as flesh at the touch of my beak if I so wished. If they would not, I was much stronger than my stature suggested, and my beak could pierce the skin of a god.

By morning this place would be my nest, and within months my brood would be ready to lay their own eggs, prepared to make the world outside our kingdom.

END

# The Murderous Grasshopper

By S.M. Dziok

The wind plucked at my clothes as I gazed at the river far below, the roar of the surging waters audible even from the high cliff. I marveled at how easy it would be to slip on the boulder and free-fall into the nearly frozen depths below. If the fall didn't kill you, then the icy water might. How long would it take to find a body trapped under ice?

How did it come to this? A woman scorned…. There are so many "what-ifs," but all I could think in that moment was: What if I'd had better hair?

Yes, if it weren't for the unmanageable mop of mousiness atop my head, I might've been consistently considered rather attractive. I mean, my face was okay, nothing too asymmetrical, no pock marks, only the occasional pimple every college kid deals with occasionally. But my hair—Christ. No matter what I did – color, cut, curl – my hair remained an awkward assortment of lumps and frizz.

Unlike the mane of my ex-boyfriend's newly exed lover. Her hair was the stuff of shampoo commercials, long and sun-shiny blonde and feathered like a beautiful bird. As the commercial claimed, *"Sometimes you need a little Finesse, sometimes you need a lot."* I needed vats of the stuff. Even at that moment, after all the turmoil, her coif looked professionally tussled. She never had a problem snagging a boyfriend—and a hot one, at that. Not the squidly guys I fumbled around with in the backseat of a Datsun out of sheer boredom or the "nice guys" with some extra pudge who used me to raise their own status and then cheated on me once they got a chance. Sheesh. Not that I was bitter or anything.

I just wished she'd stop screaming. Made it hard to have profound thoughts.

Where was I? With a prompt from Talking Heads: *"Well, how did I get here?"* Just a few months earlier, I was a bright, decent-looking young woman who was, sadly *"too shy-shy"* (thanks, Kajagoogoo). My self-confidence with the opposite sex hovered around my kneecaps. That's probably how I ended up on this cliff: Low self-esteem makes you vulnerable to jerks and creeps.

And, apparently, intergalactic grasshoppers with homicidal tendencies.

It all started about two weeks into my first semester at Highcliff University, a college of middling repute named for its picturesque location atop the river bluffs, home of the Highcliff Crickets. The choice of mascot was appropriate; a mention of Highcliff outside of our Midwestern state was usually met with the sound of crickets. What was there to do in town at night? Listen to the crickets. At least it was affordable.

My friend Deanne and her beau Ben (honest to god, that's what she called him) invited me to a little "soiree" in Ben's dorm room before going to the Hoot Hut (not making it up) to check out a campus band. Anytime Deanne "Frenchified" a word, you knew there was likely to be booze or heavy petting involved. Sure enough, when I arrived, Ben was laughing hysterically, Deanne was slurring and leaning all over him, and friends of Ben's were giggling and telling dirty jokes between shots of vodka Jell-O. Kenny Loggins's voice purred out of the boombox, and one of the dudes pointed to his crotch, stating, "This is my danger zone, baby!" Some guy handed me a cup with a noxious blue beverage in it and instructed me to drink up until I thought he was handsome.

"Not enough booze here to conjure that miracle," I replied, taking a sip anyway. It tasted of blueberries soaked in kerosene.

The usual squids were there: Freckle-Face, Shorty, Possible Molester, and Wastoid. Trust me, attention from these guys did nothing for one's self-esteem. Seriously, gag me with whatever utensil you like. Anything remotely female was fair game for them. Shorty and Wastoid were actually decent guys but not my type. Surrounded by such gentlemen, my awkwardness melted away and I became a regular Joan Rivers, as would happen when the stakes were low.

I was two vodka-cubes and one flaming blueberry drink into the pre-concert prep when there was a knock on the door. Immediately, drinks disappeared under beds and desks, lest the knocker be an RA. (RA prowls had increased since a kid went missing a week earlier. Highcliff leaders, in their awesome logic, thought patrolling dorm halls more thoroughly would somehow keep students from disappearing off the quad.)

Ben hobbled over to the door and let in the most gorgeous man I had ever seen—like, my jaw hit the floor. Gently curling, soft-looking black hair.

Eyes bluer than the Jell-O shots. He lived in the room across the hall from Ben. His name was Hugh, he said as introductions were made, the guys shaking hands and Deanne waving drunkenly from the bunk.

I shook his hand and knew that that would be it for my wittiness that evening. My mind simply wouldn't function in the presence of such beauty. I stammered out my name and tried to pat down the lump of hair above my right ear. He smiled at me.

Yep, I was done for.

Hugh joined us for the concert. That familiar combination of thrill and nausea washed over me. My usual performance anxiety.. He struck up a conversation with me—with *me!*—asking about the band and what music I liked and…

"…so what do you do when you're not in class, Lydia?"

My mind went blank. *What do I do? Do I do anything?* I couldn't remember. "Um, uh, you know. Just the normal stuff. Concerts and things," I replied to my shoes. *So lame.*

He laughed. "So you're a 'normal girl,' would you say?"

"Oh, I don't know about that. Everyone's pretty odd in their own way, no?"

He conceded that, yes, perhaps we all were odd. *Does he think I'm a freak now? A freak with lumpy hair?*

"So… um, what's your major?" I asked. *Could I be any lamer?*

"I'm pre-med, aiming to be a forensic pathologist," he said. *Oh god, save me – he's smart, too.*

The concert was forgettable, largely because I tried to appear cool and discerning the whole time. The evening ended and the gang headed back to Ben's dorm as I scurried off to my own. Hugh asked if I'd like an escort, since it was dark and there had been that violent attack on a student three days earlier, but I waved him off to show that I was a Strong, Brave and Definitely-Not-Clingy Woman. Then I resumed scurrying. Scurrying and addressing my oxfords in conversation were sure signs I had fallen in love.

It was unthinkable that someone like Hugh would be interested in me. But there he was, whenever I dropped by Ben's room. He even found me in the library one afternoon. I nearly passed out from the smile he flashed. I didn't trust what I sensed was going on: Someone I found incredibly attractive and interesting found me pretty interesting, too. It just couldn't be. I was sure to screw it up somehow.

"You'd better move in quick, Lyd," Deanne said. "The sharks are circling. Fine meat like that doesn't stay celibate for long."

"But what if I mess up, come on too strong?"

Another Dixie cup was shoved into my hand. "*Ici. Bonne courage.*"

"What?"

"Liquid lubrication. Dutch courage. Drink up and go get him."

"No," I said, "I can't show up all stinking drunk. I'll just get buzzed here and wax poetic about his eyes …."

A few wine coolers later and my toes felt fuzzy. The world was shiny. Deanne said we should go for a walk, so we linked arms and trundled over to her beau Ben's dorm.

"Hey," I slurred. "I recognize this hall."

Deanne giggled and knocked on a door.

"Hey, isn't Ben's room on the other side of the hall?" Silly Deanne, drunk again.

The door opened. Hugh answered. Deanne shoved me in and ran off.

As blurry and tingly as I was, I do remember exactly how he looked. He led me in and took a seat at his desk near the window. The afternoon sun created spots of mahogany in his black hair, his blue chambray shirt looked softly huggable, a half-smile was on his lips.

Those lips. I really wanted to kiss those lips. I may have told him that, or maybe he just guessed it. Anyway, he kissed me. Score!

And do you know what ? He did NOT call me up the next day to say it was all a mistake. He asked me out! What a gentleman he was (though not too gentlemanly, if you know what I mean). He'd meet me after each class, buy me lunch now and then. For my birthday, he brought me flowers. And when the body of that guy who went missing was found rotting in the woods and another guy went missing and all the campus was freaked out, Hugh made sure to walk me everywhere.

And the brains on that guy! It seemed the pre-med courses were too slow for him. For example, when the medical examiner's report got leaked to the press, everybody was a-buzz with one rather bizarre detail: The student's body, in advanced decomposition, was covered in a thin layer of a clear mucous-y substance. Hugh chuckled at our lack of knowledge about the human body. (Deanne and I were philosophy and English majors, respectively.)

"No, there's nothing odd about that," he informed us. "You know that gelatin is made from the collagen in the bones of animals, don't you?" (We nodded as if we knew that. Deanne is a vegetarian, so she probably regretted those Jell-O shots.)

"Well, there's collagen in human skin and bones, too. When a body starts to decompose, the cell walls break down and the collagen oozes out. With his abdomen and chest cut open, the collagen goo just had an easier time reaching the surface."

"Gross," I shivered, trying not to picture it. I didn't know the guy who died, but I had seen him in the Hoot Hut a few times. Seemed nice. Bad way to end.

"So grody," Deanne added. "Somewhere out there is a homicidal maniac. I bet that other missing guy got hacked up, too. And that chubby girl who got attacked?"

"Sylvia?" She had been in my Shakespeare class.

"Yeah. Didn't she suffer some cuts from whoever attacked her?"

I shrugged. "She did, but I heard the nurses talking about it." (That was when I had gone to the campus clinic to get some preggo-prevention pills.) "They think she might have done it to herself. Said she was, like, totally crazy and ranting when they stitched her up, talking about a giant grasshopper or something."

We all laughed then, making jokes about how Sylvia had probably had a few too many grasshoppers of the minty-drink variety. Then Deanne left, and Hugh and I got down to business, if you know what I mean.

Once we were undressed, Hugh stopped and sniffed.

"What's wrong?" I asked, doing a quick scan of any sources of odor.

"Something's … different," he said, eyebrows knitting together. "Are you wearing a different perfume?"

"No. Do I smell bad?" Trust me, that's a hard question to ask a man when you're straddling him with your bra off and panties dangling from one ankle.

"No. It's just… different," he said slowly. "I can't quite put my finger on it."

To get us back on track, I said, "Well, try putting your finger on this." (I'll leave it to your imagination what I was referring to.)

So he did, and we did, but … was it just me, or was he more mechanical in his moves? Disengaged, even. It still burned me about how I smelled different. I mean, the one thing I could criticize about Hugh, the *only* thing, was that on occasion—not that often, mind you, but from time to time—his breath stank. I don't just mean Dorito-breath or even garlic and onions. It was a hellfire of putrid meat. Did I complain? No. Did I sniff at him disapprovingly? No. Did I offer him a breath mint? You bet. I'm not a masochist, after all.

I started to worry about our relationship. Hugh was less engaged, more distracted. He was thinking about breaking it off with me, I could tell. My hair was extra frizzy, too.

Then all hell broke loose on campus. The other dude who had disappeared finally showed up—gutted and floating in the river. News vans from all over the state clogged traffic. Some chicks who were doing an astronomy project came screaming back to campus claiming they had seen some sort of alien creature that leapt after them with pincers a-clicking. The odd thing was, the university leaders didn't send them away for psychiatric treatment like they had with Sylvia. In fact, they called in a professional sketch artist. Posters appeared around town about someone who may own an insect-like costume. I saw the posters. The word "grasshopper" sprang to mind with its bulbous eyes, sharp mandibles, and insectoid claws.

That sobered everyone up. Except me. I needed numbing to blot out the question perched on my lips: "Hugh, are you planning to break up with me?"

I caught him sniffing around groups of co-eds, flashing his Pepsodent smile. They fluttered and twinkled at him. He visited different clumps of girls until he saw me peeking through the arbor vitae. He jogged over and pecked me on the cheek. I fumed and reminded him about the party that night at Shorty's, sure he would find an excuse not to come. To my surprise, he agreed to it readily.

The party was a blur. Off-brand brandy in large quantities will do that. Hugh was friendly with everyone, including me, but I resisted his charms. It was my only defense against a broken heart, I thought. Freckle-Face noticed my sour mood and punched me on the shoulder before going out for ice.

I sulked near the chip dip, hoping to save up my anger for a Big Fight with my negligent boyfriend. However, Hugh left a couple minutes later, complaining of a migraine. Possible Molester walked me back to my dorm an hour later.

The next day Freckle-Face went missing. Everyone freaked out. Most worried about their own safety, but my worries quickly turned to guilt speckled with relief. I wondered how Hugh had escaped the killer but Freckle-Face had not. If Hugh had been targeted instead, I might've lost him. Oh, my stupid plans to argue with him dramatically! That was silly schoolgirl stuff. The love of my life could have been killed. I ran over to his dorm to be consoled. He smiled sadly and kissed the top of my head.

His breath stank again. I said nothing.

City council held a meeting about the attacks. We threw ourselves into a town-and-campus effort to track down the missing Freckle-Face or the perpetrator in the weird space-bug costume. I took self-defense classes and joined the campus security panels, along with Hugh and Deanne and Shorty. Despite our intense worry about our missing friend, we were determined to be fine.

And then *she* came.

Tiffani Simcoe. Her off-campus housing wasn't safe, so she moved into Ben's dorm. Same floor, just down the hall. Whenever she sashayed past the guys, they would momentarily forget all about Freckle-Face lying gutted somewhere and start drooling over her silky blonde hair, flawless skin, ample bosom, dazzling smile, and skintight Guess jeans.

I hated her the instant I saw her.

Deanne told me she had met her when leaving with her beau Ben and the remaining squids. Tiffani barely glanced at Deanne but was all eyes for Ben, who blushed and stammered Tiffani smiled and shook hands warmly with the squids, and they all shuffled their feet and went ga-ga. As she walked away, she turned around and wiggled her fingers at them. Bitch.

"Lock up your man!" Deanne warned. "She'll have him eating out of her hand in no time."

"Hugh loves me," I protested, ignoring a cold wave of impending disaster.

It wasn't just paranoia, mind you. It was a premonition, and it unfolded right in front of me. Hugh and I were strolling on the quad one brilliant fall day when she came prancing up.

"Hi! You live in my dorm, don't you? I've seen you there," she oozed, whipping a strand of flaxen hair over her shoulder. I sported an ill-advised perm.

Hugh stood transfixed. To his credit, he introduced me but by name, not title. Tiffani flashed the briefest smile at me before turning her huge green eyes back to my boyfriend.

"You have a class in the science hall that ends at four-thirty, don't you?" she asked.

"Yes, I do. Are you there, too? I've never seen you."

Tiffani simpered and stuck out her bottom lip in a mock-pout. "I'm totally a wall-flower. I'm not surprised you haven't noticed me." I swear to god she batted her eyelashes. "I was just wondering—if it's not too much trouble—would mind walking back to the dorm with me after class? For safety's sake. With all these murders …."

"Yes, of course. It would be my honor." Hugh then remembered that I was standing next to him. "It's just a safety precaution," he told me.

Tiffani put on an innocent expression and turned to me. "You're lucky to have such a strong man by your side anytime you want. I hope you don't mind if I borrow him a couple days a week."

"I…. Well…."

"Good! Thanks so much. See you this evening, Hugh." She giggled and slithered away.

Hugh watched her every step of the way. I seethed. Then, inexplicably, he sniffed his hand, mumbled something about needing to work on a paper, and ambled away like one possessed. I stood there, stunned.

I had been Tiffanied. Just like that.

She took her time reeling him in. I guess she had to make the rounds of all the lads before selecting her target. Day by day, I watched the love of my life slip away from me in slow motion. Finally, I called him, and we officially ended things.

Deanne came over to my room afterwards with the requisite carton of ice cream and a fifth of bourbon. When the ice cream was gone, the bourbon reduced to one-sixteenth, and tissues lay crumpled around the room like snotty snowballs, it was time for the closing ceremony.

"Whaddya doin'?" Deanne slurred as I rummaged through my toiletries.

Having found the pack of pills, I held them up. Those little monsters lulled me into a false sense of security. Sure, my oven remained bun-free, but what of my heart? Hugh had shredded that to pieces. I grabbed Deanne's hand and dragged her to the bathroom.

"Wait! Don't get rid of those! Wouldn't it be better if you kept takin' 'em and just screwed whoever you want? You know, as revenge or somethin'?"

"Nope, spreading my legs opened my heart too wide. Besides, they made me break out something fierce."

*Plink.* One pill plopped into the toilet. *Plink, plunk.* There went the rest of the week.

Okay, technically the rest of the week was spent shadowing Hugh. Between classes, I lagged behind him as he jogged after Tiffani. To her credit, she made him work for it. She could be found walking with a variety of other women's boyfriends on any given day.

At night, I would pull on my parka, pour some spiked coffee in a thermos, and hide in the shrubberies below Hugh's window. It was pathetic, I know. I would cry while listening to a mixed tape of love songs on my Walkman. Then I would get angry and invent curses, my favorite being that he would become bald and impotent—and discover both things at once.

On the third night of surveillance, I did not have the luxury of sniveling in the bushes. Hugh's light went out at 9:30, and he was not an early-to-bed kind of person. Did he have company? I pushed pause on Whitney and listened for any tell-tale moans. A minute later, Hugh walked out and strode over to the student union. He stopped just outside the circle of light spilling out the windows.

A group of students burst from the union, laughing and raising a general hoopla. The light illuminated the perfect tresses of Miss Boyfriend-Stealer.

But what's this? She was arm-in-arm with another guy! Ha. Too delicious. Hugh was stalking Tiffani like I was stalking him. He trailed behind them. I could almost feel the rage pouring off him. Why, the squid Tiffani was schmoozing was totally ordinary, maybe five-nine at best, compared to Hugh's strapping six-three. The squid had a wrestler's build, with broad shoulders and a stout chest that tapered into a narrow waist. And he had red hair! I nearly peed myself with semi-tipsy chortling.

The next night, Hugh followed Tiffani and tried to woo her. She smiled at him, but then the redhead arrived and draped his arm around her shoulders. She melted into him, waved bye to Hugh, and skipped off to neck with the neckless wrestler.

So my alarm bells went off when the wrestler disappeared two days later.

Tiffani was beside herself with worry. Fortunately, several shoulders offered themselves for her to cry on. Hugh kept his distance for a while, then checked in to make sure she was okay, that she had someone to walk her back to the dorm at night.

Poor, dumb Tiffani. She fell for it.

What was I to do? Tell the police I saw Hugh follow No-Neck Wrestler toward his dorm? You bet I did just that. They informed me that they had already done a sweep of all the male dorms, looking for an insect-costume or lethal tools, and it revealed nothing. Then they asked what I had been doing there and what my relationship was to the men in question and if I was taking advantage of the tragedies on campus to frame my ex-boyfriend.

Deanne asked me the same thing. As did her beau Ben. And Wastoid and Shorty and Possible Molester. I felt abandoned.

Police found No-Neck's mucous-covered body by the end of the week. Though I didn't know him personally, I went to the funeral. In the receiving line, I offered Tiffani my condolences after re-introducing myself. (The chick had no memory for the female of the species.) Tiffani, her skin porcelain-looking in her black mourning garb, shook my hand and sniffled.

At the luncheon, I pulled her aside. After a few bullshit words about coping with loss and being there to support her, I casually brought up Hugh.

"Oh, yes. He's been a great comfort to me. Such a gentleman. You know what he said?" she asked me, forgetting I was his jilted lover. "He said he had deep feelings for me but out of respect for Clyde, he would keep his distance until after the funeral."

Ugh. "Listen, Tiffani. I know Hugh better than you do. You can't trust him. You shouldn't be alone with him." Tiffani's eyes widened in confusion. The words wilted in my throat. I couldn't tell her I thought Hugh might've killed her boyfriend. She wouldn't believe me, and she would probably tell Hugh. And then I might be in for some trouble. Maybe. Did I actually believe that? Probably not.

"Just be careful around him."

It was time to bake my half-cooked notion or get it out of the oven.

Loitering outside of Hugh's biology class, I pretended to be examining notes before falling into step beside him. "Hey, Hugh. How's it going?"

"Hey. Okay. What's up with you?"

I told him about going to the funeral, how distraught Tiffani was. How she didn't want to date anyone for a while. (My invention, of course.) Hugh's lips twitched in agitation.

"She said that?"

I nodded, and we walked on in silence. When we arrived at the liberal arts hall, he paused and looked at me with squinched eyes, nostrils flaring slightly.

"Say, are you wearing a different perfume?" I shook my head. "Ah, well. I just thought I detected something different about you. We should get coffee sometime." Then he walked away.

I watched him like a hawk after that, skipping classes and staying up late into the night to catch his comings and goings. Tiffani did not keep her distance. I didn't tell her that Hugh made a play for me, too. It was hard to resist him, but I hated being someone's sloppy seconds.

After a while, I started to rethink my theory. Had it just been jealousy? I decided to follow him one last time, to prove to myself that he was just an average college student and not some homicidal maniac.

I said to myself: *He's taking an evening stroll around campus. Nothing like a stroll to clear one's mind.* Then: *He's just people-watching, making sure that the drunk people leaving that party don't get into cars and plow into old ladies crossing the street.* Three minutes later: *That drunk guy's taking the shortcut through the woods to frat row. Hugh's just making sure he'll be safe.*

Against my better judgment, I followed them into the woods. With the moonlight, the pine trees cast shadows on the path, which twisted around clumps of trees and boulders, so once in the woods, I lost sight of the men. The only sounds were the rustling of dead leaves and occasional snatches of the drunk guy's off-key singing of "Take On Me."

Off to my right, the frat boy warbled, *"I'll be gone ... in a day or TWOOO."* With that I reoriented myself.

Then the path forked. Crap. I couldn't hear the singing, either. I listened for footsteps. Nothing. A flock of birds screeched and took flight like great black rags thrown up in the sky, causing my heart to jump in my chest.

Further to my right, then. Something had disturbed those birds. Slowly, I forced myself to put one foot in front of the other, carefully descending the slope.

Then a man cried out—screamed— and quickly fell silent.

I froze. *Do I go forward? What if I'm seen?* I looked around. There was a little ridge created by the roots of a semi-fallen tree. The boughs of the pine next to it would put me in shadow. I crouched behind the roots, gulping for air and cursing myself for not telling anyone where I had gone. *Such a fool!*

Sounds of wet smacking, slapping, sickening ripping floated back to me on the night breeze. A few minutes later, hurried footsteps approached from down the hill. I held my breath.

The footsteps crested the hill, near my spot. They passed within a few feet of me, went a few yards past, and stopped. I risked peering out from behind the pine.

It was Hugh. He zipped up his jacket and looked around. Sniffing. He swung his head around, this way and that. Then he hurried on.

I didn't dare move. He could've spotted me and been lying in wait up ahead or circling back around through the trees. I stayed put, crouched like a coiled spring.

When the sky took on a faint glow, I realized I had been there for hours. I straightened out my legs and winced through the creaking pain. Shakily, I stepped over the roots onto the path, half-expecting violent death to rain down upon me. When it didn't, I slowly made my way down the hill.

The iron stench of blood signaled I was close. There, off to the side of the path, was Frat Boy. Or, more accurately, the Late Frat Boy. He had enjoyed his last kegger. He was shiny with slime and his entrails lay curled on his abdomen like a slumbering snake.

My mouth opened but all that came out was a strangled yelp.

I had never seen a dead body before. I wanted to look away, to run, but my legs were bolted to the ground, and the face with its unfocused gaze held me fast. I puked in the bushes.

My hands only stopped shaking three hours later, after the police wrapped me in a blanket and plied me with hot chocolate in the station. Hugh was there, but he didn't see me.

I whispered to an officer, "He was there! He followed the guy and left right after the scream."

"Yes, he told us." Surprise! Apparently, Hugh had reported someone stalking him in the vicinity of the killing.

The police didn't accuse me directly, but they warned me about roaming around at night and booted me from the station.

I needed evidence and an ally. I needed Sylvia. Sylvia, the only victim who had survived an attack. The only one who might have seen something, a clue. She hadn't returned to campus yet, so I found out from one of her friends that she worked at a Blockbuster across town. I took the bus there the next day.

Sylvia glared at me over a display of *Invaders from Mars* videos.

"Sylvia? Hi, I'm Lydia. We were in the same Shakespeare class until … until …."

"Yeah, I know who you are. What do you want?"

"I want to know what happened that night. What you saw."

She sighed. "Look, I told the police all that. You can read the newspapers."

"But they thought you were crazy. I don't think you are."

She snorted angrily. "Have you ever been in a psych ward?" I shook my head. "*One Flew Over the Cuckoo's Nest* got it about right. The university ignored me until those astronomy students saw the same thing and more corpses showed up. Highcliff can go to hell. I'm transferring next semester."

Sylvia grabbed a stack of *The Goonies* cassettes to restock, but I blocked her path.

"I have an idea who it might be. The grasshopper."

She tugged at the collar of her blue polo shirt and stared at me.

"No, you don't," she said, pushing past me.

"I do! I mean, I'm not certain, but—"

She reeled around. "You don't because it's not a *who*, it's an *it*. It's an alien, a goddamned monster." Her voice rose, drawing stares from customers. "It grabbed me. It tried to rape me with a tube-like … appendage. I was out of my mind with disbelief and fear. So don't tell me you saw some suspicious dude on campus because I *know* it's not a human."

Sylvia looked worn out from an argument she'd clearly had many times before. The manager rushed over, but she waved him off and continued reshelving. I followed her into the thriller section.

"How did you get away?"

She sighed again. "I had been out jogging, so I had my Walkman. I used that to bash one of its eyes, then kneed it in the tube. It tried to chase me, but I ran fast."

I thanked her and returned to campus. This grasshopper-monster preying upon the Highcliff Crickets was not just a killer but an attempted rapist. Could that be Hugh? There was that time, earlier in the semester, when he was limping. A freak hacky sack accident, he'd said, too sore to let me touch his tube.

The next day I sat in my Shakespeare class, staring at Sylvia's still-empty seat. Her words echoed in my brain. Her wan face and Frat Boy's dead eyes merged to become Hamlet's ghostly father demanding vengeance. Something was rotten in the state of Highcliff, and I was not poor, heartbroken Ophelia in this tragedy, but Hamlet. Like the Danish prince, I wondered if a play could be just the thing to catch this killer.

The next day the fuzz showed up with a warrant to search my room. They grilled me about my connection to Freckle-Face and No-Neck, why I had been lurking outside Hugh's dorm.

Aside from a half-empty bottle of gin that Deanne had stashed under my bed, they found nothing. Still, a crowd formed around my door. My dorm-mates stared and whispered.

The whispering spread over campus. People moved away from me in halls and on the quad. Even Deanne, my erstwhile partner in crime, behaved differently.

"Look, you've been on a rollercoaster this semester. You're tightly wound. Maybe you should just, you know, take a break. Get away from things for a while."

"Finals are in ten days, Dee."

"Then take it easy on the booze, hon."

"That was your bottle in my room."

"But I wasn't the one who downed half of it, was I?" She shrugged and jangled a pocketful of quarters. "C'mon, let's go dodge Blinky, Pinky, and Inky."

"No, thanks. Tell Ms. Pac-Man hello, but I've got to get Shakespearean on my studies."

After she left, I tried studying but mostly just stared at the wall. Ms. Pac-Man scratched at something in my brain about turning the tables on your enemies.

Someone knocked on the door. Through the peephole, I saw it was Hugh. My heart stopped. Slowly, I backed away from the door and flicked off my desk lamp.

He knocked again.

"I know you're in there," he said. "I just want to talk. I've heard what people have been saying about you. The police searched my room, too. Maybe we could help each other."

A lump formed in my throat, for which I was thankful because it prevented me from speaking. I so badly wanted to sweep away the past few weeks and return things to the way they were.

"You don't have to be alone."

Oh, that was a knife in the heart. I reached toward the doorknob.... and stopped. He had killed Frat Boy, and probably Freckle-Face, too. Hell, he probably killed them all. I didn't know how or why, but I had to withstand loneliness until I either proved it or cleared him.

After a couple minutes, he left. I waited another twenty before calling Tiffani.

Somehow Tiffani's voice managed to be both breathy and cutesy when she answered the phone. She didn't seem at all bothered that the campus pariah was calling her. She probably paid no attention to the gossip, as she was the only female in her universe.

"Tiffani, listen. Hugh isn't there now, is he?"

"Hugh? No, why?"

"This may be hard to believe, but I think he's the one who killed all those people." I scrambled to remember No-Neck's name. "Including Clyde."

"That's ridiculous. Why would you think that? Hugh is sweet. He's a pre-med student, for Pete's sake. A person doesn't study how to heal people and then go around killing them." She used the same tone a child might use to explain why the Easter Bunny leaves chocolate eggs instead of rabbit poop.

"I saw him, Tiff." Not quite true, but I needed to be convincing.

"No, that couldn't be. Maybe you were dreaming?"

I wanted to pull my hair out. "I was completely awake," I growled. Having lied once, another one couldn't hurt: "And sober."

She paused. "Why should I listen to anything you say?"

"Because I'm trying to save your life."

"But Hugh's so—"

"He's not what you think, Tiffani. You must believe me. Hugh might be killing people, but I need your help to prove it or prove otherwise."

An uneasy exhalation on her side. "Look, I don't know if you're just jealous or on drugs like they say." (Now I was on drugs? Apparently, she did listen to gossip.) "But just drop it and leave us alone. I have half a mind to tell him tonight about you calling me."

"You're seeing him tonight?"

"We're going to the Hoot Hut."

"Tiffani, listen. I'm sorry. I'll leave you alone. Just please don't say anything to Hugh."

She puffed through her nose. "Well, I can't make promises—"

"Please, Tiffani," I begged. I hated that I was pleading with her to cover up for me, but I couldn't risk Hugh becoming more suspicious than he already was. We hung up and I sat for a while in my darkened room. Anger stirred within me, not at Tiffani or the cops, but at this creepy criminal preying on my friends. A Norma Rae-kind of spirit overtook me: I would have to be the one to take action.

The schedule for the Hoot Hut indicated I had an hour to prepare my plan, which largely centered on getting into Hugh's room to look for … what? The cops had already searched there. He certainly wouldn't have a space-bug outfit lying around, but maybe there was something else. A bloodied letter-opener. Some weird ooze-chemical disguised in a shampoo bottle. I had no clue. I would have to draw upon everything I learned from Scooby Doo and Nancy Drew.

Step One: Disguise self. Like a deer hunter, I showered well with the campus foam-soap to cover my smell. (What was with all of Hugh's sniffing, anyway?) Then I nabbed a grungy old sweatshirt someone had left in the stairwell. Shorty had a Boy George wig from Halloween that he let me borrow. From the depths of my closet, I pulled out a Duran-esque fedora I'd bought to hide bad hair days.

Out on the quad, I hid in the shadows, shivering, until I saw Tiffani and Hugh amble to the Hoot Hut. My panic flared—if she told Hugh about my call, I could be gutted by morning.

Once they were inside, I swallowed hard and proceeded to Step Two: Create a reason for the RA to open Hugh's door. Coming up with this part wasn't difficult. Early in the semester, a girl on my floor left a candle burning in her room. It had started a curtain on fire while she was in the cafeteria.

For my flaming entrée, I had scraps of paper, used tissues, a can of Aqua Net, and a lighter tucked into the pockets of a coat I "borrowed" from a pile near the computer room. Halfway down the hall, Ben's door opened and out he came with Deanne and Wastoid. I perused a concert poster on the wall; Deanne would recognize me from the front in an instant. They trudged by, a solemn group since Freckle-Face's disappearance.

Step Three: Start a fire. When the coast was clear, I shoved the flammables under Hugh's door. The final piece of paper I rolled into a long tube, which I lit at one end and slipped under the door. Aiming the nozzle of the Aqua Net under the door, I sprayed.

The sound of laughter bounced down the hall. Time to exit. I sprinted into a bathroom stall until conversation subsided and doors closed.

I tiptoed back to Hugh's door. No signs of smoke, so I peeked under the door. Blackened paper, mostly. One tissue was rimmed with sparkling orange, teetering on the edge of flaring up or flaming out.

Crap. Hardly the conflagration I imagined, but it would have to do. I sprayed more Aqua Net and ran to the lobby where the RA was hunched over an Apple II.

"There's smoke coming from under a door! I knocked and someone moaned, but no one opened it."

Thus began Step Four: Get in room.

"Which room?" he asked, jumping up to be the hero.

I told him and he ran into an office, emerging with keys and a fire extinguisher. He noted, as we dashed down the corridor, that the smoke detector hadn't gone off.

"Maybe the batteries failed?"

When we reached the door, he told me to stand by the manual switch for the fire alarm, just in case. He pounded on the door and tried the handle. He shouted, "I'm coming in!" People poked their heads out of their doors.

Extinguisher at the ready, he opened the door.

"What the—?"

I ran up behind him and heard the extinguisher go off.

"Is anyone in here?" I asked the RA.

"Doesn't look like it, but I don't understand what he did here." He stomped on the detritus of my little bonfire.

"That's so strange," I said. "I clearly heard somebody. Maybe he's in the closet or went out the window?" I cracked the window, which was Step Five.

"Hey, uh… I don't think you should be touching things. I'll write up a report on this guy, so thanks for your help—"

"Of course. Sorry. Your responsiveness was awesome," I cooed before dashing out the door. He was kind of cute, and I was flirting openly because I was in disguise, not being myself. Note to self: Consider wigs as a viable hair option.

I secreted myself in the shrubbery beneath Hugh's window. Through the gap in the window, I heard a camera clicking as the RA took photos for his report. When the lights went off and the door shut, it was time to launch Step Six: Get in again. I popped out the screen with a butter knife (thanks, cafeteria!), slid the window open further, and squirmed inside.

Books and picture frames fell to the floor as I crawled through the window onto his desk.. I restacked the textbooks and replaced the photos. In the weak beam of my flashlight, I saw his sickeningly attractive family, which made me angrier. Why should such a creep get to have such gorgeous parents and a cute-as-buttons younger sister?

Thus began Step Seven: Investigate. I had been in his room several times before, of course, but I'd only had eyes for Hugh then. I hadn't been looking for evidence of his being a crazed killer. I sniffed his hair products and cologne—all normal, though they evoked a confusing mix of arousal and disgust in me. I scanned notebooks for any weird stuff, doodles of eviscerated bodies or something, but there were just science notes. None of the sharp objects in his room (pens, mostly) appeared blood-stained, nor did his clothes.

I looked back at the desk, at those annoying, gleaming smiles of his family. Were they psychos, too? They had money, surely. They probably all went skiing in Vail or St. Moritz, judging by the pic of his parents. I pulled off the back of the frame to fuel my envy but instead found something puzzling: The photo had been cut out of a magazine. Either his parents were famous or ….

I pulled off the back of his sister's photo. Hers was the picture that came with the frame.

Icy fingers tickled my spine. Until that moment, I hadn't *really* believed in my core that Hugh was unhinged. Yes, he'd been near a victim, but who puts up fake family pictures? This level of attention to deception unnerved me.

The glowing face of his clock showed I had another twenty minutes. Nothing was left unsearched: his garbage can, the undersides of his desk and bed, interiors of pillows. Oddities I uncovered:

- A suitcase filled with brand new shirts and pants, all duplicates of clothes already in his closet.

- A surprising lack of normal guy stuff. Had I been so love-stricken I hadn't noticed? No boombox, action figures, or magazines. No posters of bands.

- A calendar tucked into a drawer. Normal, except that it was full of odd markings.

I flipped through the calendar. Early in the semester, he'd marked a couple days in blue, two weeks apart. One of the days had a slash through it. Shortly after we started going out, he began adding red circles to the calendar. The circles got bigger day by day until he colored them solid and they shrank before regrowing. Later that month, the red gave way to green question marks. The blue marks were more random.

After a few weeks of green question marks with intermittent solid red circles, the other red circles reappeared. "Tiffani" was written over the first one.

Oh, hells. I knew what I was looking at. Any girl from my sixth-grade sex ed class could name it: a menstruation-ovulation calendar. Sure enough, the solid red circles lined up with the monthly visit of my Aunt Flow. The green question marks were when I was on the pill. I flipped to the current month. My circles reappeared. Apparently, both Tiffani and I were having our periods in about two weeks.

Maybe instead of pathology, Hugh was going into gynecology? I tucked the calendar under my coat, peered through the peephole 'til the hallway cleared, and ran back to my room, where I paced and chewed my thumbnails.

I jumped out of my skin when the phone rang. "Hello?" I whispered.

"Hi, it's Tiffani. I'm not sure I should be calling you, but ...."

"What is it, Tiffani?"

"It's just ... Could we meet sometime? To talk?"

Alarms bells went off. "Why? What do you want to talk about?"

She paused. "It's Hugh. It may be nothing, but—"

"Isn't he with you?"

"No, he left early, said he wasn't comfortable." She gave an anxious sigh. "Could I come over? Now?"

Perplexed, I agreed. I stashed my costume in the closet. When Tiffani arrived, her big doe-eyes glanced all around, never resting on one object too long.

"So, what about Hugh, Tiffani?"

She twiddled her fingers and took a step back toward the door. "I don't know. It's probably nothing. I shouldn't have come."

She was about to open the door, when I asked, "Are you expecting your period on the 18th?"

Tiffani stopped. "What?"

"Your period. The 18th?"

She cocked one eyebrow. "Thereabouts. How did you guess?"

"I didn't. Hugh told me." I opened the calendar. "This was stashed in his desk."

Like a fawn taking its first steps, she inched closer. "You were in his room?"

I ignored the question and turned to the earlier in the semester. "Here's me. The solid parts line up with my monthly visitor. The green is when I went on the pill."

"You slept with him? How long had you known him?" Was that disdain I detected in her voice?

"Here's where you start seeing him." I pointed out her name. She was silent for a moment.

"But why would he mark such a thing? *I* didn't have sex with him!"

I bit my lip. This wasn't a time for Prissy Pristine. I called her attention to the blue marks. "I'm wondering if these marks line up with the attacks."

I pulled the campus newspaper out of my garbage can. A blue date aligned with the night Freckle-Face disappeared. Tiffani's face blanched. She stared at a blue date in November.

"That's the day Clyde was killed," she whispered.

I sensed we were on the verge of something important.

"You didn't make that calendar yourself, did you," she said. It was not a question. I assured her that I had no interest in tracking her menses. She sat down heavily on my bed.

"Hugh got upset tonight. I caught him in, well, it was either a lie or he was pretending to know something he didn't. It struck me as odd, so I pointed out that he was mistaken, and he got angry and left."

"Explain."

She pulled off her woolen cap. Her hair was still a perfect blonde waterfall. "There were some wrestling guys at the Hut, friends of Clyde's. They came over to chat." She turned a pleased smile toward me. "I think they're jealous on Clyde's behalf that I've been going on dates with Hugh."

I swallowed my bile.

"They brought up that coroner's report about his ... his body being covered in a gelatinous substance." Her voice quavered, so I handed her a tissue. She dabbed at her eyes.

"Hugh scoffed at them for thinking it was so bizarre."

I interjected, as I'd had the same Hugh lecture. "Right. Collagen in the body, when exposed to air, comes to the surface."

Tiffani looked at me like I'd grown a second head.

"That's not how it works!" she cried. "Hugh pointed out that they had never seen a body cut open. Not like he had, being pre-med. He said it depended on the depth and magnitude of the cuts and the age of the person, but that a certain amount was normal."

"Isn't it?" I wished I'd paid more attention in biology.

"No! That's nonsense. I told him as much. I grew up on a farm, see. I've seen hogs, cows, sheep, all sorts of animals completely sliced open. Some were attacked by coyotes, and we didn't find them for a couple days. No collagen ooze. Someone going into medicine would know that."

I tried to picture perfect Tiffani beside a slaughtered pig.

"What I have seen, though, are certain amphibians and insects that inject an enzyme into their prey to break it down and make it easier to digest. Collagen reacts to that, in some cases."

Now it was my turn to stare at Tiffani like she'd grown a new head. A much smarter and more science-filled head.

"What's your major, Tiffani?"

"Undecided. Either veterinary medicine or entomology."

Something inside me twisted in despair. Beautifully feathered hair, and yet there's more than a feather-brain underneath. So unfair.

"Anyway, this calendar is evidence of ... something. Not sure what." She gasped. "Now your fingerprints are all over it. You shouldn't have taken it from his room."

I brushed that aside. Something else was niggling in my brain. "Wait a minute. Injecting an enzyme into prey? Are you saying that Hugh, or whoever is doing the killings, is a *creature*?"

"No, that would be a ridiculous thing to say. Sheer lunacy."

I took a seat next to her. Behind her emphatic denial lingered some doubt. "Two hours ago, you said it was ridiculous that Hugh was a killer. Then you told me he's been lying about basic science."

She squirmed. "I'm not saying he's the killer. He's an odd person. That's all."

It was a start, a tiny concession. I let her words hang in the air for a moment.

"Tiffani, he's tracking our menstrual cycles."

She jumped up and started pacing. "Why is he doing that?"

"Maybe he wants to impregnate us," I said, thinking of Sylvia's story.

"I haven't even let him get to third base!"

"You're not on the pill, are you?"

"Of course not. I'm not that—"

"—kind of girl. Right. You've said."

An idea was forming in my head, an impossible, crazy idea. I told Tiffani to keep her distance from Hugh but not act like she was keeping her distance—*Fly casual,* as Han Solo said. Stay in groups, don't be alone with Hugh. I walked her to the lobby where the RA called for an escort for her.

Before leaving, she asked, "What are you going to do?"

"I don't know. Is there anything we can do?"

Her mouth pulled to one side, giving her the cutest dimple in one cheek. "Well, I read that scientists started doing DNA testing last year, so if the police took samples from the bodies…."

I waited for her to complete the thought. "Yes, and?"

"Well, then they could compare evidence from the bodies with Hugh's DNA. I'm sure they'd find he's not a match at all, and then we can drop these accusations.."

I could tell she wanted that to be true. Did I? Not sure, but I noted her use of *we*. "But where is the nearest lab for that? How long will it take? And how do we get Hugh's DNA?"

She shrugged. "No clue. And the police probably wouldn't tell us anyway."

I gripped her arm. "But we have to try. One way or another, we have to know. And according to Hugh's calendar, we'll be most alluring to him in the next two days."

We needed to get Hugh's DNA, ideally blood because his human guise could be artificial. (Tiffani rolled her eyes at that.) Given the scope of the killings, the police were probably coordinating with the feds—people with access to DNA testing. Maybe they'd already run tests. Maybe some of Hugh the Alien's blood was on the victims, and the lab dismissed it for not being human.

The next day, as my ovum ripened, I hatched a plan. I needed someplace private, yet close enough to civilization to get help quickly if things went pear-shaped. Tiffani needed to act the role of her life.

"You want me to *what?*" she shrieked into her phone. "I thought you said I should keep my distance! That's the very opposite of keeping my distance."

"You don't actually have to have sex with him. Just, you know, make him think you're going to."

"How is this going to solve anything?"

"Tiffani, we have to figure out why Hugh's tracking our cycles and marking dates that people got killed. Your baby-oven is already pre-heated. He'll have a hard time resisting if you suggest you'd be keen for some naked fun time." It was hard for me to put a notorious Jolene into the arms of the man I once loved, but desperate times....

That day the sky was devoid of all color, matching my complexion. If I were wrong about Hugh, I would be in serious trouble, and my reputation would be utterly destroyed—no friends, maybe expulsion. If I were right but unsuccessful, I would probably be dead.

A path stretched along the perimeter of campus and followed the river into town. Along the way, there were little three-sided shelters for protection from the rain or beating sun. Kids mostly use them for woodsy make-out sessions or to smoke weed.

I staked out a shelter two hours before the appointed time and shooed away the potheads. To ward off the chill and calm my nerves, I had a thermos of rummy coffee. As it emptied, my bladder got fuller. I couldn't risk peeing in the woods, so I crossed my legs and waited.

Eventually, familiar voices approached. A tinkle of laughter. (Tinkle? Urination on the brain.)

Soon Tiffani came into view, arm-in-arm with Hugh. If she was play-acting, she was doing a good job. He whispered into her ear, and she shrugged shyly and curled into him.

That worried me. Had she reconsidered?

They walked to the shelter behind which I was hiding. More giggling and cutesy talk. I wanted to barf. Finally, there was just the moist smacking of lips and occasional groans.

A little piece of me died. Hugh used to make those sounds with me.

Tiffani and I had a pre-arranged signal. When enough of his skin was exposed, she would say, "Oh, Hugh, I love the way you feel." That was my signal to leap out, sterile lancet in hand (lifted off a diabetic classmate) and nab some of his blood before sprinting away. With his pants around his knees, he wouldn't be able to pursue me right away.

That was supposed to be how it went. You know what they say about the best laid plans … if someone else is getting laid, your plan's not the best.

Tiffani interrupted her (hopefully) fake sighs of pleasures. "No need for speed, hon."

A few seconds later: "Slow down there, buddy."

Her tone pitched up. "Hugh, not so—" Her voice became muffled. I heard thrashing on the bench. She should've given the signal already.

"No! Stop," she cried.

That was a signal of an entirely different nature. I raced around the corner. Hugh's pants were down, and he had both of Tiffani's wrists pinned to the corner of the shelter. One hand covered her mouth. She struggled against him, trying to push her skirt down over her hips.

I was paralyzed by what I saw. Of all the things I thought Hugh was, a rapist was never on the list. The "r" word sliced through my fog and forced me into action.

"Hey," I shouted, pounding the side of the shelter. "Get off her!"

Hugh whirled around, loosening his grip on Tiffani. She screamed and ran. He tripped on his jeans, and I jabbed his bare thigh. He growled and swatted my hand before scrambling to his feet and shuffling after Tiffani.

I sprinted down the path as fast as my bladder would allow, but my mind was still rooted back at the shelter. Were those *pincers* I had seen in his mouth?

Tiffani's cries stopped me. I couldn't just leave her to ward off an attacker. I followed her voice toward the river bluffs. The sun had dipped below the line of trees, making it hard to judge depth and distance.

She stopped screaming—not a good sign.

The path opened onto the cliffs with large boulders marking the ridge. Tiffani backed her way up the tumbled rock to the top of a boulder. She held one hand up in front of her to fend him off.

Hugh, jeans now secured, approached her, his hand held out.

I stopped. Neither predator nor prey had noticed me. I crept closer, looking around for a weapon.

"Tiffani, please come down. I'm sorry I got carried away. I promise that won't happen again."

Tiffani shook her head emphatically, her lips crumpling to hold back tears. Hugh moved closer, mounting the bottom stone.

"I would never try to hurt you. You have to know that. You're just so beautiful. I hate myself for scaring you like that."

Tears streamed down her face. She scrambled to the edge of the boulder. She shot a look over her shoulder, down the steep cliff to the river. She was running out of room.

"Tiffani, baby, listen to—"

"You were forcing me!"

Hugh stopped in his tracks. My hand found a rock that fit into my palm.

"I'm so very sorry. I've just wanted you so badly."

I couldn't take any more of this. Stepping out from the woods, I shouted, "What are you, Hugh? We know you're not human."

Hugh whirled around. "What? What are you talking about?"

"You killed all those people." My voice shook.

He laughed. "What are you even doing here?" he asked, as if addressing doggy-doo on his shoe.

I was used to apathy from him, but this was outright disgust. I braced myself.

"You've been killing people and you wanted to impregnate us," I shouted. "You are not human." My vocal cords rasped. Warm wetness spread down my legs.

Hugh sighed. "How drunk are you?"

"I haven't been drinking," I roared, unconcerned about truthfulness or my pants now.

He turned to Tiffani. "She's gotten into your head, hasn't she?"

Tiffani paused before shaking her head. "No. No she hasn't." She really was not a good liar.

"She's been planting ideas in your head, Tiff, and she's been stalking me." Tiffani's frown indicated that she knew. "She even broke into my room. She's upset that our relationship ended, so she's poisoning you against me."

Tiffani sniffled. In a feeble voice, she asked, "But what about the calendar?"

"What calendar?"

"The one she found in your—" Tiffani's mouth rounded into an O. She stared at me with a crease forming between her eyebrows. "She *said* she found a calendar in your room." She bowed her head. "Oh, Hugh. Maybe I have been silly...."

Hugh reached the top of the boulder. Tiffani let him approach. Gently, he pushed a strand of hair from her face. Anger nearly blinded me as I rushed toward them.

"No! Listen to me, Tiffani. You know Hugh's been lying about the ooze. I saw him when Frat Boy was killed. I swear the calendar is his. You can't believe him."

Hugh guffawed, exasperated. "Tiff, do you trust her? I can smell the booze from here. She's jealous and making up ridiculous tales about me. The police even had to warn her about that. It's sad, really. Look at her. She peed herself! Couldn't even manage to comb her—"

All my old gym teachers would have been amazed. I threw that rock with all my might and hit Hugh right in the strike zone. He stumbled in surprise.

"You bastard!" Fury clouded my eyes. I launched myself at him, a blaze of knees and fists.

Then I struck empty air. For a split second, Hugh was suspended above the cliff, his eyes wide, arms flailing. Then he was gone.

Did I push him? Maybe he tripped. It was a long, sharp fall to the river. From that height, in the waning light, I couldn't tell if it was his coat floating off swiftly or a broken sheet of ice. I followed it with my eyes until the dark rapids pulled it under. There went the love of my life, the one who really was too good to be true.

And maybe, just maybe, I killed him. Could spell trouble for me.

But who knows? I wasn't going to stick around to find out if gigantic alien grasshoppers could swim.

# The Velvet Hammer

A Misadventure of Braxton Hicks

By: William Joseph Roberts

Whenever I know I'm going to be passing through where an old friend or colleague just happens to be, I'll try to swing in to snag a meal or a beer and maybe, depending on the person I might have a little something for them that I make sure to carry along with me for the trip.

After a dull and boring three-week job out in Arkansas, I'd already planned to swing through Memphis on my way back home to Chickamauga to visit my good friend, Pierce Maggert, who also happened to be a subject matter expert on just about anything strange, rare, or occult related.

We met several years ago while I was information gathering on this particularly nasty possession case, where we were both seeking the same item and it worked out to both of our benefits to work together in order to find the cursed item causing the problem.

Now, I know what you're thinking. Possession is a bunch of bullshit. And normally I tended to agree with that opinion, but to a certain degree, yes, possession is a real and true thing that just doesn't have an explanation yet. I hadn't personally come across any evidence to prove or disprove the existence of angels or demons one way or the other. What I can say for a fact is that there are dark, malicious things that lurk in every corner of our world. Things that thrive on harming others. And those dark things have a varying degree of power and influence over the human mind. Now, some say that this is proof that emotion and energies are imbued into the things around us or the things that we care about or cherish. This is exactly the kind of explanation that Pierce had given me on this particular little music box we were both hunting. The worst of all was trying to figure out why this family had taken turns being the batshit crazy entity that called itself Foster.

Well, once we found the box and neutralized it, things returned to normal for the family. It happens. The father picked it up in the estate sale for his oldest daughter with no idea it was tainted. He just knew he'd gotten a cute little music box that his daughter would love.

Upon that first meeting in Assumption Parish, Louisiana with Pierce many many moons ago, I thought he was Mike Tobacco, the male lead played by Grant Kramer in Killer Klowns from Outer Space. And to this day, he swears it wasn't him, but damn if they don't look an awful lot alike.

Since then, we'd become damned good friends. While I continued working the weird and odd jobs for the government, Pierce had settled down and come into possession of an old mansion in Memphis Tennessee. Originally built by a wealthy wildcatter and homesteader back in the early 1800s before Memphis was incorporated into an official city, the building was renowned for its opulence.

At one point in its sordid past, it had been owned by a very wealthy businessman who abandoned the mansion during the Battle of Memphis in June of 1862, subsequently leading to the occupation of the city by Union forces for the remainder of the Civil War.

Seeing an opportunity amid the chaos of war, a bright and opportunistic young lady, turned the once prestigious mansion into a brothel before Union soldiers could occupy the city. By recruiting girls from other houses and those working independently on the streets, Madam Jobe cornered the market.

Pierce, being the historical nerd that he was, decided to restore the extravagant, four-story structure to its pre-Civil War glory he named the Velvet Hannorah, but most locals just called it the Velvet Hammer.

He turned it into a high-end bed-and-breakfast-style gentleman's club; complete with all manner of vices that you would expect and several that you wouldn't, including several exclusive, off-menu *private* offerings available for those who knew how to properly *order* them. Even though it was technically illegal, I really couldn't care. What two consenting adults did behind closed doors was entirely their business as far as I was concerned and not for me to judge.


Pierce was an Eclectic one, to say the least. Besides being an avid historian, he was also borderline obsessed with the occult and all things odd, strange, disturbing, and weird. And he decorated the place as such. While keeping most of the original furniture remaining from Madam Jobe's time, he added any oddity that he could get his hands on; ancient electric chairs, electroshock units, fully articulated skeletons, pictures of Sideshow freaks, specimen jars, and other macabre oddities.

Anytime I came across something that fit his strange tastes that didn't break the bank I'd try to pick it up for him. Hell, it was the least I could do to show my appreciation for him putting up with all of my stupid questions over the years. It never failed that he'd have some sort of answer that pointed me in the right direction on the really weird jobs. So, getting him a small gift was the least I could do.

I turned off the main street and down the driveway, sliding between the mansion and the modern monstrosity next door. There was only one car in the parking area when I pulled in, but that wasn't a surprise. Most of the regular patrons either parked elsewhere and walked or were dropped off at the front door. Even the girls who didn't live in the Hammer parked elsewhere or called a taxi to take them home at the end of the night.

I knew Pierce was in because the one car in the parking area was unmistakably his. For a man with all of his eccentricities, you'd think he could get more creative and drive something a little more flash and style, like an old Rolls-Royce. I could see him riding around in something like that considering his love for fancy vests and suit jackets. But no… Pierce could not be parted with his beloved *classic*. I called it a god-awful eye sore that needed to be sent to the crusher, but he wouldn't have anything to do with it. No matter how many times I mentioned getting the car restored he refused without a thought otherwise. He argued that he'd lose that *classic* aged look that he cherished in his collected things.

The faded, baby-shit yellow 1973 Oldsmobile Delta 88 sat there, almost seeming to glower at me and the rumble of Valerie, my trusty motorcycle. Valerie wasn't much, but she got me where I needed to be, and she was stupid cheap on gas after I re-jetted the carburetor.

I pulled up next to the god-awful ugly turd of a car, dropped the kickstand, and shut Valerie off. I fished a small package wrapped in simple brown paper from the saddle bags I'd brought for Pierce. It wasn't much, but it was something I'd came across that I knew Pierce would appreciate.

Passing through the heavy wooden gate that separated the parking area from the small sitting Garden, it almost felt like I'd stepped back in time. Originally intended for early morning or a proper high tea for the patrons that followed that sort of thing, *the garden*, had all the vibes of Victorian high society, from the wrought iron furniture to creepy cherub sculptures.

I took the stairs to the veranda and entered through the double doors into the upper parlor, which Pierce tended to keep reserved for special events that required a bit of *extra privacy*.

Almost every surface was covered in something decorative; stained hardwoods, tapestries, beautifully woven rugs, and decorative wallpapers set the mood. It had that Victorian feel mingled with *The Addams Family* vibe thanks to all of the macabre oddities decorating every available surface in the house.

I stepped through the parlor's posh mahogany interior doors to the upper balcony that overlooked the primary parlor and entertainment room. There, in a high-backed chair upholstered in red velvet near a front window, sat Pierce, reading the morning paper with his afternoon tea. Pierce wasn't anything if he wasn't a creature of habit.

"It's good to see that things don't always change."

Pierce glanced up and smiled. That smile right there, could light up a dark room, and I knew for a fact it had gotten him into more trouble than he ever bargained for over the years. He had the look and carried himself like a Baron or Lord from the movies. Pretty boy looks and build, combined with a head full of dark hair that had only recently started showing signs of salt and pepper creeping in at his temples only accentuated his debonaire, lordly charm. That charm sometimes got him into trouble. Pierce was known to woo and swoon nearly about any female he encountered with little effort, but there were several he'd told me about that had nearly cost him his life. He'd just shrugged it off as bad luck.

"Braxton, you dirty old dog!"

Pulling off the black-rim glasses he wore, Pierce sat them on the side table, then stood and straightened his tweed hunting jacket.

Pierce clapped his hands together. "I am so glad you stopped in, Braxton. You've been on my mind of late. And besides, it has been much too long since your last visit, old friend."

"Naw, are you kidding me?" I made my way down the narrow spiral staircase that sat against the outer wall of the house. "It seems like only yesterday we were hunting down that supposed succubus working the streets of Hollywood."

"That was two years ago, Braxton."

"Really? It doesn't seem like it."

"Really."

"Well, sometimes life just gets busy as hell, I guess."

"Maybe for you, Mister Hicks. Time ticks by at an acceptably slow pace for me these days, especially since I left the hunting business to younger, more eager individuals such as yourself."

"That sorta news doesn't hurt my feelings any. It just means more gigs for me."

"Life is never boring for you, is it?"

"Nope, not really."

"Don't you ever take a break?"

"You know, that's a damned good question that you should probably be directing toward the universe instead of me." Pierce gave me one of those confused puppy looks, tilted head and all.

"How So?"

I figured I'd let him in on the inside joke. "It never fails, that any time I try to take a break, shit goes sideways. I stop in to see an old friend, have a few beers, maybe toss in a fishing line or two, and relax a bit. But, oh hell no— that's when swamp ghouls and an undead necromancer decide to pop up out of nowhere to harsh on my calm."

"Wait, are you serious?"

"The universe has this fucked up sense of humor. No matter where I am or who I'm with, it throws me some new curveball to deal with and harshes on my calm." I stopped a pace or two from Pierce. He shook his head like he was at a loss for words. "It's good to see you again, Pierce."

He nodded, snapping back to the conversation, and smiled. "It's great to see you again, old friend." We locked hands, shook, and brought it in for one of those brotherly shoulder hugs. "What's this," he asked, pointing down at the brown paper-wrapped gift I held in my left hand.

"Oh, this…" I said, holding it out to him. "This is a little something I picked up on the side, working an estate job down in Miami. There was this collector who had a few too many dangerous items that I had to confiscate and document. This just happened to get classified as a dangerous item when really it isn't, but as soon as I saw it, I knew it would be something you'd cherish."

Pierce continued to stare at me and blinked several times like his brain had decided to shut down and do a reboot. He shook his head and eagerly accepted the package. Unraveling the rough twine tied around the gift, he ripped away the dull brown paper and exposed a wooden frame.

The small ebony black picture frame, as small as a large index card held what looked like a desiccated piece of rough cured leather suspended and centered in the frame by hair-thin wires.

He rotated the frame ninety degrees at a time, trying to evaluate the item from different angles before flipping it over and examining the item through the rear glass.

Pierce glanced back up at me in total confusion. "What is it?"

"That my friend," I started, "is a one-of-a-kind specimen. You're an intelligent, educated man. What could you deduce that it is?"

"Some sort of cured leather, but no clue as to what." Pierce grabbed his glasses from the side table and looking down the bridge of his nose through the extra eyes like some sort of upscale grandpa, he took a closer look at the gift. "The coloration suggests extreme age, poor preservation techniques, or something I'm just not familiar with."

"What class of creature would you put it into?"

Pierce glanced back up at me, then back to the specimen several times before shaking his head. "I have no idea. By the texture alone, I would guess it was from something like an elephant, hippo, or possibly rhino."

"So, class Mammalia?" He gave me an even longer look of confusion, probably because the dumb biker used a big word meant for brainiacs. He slowly nodded.

"Yeah, mammal," he answered.

"And you'd be completely wrong, Mister Maggert."

He cocked his head to the side again, curiosity painted across his face. "Then what is it?"

"Reptilia." I smiled. He looked back at the specimen, examining it even closer then looked up at me over his glasses. "Do you know the possible genus or family?"

"Sauropod."

His eyes went wide before he stepped closer to the room's large front windows to get a look at the specimen in better light.

"What do you mean sauropod? Is this from some Siberian expedition where they passed off preserved mammoth flesh as something it isn't?"

"Nope," I said smugly, shaking my head. "That my friend, is a piece supposedly acquired by a German explorer hired by the King Leopold II of Belgium and tasked to survey his latest personal acquisition, which just happened to be the Congo Free State at that time."

Pierce started to speak, stuttered, then stopped and composed himself. "King Leopold and the Congo Free State," he mumbled, more asking than stating. His eyes rolled back and forth in their sockets as he thought. "You're talking the mid-1880s."

"1885 to be exact."

Pierce stood straight, taken aback, and smiled. "Well, go on. Don't hold out on me."

"This particular piece, acquired during that expedition into the territory interior and preserved as well as could be in the middle of a tropical jungle, was brought back to Belgium, where it was sold as an oddity to an interested buyer due to its connection to a local legend of the Congo."

Pierce shifted in place, smiled, and let out a nervous laugh. "Okay, and? Listen, you're killing me with this suspense. Just tell me, already."

"From there, it traded hands several more times over the years, finally finding itself in the hands of a rare oddities collector from Providence, Road Island, who eventually moved down to Miami where the collection, including this piece, was passed down to the heir upon the death of the previous collector. This is where I happened to come across the piece and realize just how much this particular thing would mean to you. I figured you'd cherish it well above any of these other trinkets you have decorating this place."

"You do realize, I know karate. I could hurt you in several ways that you wouldn't like."

I waggled my eyebrows at him. "Are you sure about that, big boy?" I smiled.

Pierce glared at me, almost smoldering, then took a step forward.

"Alright, alright." I took several steps backward, both of my hands up in the air, defensively waving him off.

"Supposedly, this is a piece of flesh that was torn away from a Mokele-mbembe that one of the local tribes had trapped by accident, but it managed to escape before the German explorer could lay eyes on the creature itself."

Pierce looked back and forth from me to the specimen several times while he tried to catch his breath and form something resembling a real word.

"Mokele-mbembe? *The* Mokele-mbembe? Are you fucking serious?"

I shook my head and defensively held my arms out to the sides. "I can't guarantee anything, man. I'm just relaying the info I picked up with the piece."

Pierce's smile suddenly faded, and he handed the specimen back to me. "I can't take this."

"Why not? You've got it."

"It's stolen."

"Now…see, that's a seriously grey area there." I pushed the specimen back to him. "Technically no, it isn't stolen. Not only was the previous owner, who, as a side note, never cared about his father's collection in the first place, was handsomely compensated by the federal government for the piece."

Pierce laughed. "What, they paid the guy a few hundred bucks?"

"Pretty much."

"Do you realize how rare this could be if it were real? According to reports from several interviews with villagers in the Likuoala swamp region, the last Mokele-mbembe supposedly died sometime in and around the 1990s."

"Yeah but it only has value to somebody who knows what it is and values it as such," I countered. His smile easily beamed from ear to ear. In all the years I'd known Pierce. I don't think I had seen him this happy before now.

Well…, unless you counted that time in Vegas on New Year's with the Sandusky triplets. Each of them were no less than five foot six with long wavy blonde locks and stacked as thick as a brick shit house.

Triple the pleasure, triple the fun.

Pierce quickly rearranged a few other antiquities on the mantelpiece and made space for the new specimen, then took a step back to admire it. He suddenly sucked in a breath and turned back to me with a snap of his fingers.

"That reminds me. I have something I've been holding onto since I last saw you. Go on ahead into the bar and tell them to pour you a drink on the house."

"That's much appreciated, Pierce. I didn't know you were so generous," I said and smiled.

"Just don't tell the general populace about it. It'll ruin my reputation as a curmudgeon." Pierce hurried up the spiral stairs I'd come down. "It's damn good to see you, Braxton. Make yourself at home. I'll return momentarily."

I turned and slowly made my way into the foyer. The deep rich wood and velvet continued throughout this part of the house. Dark polished wood furniture sat along the walls. Antiquities and late nineteenth-century photographs decorated any available spaces. It looked like something straight out of a movie set depicting a Victorian-era brothel. The room was complete with stained glass lamps, red velvet chairs, and lounging couches. A polished Mahogany bar top and intricately carved back bar complete with what looked like hand-blown mirror panels took up the back wall of the room.

No sooner had I walked in than a half dozen *gentlemen* turned to look at me. The scowls on their faces told me exactly what they thought of a dirty biker walking into their private gentleman's club.

Now, most of the gentlemen's clubs I've ever been in were nowhere near this classy. And generally my attire fit, but not with this bunch. Several of them were wearing high-dollar three-piece suits that probably cost more than a year's pay for me.

For that kinda cost, it was my understanding a patron of the establishment could get everything from cheap wine to expensive top-shelf cognac, fine cigars, and exotic mixtures for the many hookah and water pipes placed around the Lounge. You could even get exclusive extras like a private massage, bath, and laundry services, or a little personal companionship. And if the eye candy scattered around the room was any indication, it was some kinda high-dollar premium package that Pierce was offering.

I smiled and waved at the folks in the room. "How y'all doin'?" I said then sauntered my way up to the bar. "Give me a shot and a beer, preferably something dark and chewy."

Pierce had done well setting this place up for the feel of what it once was. It's like I'd taken a step back in time minus the electric lights and other modern amenities. And of course, Pierce being Pierce, the house had something to do with his collecting habit.

The house had a *history*. Rumor had it the original owner was t an occultist who dabbled in devil worship and things like demon summoning; possibly worshipping the great old ones. Pierce mentioned there were several times throughout the house's history that strange disappearances had happened. He'd rattled off the number to me at one point, but I couldn't remember. He was so excited when he signed the deal for the place.

Lucky for me, I spotted one of my favorite cigar brands sitting in the small humidor of the back bar.

"Hey, buddy, how about one of those sticks too, while you're at it?" I said, pointing at the humidor. "Bottom row second from the left."

The bartender was as stoic and statuesque as a marble carving. From his lack of response, I started to wonder if he wasn't maybe one of the antiquities that Pierce had collected for the place.

"Can I help you, sir?" The bartender asked in a proper British accent, then straightened his round Poindexter glasses and bow tie.

"Yeah, man. I said, give me a shot of whiskey and a beer, preferably something dark and chewy, plus one of those tasty smokey treats in the humidor over there."

This guy had no chances ever in a poker match. His eye roll and body language said everything I needed to know about his attitude. Tired, exasperated, and difficult.

"I am afraid I have to ask you for your proof of membership, sir."

This little shit stain was about to start getting on my nerves. "I don't need a membership. I'm friends with the owner."

The guy scoffed in that pretentious, British way. "I am sorry, sir, but everyone simply must have a membership."

Yup, and there it was. He was dancing on that nerve. "Well, I'll tell you what, buddy. You give it just a few minutes and your boss Mr. Maggart will be back down here. Trust me, you're gonna want to go ahead and pour me that drink, bud."

The doofus reached into his pocket and tapped away on his phone, content with ignoring me.

"So where the hell is Billy Joe?" I asked. "The last time I was here he was running the joint and didn't give me any trouble at all."

The little prick did his little scoff again and smiled at me with one of those knowing glares. "Unfortunately, sir, Billy Joe is no longer employed by the establishment, and has not been for quite some time."

"Well, what happened to him?" I inquired, sliding onto one of the fine leather bar stools.

"I am not honestly sure, Sir. He simply disappeared several weeks ago and has not reappeared, so we do not speak about Billy Joe."

"Was he having lady troubles?"

"Afraid I do not know, Sir. Again, we do not speak about Billy Joe any longer."

"There you are," Pierce said as he hurried into the lounge "Did Nigel have something to suit you on tap?"

I turned to him and shrugged. "I don't know. He won't pour me a drink. Says I need to show my membership credentials first."

Pierce turned back to the bartender and waved at the back bar. "He's a friend, Nigel. Pour him whatever he wants."

Nigel let out one of those disappointed British huffs. "Very well, sir," he said, then turned around to grab a bottle of Jack Daniels.

"Oh, no, no, not that one," Pierce said, waving him off. "Pour three fingers of the Rémy Martin Louis XIII Cognac for each of us, if you would please."

"Straight, no ice," I added.

"As you wish sir," Nigel said reluctantly and moved a step stool to retrieve a beautifully blown glass bottle from the top shelf. He poured three fingers worth of the dark amber liquid into glass tumblers, followed by a draft pour of a dark beer with a foamy head on it.

Pierce picked up his glass and held it up in salute. "To good health and a long life. Cheers."

I picked up my glass and clanked it against his. "Sláinte!" Tipping back the glass, I was thoroughly impressed with the flavor. Better than most bourbons or whiskeys I'd ever had.

"What did you think?"

"That is damned tasty."

Pierce chuckled into his drink. "It better be, for what I paid for that bottle."

That side comment piqued my interest. I turned to him and asked, "So how much did a bottle of this stuff run you?"

"What do you think it cost me?"

"I dunno," I said, shrugging. "Hundred bucks maybe?"

He let out a deep belly laugh and took another drink. "Nope. Not even close, my friend. Do you really want to know?"

"Hell, yeah. You got me all curious now."

"Well, the bottle cost me roughly four thousand dollars, it's a 750ml bottle which is roughly sixteen shots, and a three-finger pour is equal to two shots, so each of these glasses are worth about five hundred dollars each." He smiled and took another drink.

"I'm glad I didn't just slam it back, then," I said and took another drink myself.

I motioned again for one of the cigars, and Nigel was nice enough to oblige me by bringing me two of them. He even cut the tip and lit one for me. The second one I tucked into the breast pocket of my kutte, then puffed on the lit cigar a few times and took another sip of the rich amber liquid. Man was this ever good, but I was glad it was on the house, cause damn if it wasn't too rich for my country blood.

I noticed Pierce nervously fidgeting with his glass.

"What's up, man? You look like something's bothering you."

"I acquired a little something that I think would benefit you more than myself, especially now that I've gotten out of the hunting business."

"Okay," I said around the cigar, taking another puff. "You're just full of surprises today, ain't ya?"

He flashed a wide smile and continued. "It has quite a history, but in your line of work, it could be extremely beneficial." From his right trouser pocket, Pierce produced a silver fob watch on a chain. Beautifully intricate designs of geese and ducks decorated its highly polished surface. The blue crystal glass covering the face of the timepiece gleamed in the dim light of the lounge.

"This is *Saint Aaron's Blessed Timepiece of the Sacrament*," he said as he delicately handed it over to me. "It is said to contain the finger bone of Saint Aaron of Trakai within a vessel of holy water that was blessed by the Pope himself. It is said to protect the wearer from possession and harm from evil."

I glanced down at it and then back to Pierce. "Are you sure you wanna give me something like this? The thing looks like it's made of pure silver."

"It is," he confirmed.

"Then it's gotta be worth a small fortune in scrap value alone."

"Don't ask. You don't want to know."

I tried to hand it back to him but he immediately slid his hands into his pockets. "We saw a lot of weird stuff back in the day. In your line of work, this has a far better chance of protecting you than anything I might do with it. We have been friends for a very long time, and it might just save your ass one day. So, it's yours."

I stared at it for a long minute. The face popped open when I pressed a small button on the side of the timepiece. The gear works were exposed in the back, but in the front, through the blue crystal face, you could see something that resembled a small finger bone suspended in a liquid.

"I don't know, Pierce. This is kind of above and beyond."

"All the times you've helped me, not to mention what you just brought me. It is well worth every penny to me. Consider it a token of our friendship."

"Why is it blue? Almost looks like it's full of glass cleaner or something."

"The facing is a polished piece of sapphire."

"Bullshit. I thought sapphire was a dark blue or purple."

"It is, but it can come in many shades, including greens and reds like any beryl. It just depends on where it comes from. This particular sapphire is thought to have originated in Myanmar."

"Are you sure?" I intently stared back at him.

"Positively."

"Do you think it actually works?"

"Whether it does or not, I don't know, but it wouldn't hurt to have, just in case. Remember, I know how pivotal the right tool can be to give you an extra edge when dealing with the weird and strange."

"Well, thank you, Pierce. I appreciate it much." I tucked the watch into the fob pocket of my kutte and strung the chain over to a buttonhole.

I grabbed the tumbler and held it up for a silent toast. We clanked glasses and took another drink together.

The glassware decorating the back bar suddenly shook and clinked to a rumbling that reverberated throughout the building. I could feel the low vibrations through the soles of my boots.

I turned back to Pierce with a questioning look. "What in the hell just happened? Did we cast some kinda spell or something?"

Pierce let out a gut chuckling chortle. "No, no, nothing like that. The old boiler system down in the basement is acting up again. One of those things I've been meaning to replace but it keeps working, so I haven't."

I took a long drink from the beer, finishing it off in three big gulps. "Well, give me a few minutes and I'll go see what I can figure out on it."

"You know how to work on boilers?"

"I know enough to know how to work on a little bit of everything. Boilers ain't nothing but big water heaters. Fuel, fire, water, exhaust." I shrugged. "I mean, what's the worst that can happen? You'll still have to call someone else out?"

"This is very true," Pierce replied.

"How do I get down to the basement?"

"The stairs are at the back of the kitchen. Here," he said, standing. "Let me show you where it's at."

I followed Pierce through to the back of the house and into the kitchen where he turned a corner and opened what looked like a door to a coat closet, revealing a steep set of narrow stairs. The smell of old motor oil and French fries smacked me in the face as soon as he opened it.

Reaching the bottom, he flicked on the lights that barely did anything to drive back the darkness.

The boiler clicked as if on queue and the blower roared as it tried to ignite the main burner. It suddenly clicked off and the blower spun down. Another click, rumble, and blower running but was left with the click click click of the ignition module. The air was heavy with the stink of motor oil fries now.

"What kind of fuel is this thing running off of?" I asked as I looked over the controls and piping.

"It runs off of waste oil. So it can burn anything from used motor oil to diesel, or whatever we can get our hands on. I managed an agreement with several of the larger chain restaurants around town for their used fryer oil and several of the auto shops for the used motor oil they have to get rid of from oil changes. It's a lot cheaper than buying fuel oil and has worked like a charm for years.

I really couldn't argue with that reasoning. Anything to do with oil was expensive these days.

The unit clicked again as it attempted another ignition sequence. I could easily hear the fuel pump kick in, spraying oil into the combustion chamber. In essence, it wasn't any different than any internal combustion engine. Suck, squeeze, bang, blow. Only in this case, you added fuel and air together, skip the squeeze part, just go straight to burning, and boom, you've got heat.

I turned back to Pierce. "Got a flashlight?"

"Oh yeah. Right here," he said, grabbing one from a shelf near the stairs.

I cut off the main power and opened the control box, exposing an awful tangle of ancient wires and relays with a single fuse in the middle of the mess. Nothing looked out of place. I shook the relays to check them and nothing rattled like they'd broken, so I put it all back together, cut the power back on, and adjusted the temperature to a higher setting so it wouldn't take so long for it to kick back over.

Again, the blower started going and you could hear the fuel pump followed by the ignition sequence, and the click click click of the ignition module was unmistakable.

I peeked into the viewport on the front of the boiler and couldn't see any sort of spark even though the module was clicking. Finding a pipe wrench lying on top of the control panel, I grabbed it and tapped at the side of the control module. For a moment there was a spark and the flurry of ignition. It popped from the excess fuel sitting in the bottom of the combustion chamber.

"Come on, you hunk of shit!" I shouted and kicked the side of the boiler. The boiler roared to life like an angry beast awakened from its millennia of slumber. Flames spilled out from every seam as the casing expanded and rippled. It rumbled with a reverberation that shook the foundation of the building.

"That doesn't look good," Pierce said, backing away.

"Nope, that probably isn't good!"

Before I could back away from what looked like a critical failure, something hooked my ankle, pulling my foot out from under me. I fell backward, landing hard on the cobblestone floor of the basement.

The boiler rumbled, then shifted to the side. The manway on the front end flew open, exposing rows upon rows of razor-sharp teeth. It shifted again to the other side, jerking like it was trying to pull its feet out of thick mud. Telephone line thick tentacles wriggled free from around the concrete footings and shot out in my direction. Hot steam roiled out from what seemed like hundreds of leaks across the boiler beast's shell.

"Pierce! What the hell is that?" I shouted, backpedaling.

"Your guess is as good as mine!"

I turned to run and found that Pierce had already sprinted for the stairs. "You mean you didn't *collect* it?"

"Not this one. The boiler came with the house."

I followed him up the stairs. Droplets of what looked like condensation had started to collect along the floor joists, walls, and ceiling. We both rushed up the stairs and slammed the basement door shut behind us.

"Okay, so if you didn't collect that thing, then what the hell is it?" I asked, and that's when we both heard the screams. Some sounded like honest panic, others like horrific pain and suffering.

We rushed to the front of the house and found the suit-clad patrons, the bartender, and several of the girls gathered, struggling to open the front door. The walls and ceiling began to drip with a viscous yellow liquid. One of the older gentlemen picked up a nearby chair and threw it against the large window alongside the door. It merely bounced off the glass and landed at the man's feet.

Something plopped on the back of my arm. It burned, like battery acid or a bad chemical burn. I hurried to wipe it off on my jeans.

"Pierce," I said, shouting over the panicked complaints of the crowd. "Is it possible that a house could be a cryptid?"

"What?"

"I'm serious. Look at this," I said, motioning around the room at the dripping walls. "It burns like battery acid. What if it was more like stomach acid?"

Pierce snapped his fingers, excitement lighting up his face. "That could explain all of the past disappearances."

"How far apart were the other disappearances?"

"Roughly," he said, mumbling to himself. "About every sixty-seven years or so, give or take."

"Then yeah. I'd bet you're right. It wakes up to feed, then back to being a house again. Ever heard of anything like it before?"

"The only thing that comes to mind is a Gardinel, but I thought they were fiction."

"Apparently not. Now how do we get out of here? Do Gardinel's have any sort of weaknesses?"

"I don't know...," Pierce said, drifting off into thought.

"But, weren't there survivors?"

The grim look on his face told me all that I needed to know. He shook his head slowly and mumbled a dismayed, "No."

I pulled my phone out of my pocket and dialed Mandy, my silent partner in crime as well as the proprietor and sole owner of Karatech, a multi-disciplined business housed in what used to be an old-school Pizza Hut in an outdated shopping center. She handled the heavy research for me when I was on a job.

"Yeah, Brax. What's up? I thought you were on your way back from that gig out west?"

"I am, but I stopped to see an old friend in Memphis. Listen, I don't know how much time we've got. I need to know anything you can find out about a cryptid that is also a house."

"So, like a mimic, but house-sized?"

"You got it. And Mandy, make it quick. Pierce said it might also be called a Gardinel."

Several blood-curdling screams came from one of the upstairs rooms.

"That sounded like Emmy," Pierce said, then sprinted for the stairs.

I followed right behind him, sprinting two steps at a time. "I specifically need to know how to kill one."

"What was screaming and why do you need to know this all of a sudden?"

"Don't worry about that, just get me the info ASAP."

"Keep your pants on," she grunted. "Okay…Oh, that isn't good." She suddenly sounded concerned, which was probably for good reason. "The only thing I'm seeing is mentions in fiction, primarily by Manly Wade Wellman starting in… 1946. On a quick search, the only reference to hurting one of these things is by burning or full-on demolition."

Yeah…, that didn't bode well at all. "Thanks for all the help you give me. I appreciate you and everything you do."

"Um… Okay. Thanks, I think. Brax, what's going on?"

"Nothing you can do anything about. Oh, and Mandy…"

"Yeah."

"I never stopped loving you," I said, then hit the end call button on my phone.

We arrived at the second floor and Pierce hurried to the end of the hall. The corridor flexed and bowed like some distorted thing out of a horror flick. Pierce grabbed the doorknob, then quickly jerked his hand back and wiped it on his pants.

"What happened?"

"It burns," he said, then opened his palm to show me. Sure enough, I'd been burned enough times from pouring concrete or cleaning it with muriatic acid to know what a chemical burn looked like.

Luckily I had tucked my riding gloves in my back pocket. Quickly I slid them on, grabbed the doorknob, and twisted. I pushed, digging my feet in as best as I could on the damp hardwood. I slammed my shoulder into the door several times but it still wouldn't budge.

"Help me," I said over my shoulder to Pierce. On the count of three, we both slammed our shoulders into the door, forcing it open, but at that moment I really wished that we hadn't.

The room was a disaster. Furniture, decorations, and anything that had been in the room looked like it had been tossed into a drink tumbler and mixed thoroughly.

Including the people.

Blood-spattered bones that looked like they had been picked clean were scattered around the room. It stank like the acrid stench of stomach bile after a night of binge-drinking cheap beer and tequila shots.

"We seriously need to get out of this house," I said, then hurried back toward the stairs.

"What are we going to do?" Pierce asked, following close behind.

The guys in the suits had picked up a wooden bench from the foyer, attempting to use it as a battering ram.

"No… not my John and Thomas Seymour bench," Pierce whined.

"Who cares, it's a bench. And I don't know what we're going to do. Got any books that might have something on this thing?"

"Maybe, but it would be back in the library."

"Then let's get to it. We have zero time to waste." I shoved him ahead of me, directing him toward the library while I fished my phone out of my pocket again. I thumbed through the contact list as I walked. Finding Agent Jessie Carter's number, I hit the call button.

Me and Carter went way back. Not quite as far back as me and Mandy, but far enough. She'd been a pain in my ass for years, both in the military and afterward. Damned officers just seemed to have a knack for fucking with a good time. And I had to admit that she was a damn good agent. Probably one of the best friends I ever had, not that she would ever admit to it.

The phone rang and rang and rang. I thought it was about to go to voicemail when it clicked and an exasperated "What" came across the line.

I let out a sigh of relief. "God dammit Jessie, it's good to hear your voice."

"Hicks? Are you drunk or something?"

I barked out a laugh. "By the gods, don't I freaking wish."

"You called me Jessie. You always call me something stupid, like Daisy or Buttercup. What's wrong?" I could hear the concern underlying her bad-girl voice.

"I just wanted to let you know, that I may have given you hell all these years, but that doesn't mean I don't respect you and your skill as an agent.

You're damn good at what you do. Don't let any of those corporate-type sniveling asshats tell you otherwise."

"Okay, either you're high or something really bad is going on."

"Just remember what I said and keep up the good work, Carter." I ended the call and muted her number before I continued into the library with Pierce. I grabbed him by the collar of his shirt and dragged him back into the foyer a split second after he opened the library door.

The room dripped and oozed with whatever the hell it was that had burned me earlier. The walls moved and undulated like some sort of muscle spasms.

"How about we not go in there and say we did." I slammed the door shut.

"All right," Pierce said, turning to me. "What do we do now?"

Ya know, it's at times like this that I really wish people didn't put a lot of faith in me, because I wasn't sure what the hell I was supposed to do. I'd always just kind of winged this thing as I got the gigs.

But we were all seriously fucked if I couldn't think of something really quick like. Mandy mentioned burning or demolition. So that meant that these things weren't immortal or impervious. Just seriously tough. Maybe we could start a fire and smoke our way out, but that could just as well suffocate all of us before we could escape.

I hurried back into the lounge and took a quick look around the room. Pierce had all sorts of antiques hanging on walls and sitting on shelves, but hanging over the mantle in the lounge were a pair of axes that looked like something out of a sword and sorcery flick.

"Are those real?" I asked, pointing at the axes. "Or are they just those decorative Bud-K pieces of shit you can get for cheap at the flea market?"

"Oh, they're real all right. And they're about a hundred and fifty years old at least. They were once part of the Danish guard's dress uniform for a short period before they discontinued it in favor of sabers."

"That sounds perfect to me." I reached up and wrenched both the axes off the wall. They were hefty for their size, but solid and looked like something you'd see in a fantasy movie or maybe what a Viking berserker would carry in battle.

"Let's see if we can't blow this popsicle stand," I said and hurried back to the foyer. I reared back and swung the axe in my right hand with all of my might. It struck the heavy wooden front door and dug in deep. Black ichor gushed forth when I wrenched the blade free.

The entire house shuddered and an inhuman aethereal roar echoed throughout the structure

I struck again with the left, pried it free, then again with the right. Dark purplish flesh fell away from the door frame. Ichor oozed down from the wound, pooling on the floor.

The house screamed, sounding like it was in excruciating pain. The walls flexed and undulated, knocking pictures and other decorations to the ground, and then it bucked, striking out. Tentacles emerged from the base of the grand staircase, and a toothy maw opened up where the stair steps were. Rows upon rows of jagged sharp teeth gleamed in that massive ephemeral mouth.

The door struck back before my next swing could land. Everything went suddenly dark. It felt as if I were floating, soaring through the air. Then something struck me hard from behind.

"Braxton." I heard Pierce shouting from somewhere beyond the darkness. "Braxton! Hey! Tell me, you are okay! You aren't allowed to die on me that easy." He shook me, holding me up by the shoulders.

I shifted and flexed, checking myself for any broken bones before I opened my eyes. Blotches of color floated in my vision. I shook my head to clear out the stars.

"This fucking thing is not going to beat me." I shouted, letting out a primal roar. I did not want to give up. And I would fight until my last fucking breath to get us out of the belly of this beast thing. I leapt to my feet and charged at the front door again. The blades flashed in the flickering lights and struck hard.

Screams erupted from behind me. Two of the old dudes were wrapped in the coils of thick purple tentacles. They had little chance of fighting against the Gardinel, and were quickly dragged beneath the stairwell. I hacked and chopped at the door with everything in me, blocking each strike the house took at me.

The light of day finally appeared through a small hole I had carved through the fleshy doors.

Someone shouted something from behind me, but the words didn't translate. I swung again, but the blade of the axe stuck fast into the heavy aged wood of a solid oak door. Bracing my foot against the door I yanked, splintering the aged wood. The door limply swung open on its own, revealing the world outside.

The rumble of the house ceased, replaced by an eerie silence that washed over the room. Panicked whispers and whimpers from behind me found my ears. I turned to see the patrons and employees of the Velvet Hammer, huddled in the middle of the foyer floor. The walls no longer oozed and seeped. The stairwell was once again a stairwell, not the jagged maw of a malformed beast.

I lost count of the bodies that rushed by, escaping the building as I stood there at the open door. One after another fled the scene, among panicked shouts and chaotic ramblings.

"Braxton. You did it. You got us out," Pierce shouted into my ear, shaking my shoulder once again.

I dropped the axes and stepped through the threshold of the front entrance into the dimming evening light. Just to be on the safe side, I headed down the sidewalk, getting myself as far away from the porch as possible. I didn't want to take any chances on this thing waking back up, or catching me off guard because it was playing possum. I sat on the curb and pulled the extra cigar Nigel had given me earlier from the breast pocket of my kutte, then bit off the tip.

Pierce dropped onto the sidewalk sitting next to me and slapped me on the shoulder. He was grinning ear to ear like an idiot.

"Would you have ever guessed that thing was alive?"

I looked at him like he was a crazy man, but he just continued to beam with excitement.

"You're going to keep the place, aren't you?"

He nodded with a shit-eating grin and gave me an affirmative, "Uh huh."

"How are you gonna explain the missing persons? You know I can't do anything to cover that up for you."

"I'll figure something out," Pierce said, smiling back at the house. "If all the old tales hold true, it's fed and good for another sixty-seventy years. I'll just have to make sure that things are…um…prepared for that moment."

He had that gleam in his eye like nothing was ever going to change his mind.

"People think I'm bat shit crazy most of the time, but you really take the cake, Pierce."

"Well, I know what I like." He flashed his best toothy grin before he dialed his lawyer to deal with the insurance company.

I lit the cigar and took a long slow draw, enjoying the flavor of the expensive stick, then turned back to look at the old Victorian mansion. It was beautiful architecture that was beyond reproach, but I don't know that I could ever step foot in the place ever again, especially after the day we'd just had.

My phone vibrated, and I remembered I'd muted it earlier. I pulled the phone out of my pocket and found several dozen texts from Mandy and Carter flooding my inbox. I turned the ringer back on and dialed up Carter.

"Braxton." She yelled into the phone. "What the fuck is going on? Don't you ever cut me off like that again!"

"Aww," I said in as loving a tone as I could. "Agent Carter, I didn't know you cared." She let out one of those shocked, *how dare you* gasps. Before she could get a word in, I continued.

"Daijoubu, Carter."

"What? Speak some sense, Hicks."

"It's all good, baby doll…," I continued. "We're all just golden. Life is shiny and good again, Buttercup. Suppose it's just time for the next gig, is all."

We hope that you enjoyed this title and look forward to many more to come. Please, leave us a review! Reviews matter to all of our authors.

And don't forget to check out the latest edition of **Car Wars**

http://www.sjgames.com/car-wars/

Or the other amazing titles from
Steve Jackson Games

http://www.sjgames.com

...or the latest in the Car Warriors: Autoduel Chronicle fiction series.
https://threeravenspublishing.com/car-warriors-autoduel-chronicles/

Take a look at some of our other award-winning series at
https://threeravenspublishing.com/series-universes/

Visit us at https://www.threeravenspublishing.com and sign up for our newsletter for the latest and greatest news on upcoming titles and events.

Other series and titles you might enjoy.

DECLAN FINN
DECLAN FINN
DECLAN FINN
DECLAN FINN
Demons are Forever
HONOR at STAKE
Live and Let Bite
Good to the Last Drop
The Dragon Award Nominated Series
FREE on Kindle Unlimited!

AVAILABLE ON
AMAZON
JOINT TASK FORCE
13
HOLDING THE LINE
BETWEEN HEAVEN AND HELL

MYSTERY,
MAGIC &
MAYHEM
WITH A TWIST
OF ROMANCE
J.F. POSTHUMUS
ON AMAZON
FIND ME
B.E.N.T.
BIOLOGIC    ENHANCED    NASCENT    TALENT

THE RAVEN
AND
MICHAEL K. FALCIANI
THE CROW
FIND ME
ON AMAZON

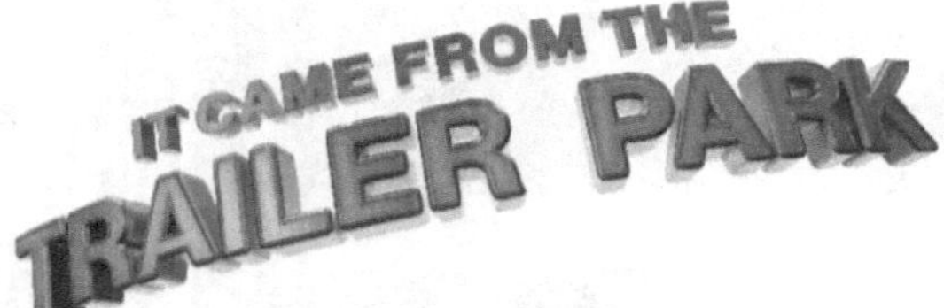
STARFLIGHT

IT CAME FROM THE
TRAILER PARK

Three Ravens Publishing
Are you looking for fun, new fiction?
The Written Word Will Never Be The Same…
https://www.threeravenspublishing.com
Veteran Owned and Operated

You can also keep up to date with our latest release announcements on Scifi.radio and get some of the best fandom programing on the planet.

Scifi for your Wifi

And don't forget to check out our other Sponsors and Affiliates

A southern Appalachian jewel for craft beer lovers, Buck Bald Brewing offers something for everyone. With delicious, locally brewed beverages from across the spectrum, Buck Bald Brewing offers craft brews that are consistently amazing.

From the dark and smooth Shesquatch Scottish ale, to the intense hops of Hippibilly IPA, to the puckering sour of the blackberry and cinnamon in Berry My Heart at the Trailer Park, and more than 60+ rotating brews, you'll find what you're looking for and more.

With smiling faces behind the bar ready to help you find your next favorite brew, a constantly rotating selection of delicious craft beverages, toe-tapping tunes always playing, and the biggest games on TV, you can kick your feet up in either Copperhill, Tennessee or Murphy, North Carolina and immerse yourself in the Buck Bald Brewing experience. So, come out, fill a pint, fill a growler, and fill your mind at your new favorite family-owned craft brewery.

To discover more visit us at buckbaldbrewing.com or follow us on Facebook @buckbaldbrewing and @buckbaldbrewingmurphy.